THE
HAUNTING
OF
SORROW'S LEAP

CHRIS SORENSEN

Chris Sorensen — First Edition

ISBN: 979-8-9939059-1-4

And I'm haunted
By the lives that I have loved
And actions I have hated
I'm haunted
By the lives that wove the web
Inside my haunted head

"Haunted" by Poe

1

The teenager in a Jason Voorhees T-shirt approached my booth as I was rearranging the unsold crystals and charms in a quixotic effort to make them more appealing.

"You write this?" He picked up a copy of my book, *Voices from the Other Room.* "You Ellen Marx?"

"Yes, on both counts," I said. His face was a constellation of pimples. I could trace the Big Dipper on his forehead.

He flipped through the pages with all the enthusiasm of someone killing time at a dentist's office. *Voices* had been my last hurrah, self-published eight years ago and currently selling just enough copies to remind me it existed. I'd been twenty-seven when it made its unremarkable debut, and I hadn't written since. There was no point. The voices had gone silent.

"How much?"

"Ten bucks. Cash." It had to be cash since it wasn't part of the official merchandise. The Sisters wouldn't reimburse me if I used the card reader.

The kid returned the book to its pile and snatched up a grasshopper encased in a liquid-filled glass vial.

"How much?"

"It should say on the sticker," I replied.

The boy twirled the vial, causing the dead insect to spin in the alcohol.

"It doesn't have a sticker."

I sighed and leafed through the pricing sheets. The lists were well organized, of course. Weird Sisters, Inc. was nothing if not efficient, a reflection of its owners who had opted out of attending this particular event. Apparently, the Secaucus Hooky Spooky Convention was small potatoes in their eyes. Best to send the hired help.

I ran a finger down the list of charms. After sifting through prices for everything from bottled cows' teeth to something disturbingly labeled "Baby Fingers," I located the item in question.

"Twenty-seven dollars," I said.

His eyebrows climbed toward his hairline. "For this?"

I dove into sales mode. Mythological improvisation was my strong suit, and I had no qualms about embellishing—downright inventing—the qualities or provenance of the crap I sold.

"That's cheap for such a powerful love charm. The Weird Sisters harvested that critter beneath a full moon. And the vial? Vintage. Recovered from a suspicious factory fire down in New Orleans. If it doesn't sell, I'm keeping it for myself."

The boy turned it over in his hands.

"Pass."

He set the vial back down among the crystals and amulets. I didn't blame him. The stock they'd sent me here with was crap—second-tier baubles they hadn't managed to unload back at the shop in Iowa City, a shoddy collection of stale sage, witchy earrings, and charms, charms, charms. But inventory was inventory, and the Sisters had inventory to spare.

As the boy retreated, I surveyed the scene around me. Fifty or so booths played host to the sparse October crowd. The Meadowlands Conference Center was the nadir of New Jersey venues, and the cramped East Room they'd stuffed us in had been untouched since the nineties—its puke-beige walls and worn, patterned carpet made it feel like a casino from which all the slot machines had fled.

Mine was one of the skimpier setups, wedged between a woman selling "magical" feathers and a guy handing out samples of a Houdini-themed energy drink. Magic Feather Lady enthusiastically flapped her lips while Energy Drink Boy poured shots like a Saturday night bartender.

A gaggle of teenage goth posers passed by, trailing their leader, a young woman dolled up like some Tim Burton princess. She'd stolen Cruella de Vil's trademark black-and-white hairstyle and wore a sash proclaiming herself, "The Halloween Queen." Phones up, they filmed everything and saw nothing.

"Who the hell is that?" I asked Magic Feather Lady.

"Some influencer," she sighed. "Here to use the convention as a backdrop. There's more of them every year. They breed like cockroaches."

The Queen and her retinue sidled up to one of the more

popular booths—it had been swarmed since doors opened. A professional banner touted the newest book by William Quan, Medium, featuring a photo of a young man with piercing eyes and spiked hair. He looked like an indie rock star, which explained the swarm of females buzzing about his booth.

There was a time when I could have rocked a con like young Mr. Quan. Ten years ago, I'd rid a shopping mall of a particularly nasty poltergeist. Today? I was just another of the bungled and the botched haunting the Meadowlands Conference Center. Whatever gifts I'd had bid me sayonara that afternoon in late August when...well, like I said, those days had passed.

I picked up the vial and stared at the bug inside. One day, he was hopping around in a field; the next, trapped inside a glass tube. I wasn't sure which of us had drawn the shorter straw.

Quan's harried assistant stood on a folding chair and waved his arms, begging the crowd's attention.

"That's it, folks. Bill has signed his last book of the evening. But don't worry, he'll be back tomorrow."

The bevy of fans let out a collective sigh of disappointment. The kid had it good; he had them eating out of his hand. *Keep ridin' that Apple Pay Express as long as you can*, I thought.

My phone chirped, and my heart sank. The Sisters weren't just calling; they were attempting to FaceTime. The first day of sales had been anything but brisk, but of course, they already knew that—they were getting up-to-the-minute updates on my lack of sales via the traitorous card reader.

I tapped my phone, and the Sisters appeared: two blond gals in their twenties who'd had more work done than women twice their age.

Mika, the one I secretly thought of as "The Scarecrow," spoke first. "These numbers are pitiful," she slurred, already deep into her daily bottle of chardonnay.

"Hello to you, too," I said.

"We never should have sent you on this trip. This whole thing's going to be a wash."

The image jittered as Jamie took charge of the phone. Jamie was younger than her sister, but you wouldn't know by looking at her. While Mika guzzled wine, Jamie mainlined worry.

"Are you pushing the crystals, Ellen?" Jamie whined. "You gotta lean into the crystals."

"I'm leaning, I'm leaning," I replied, seriously considering slitting my own throat.

"Push the crystals and hand out cards. I don't want you bringing back a single business card, do you hear me?"

I was about to tell her where she could stick her business cards when a loud crash echoed through the room. My thoughts flew to the kid in the Jason Voorhees T-shirt. He'd definitely had school shooter vibes. But no, he was currently haunting a booth hawking steampunk attire.

"Ellen? You there?"

Laughter rose from the crowd, and I craned my neck to see what was going on.

"Ellen?"

"Call you right back." I switched off the phone with pleasure.

I scanned the room, homing in on the source of the commotion.

A chunky guy in thick-framed glasses and cargo pants lay sprawled on the floor just inside the entrance to the East Room, DVDs from his burst backpack scattered around him. The guy had stumbled over the tripod base of one of the loudspeakers spewing witch house music, bringing it crashing down. Now, he lay like a bug on its back as the crowd stood by and gawked.

The tittering onlookers brought acid to my throat.

I charged the scene, throwing elbows to part the crowd.

"Move it, move it!"

Chunky was frantically gathering his DVDs, like a poker player fearful he might lose his chips.

The Halloween Queen and her entourage had arrived as if on cue, drawn to the drama like moths to a flame. The Queen knelt and plucked up that which was just beyond Chunky's reach: a child's threadbare stuffed animal.

"Isn't this just delicious?" she said, turning it over in her hands.

The toy had probably been a dog once upon a time, but age and flame had made it almost unrecognizable. The beige creature was balding, its mournful eyes turned upward, half of its fur melted black.

The Queen gazed upon it covetously. "How much do you want for it?"

"It's not for sale," the young man croaked.

"Oh, honey," one of the Queen's waifish followers crooned. "Everything's for sale."

"Give him to me!" Tears welled in Chunky's eyes.

"Just a few more shots," a member of the entourage said, snapping photos. The Queen held up the stuffed animal, posing with mock horror on her face. *Snap-snap*.

I ripped the dog from the Halloween Queen's hands and locked eyes with her, feeling that unpleasant buzz. For me, full eye contact was something akin to French kissing a nine-volt battery.

"You're what's wrong with the world, you know that? You and the rest of these assholes." I swung the dog at the gathering crowd. "You think you're special because you play dress-up and muck around with tarot cards. The internet is littered with your cosplay nonsense. If you ever came face-to-face with an honest-to-God ghost, you'd piss your pants. You're nothing but a bunch of self-absorbed, self-deluded, sage-burning crystal-clutchers. That's right, can't forget those crystals, gotta *lean into* those crystals. Well, today's your lucky day. We've got a shit-ton of your favorite crap over at Booth 38. One-stop shopping for gullible goons."

I paused, fully intending to continue my tirade—it felt fucking great to get all that poison out of my system—when I noticed the wall of upraised phones pointed in my direction.

The Queen reached out and lifted the ID hanging around my neck.

"Booth 38. The Weird Sisters." A tense smile crossed her lips. "I'll have to stop by and give my followers a peek." She turned to her pack, and, with a click of her fingers, they were off, all whispers and giggles.

"Wow," the young man with the backpack said as he rose to face me. "That was...that was something."

"You caught me on a weird day."

"Anyway, thanks for stepping in." He held out his hands. "May I?"

I was still holding the disfigured dog. "Sorry. Here you go."

"Sorry, Jersey," he said to his pup before stuffing it back into his pack.

I helped him gather the rest of his merch.

"I thought DVDs were dead," I said.

"Yeah, well, when you've got thirty boxes sitting in storage, you sell what you got."

"Fucking inventory."

"You got that right." He wiped the last tears from his baby face and smoothed down his strip mall haircut. "The name's JJ."

"Ellen."

"Thanks again, Ellen," he said, sticking out a pudgy hand I reluctantly took.

"No problem."

A door deep inside my head rattled.

The boy is crying.

Something wanted out.

JJ winced. "Hey!"

The boy is screaming.

The door's hinges groaned.

"Could you let go of my hand?"

Screaming.

I tried to pull away, but my hand wouldn't release its grip.

My fingers twitched with a faint electrical charge, causing them to tighten, release, tighten, release.

The door began to splinter. To crack. The pressure threatened to shatter my skull as well.

I yanked back my hand, that raw electric hum still dancing through my digits.

"Are you okay?" JJ asked. "You need some water or something?"

"I'm fine." But that was a lie. For the first time since my mother's death, for the first time since that other world had gone silent, I'd felt a touch of the old magic.

A voice squawked from the toppled loudspeaker, scaring the hell out of me.

"Witches and warlocks, this concludes the first day of the Hooky Spooky. We hope you had fun. Vendors, please remain at your booths until our team checks in with you. And have a very *hoo-ooky spoo-ooky* night!"

I retreated to my booth, my heart pounding an alarm. I gripped the table's edge and clenched my eyes shut, willing myself to calm the fuck down.

Get ahold of yourself, get ahold of yourself, get ahold of yourself...

When at last my breathing slowed and the buzzing in my head stilled, I opened my eyes once more.

My attempt to arrange the Weird Sisters' trinkets into a pattern more pleasing to customers may have failed, but as I stood there staring down at the collection of cards and crystals and coins, I thought I read a message in the mayhem.

Danger.

2

I secured the booth for the night and bolted for the conference center's main lobby, sidestepping vendors, vamps, and various hangers-on. The Meadowlands Lounge was as packed as an airport bar in a snowstorm, the crowd greedily buying up the neon shots the servers had on offer. One of the more popular drink-slingers wore a tight top stating, "I Want Your Hex."

Hell had nothing on the Meadowlands Lounge.

I sensed a migraine bearing down, and I scurried for the elevators, passing waves of goth-wannabes making out, drinking up, and letting loose. I just wanted to get back to my room, check in with the Sisters, and fall asleep to an old movie. If the hotel didn't have TCM, I might hurl myself out the window.

I rang for the elevator, eager to ride it up, up, up and away. My room was on the fourth floor; I'd requested a move up to the top floor so I wouldn't have to endure the sound of people partying overhead, but alas, no cigar.

When the first elevator car came, I handed it off to a shell-shocked family of four who were just realizing they'd picked the wrong weekend to book a room at the Meadowlands. I grabbed the next, stabbed the button for my floor, and breathed a sigh of relief. I had it all to myself, had time to slow my breathing. My inner radio had been silent for so long that it was unsettling to have to suddenly switch back on at full volume.

Unsettling? It was fucking horrible, that's what it was.

"Hold it!" a voice cried, and a hand slipped between the closing doors. Chunky, aka JJ, wrestled with the elevator until it cried uncle and allowed him entry.

"Good, it *is* you," he huffed, shifting the weight of his monster backpack. "With everyone wearing black from head to toe, I wasn't quite sure."

"I only wear black when I'm working. It's the official uniform," I said, annoyed at being lumped in with the rabble downstairs.

I'd stopped dressing in dark clothing after I woke up one day expecting to see a short girl with black lipstick and gothy gear in the mirror and instead saw a short woman pushing thirty dressed like an employee of Spirit Halloween.

"It suits you."

Damn. Was he hitting on me? I had no idea, and it pissed me off. Wasn't it enough I had to share the ride with this guy who'd shaken my psychic senses awake without having to navigate my social blind spots?

"Not interested," I said curtly, reciting my two-word escape hatch.

"What? Oh. No, no, I just..." Those bubble cheeks of his turned red. Now it was his turn to feel awkward. Good. "I just wanted you to have this. You know, for helping me out."

He held up one of his DVDs, and I got a clear look at it for the first time. The title on the front read, *JJ Gadzinski: The Boy Who Went to Heaven.* A clipart child adorned the cover, arms upraised to the sun.

"Pass," I said, channeling the kid in the Jason T-shirt.

"Pass?"

"The last time I owned a DVD player was during the Obama administration."

He grinned and flipped the case around, revealing a QR code on the back. "No worries! You can stream it."

"If I can stream it, why do I need the DVD?"

"Uh..." His face twisted into a question mark.

"Fine," I said, already exhausted by the conversation.

I grabbed the DVD.

The boy is burning.

The thought struck cold and final, like metal against bone. My fingers gripped the case tight. The disc inside snapped like the bones of a small animal.

"What the hell?" JJ cried.

I shook my hand furiously, but if anything, my fingers only tightened their grip.

The air in the car was suddenly thick with smoke. The sharp scent of gasoline hit my nostrils, and heat rose from the floor. The lighted buttons on the control panel flashed in rapid succession—*three, one, five, three, one, one, two, three...*

The clamshell case folded in on itself as my muscles began to cramp.

The first flickers of flame reflected in JJ's glasses.

We're gonna burn. We're gonna burn.

The elevator shuddered, its machinery missing a beat, lurching the car with a single jolt.

Everything went still. A chime sounded, and I glanced up. Fourth floor.

The doors parted.

I brushed past JJ and escaped into the hallway. He was shouting after me, but I didn't hear a word.

I reached Room 403, fumbled for my key card, and pressed it against the sensor. The lock clicked. I swung open the door and slammed it shut behind me.

3

I downed two bowls of cereal before coming up for air, shoveling spoonful after spoonful of Lucky Charms into my mouth.

I stared at the mangled DVD case sitting on the desk. My first impulse had been to toss it out the window and be done with it, but apparently the Meadowlands frowned upon encouraging jumpers—the window was sealed shut.

What had caused the door to open? That much was obvious: it was JJ, of course. But I'd had visions before, countless numbers of them, yet this was different in a way I couldn't put my finger on.

It just tasted off.

I grabbed my phone. As expected, multiple texts from the Sisters awaited me. No doubt they were eager to badger me in an end-of-day call. Too bad. I powered down my phone and set it aside—the Sisters would have to wait.

I moved to the desk, opened my laptop, and showed its camera the code on the back of JJ's DVD.

The Sacred Shore Productions website popped up. SSP specialized in distributing "films to inspire," including such classics as *The White Light Promise, Angel at My Table,* as well as *JJ Gadzinski: The Boy Who Went to Heaven.*

The movie was pablum. Mike Walker, a certified "religious expert" with a syrupy voice, laid out the basics of JJ's story while serving up Bible verses and meaningful nods. Long and the short of it: JJ died, JJ came back, yay God.

I gave the movie ten minutes, then shut it off.

I poured another bowl of cereal and dove into Google. A few searches later, I had JJ Gadzinki's life story laid out in front of me.

The first item was an archived news interview. A five-year-old JJ and his parents sat in their living room fielding questions. The year was 2003. JJ's near-death experience had occurred the year prior.

"So, tell me, JJ, what was it like?" the reporter asked.

Little JJ, a tub of a kid clutching his threadbare doggy, looked as nervous as if he'd just been asked to spell "bourgeoisie."

"Well...Dad crashed the car—"

"We skidded on some ice," Dad amended.

"And we hit a truck."

"There was no salt on that road," JJ's mother said. "Jerry couldn't help—"

The reporter pressed on. "There was a crash. What happened next, JJ? What did you see?"

I felt for the kid. He looked like he'd rather be outside playing, upstairs reading, anywhere other than sitting on that cheap sofa getting peppered with questions.

"Fire," the boy whispered.

"And the people with wings?" his mother prodded. "Remember?"

"Yeah."

The reporter grinned—this story was gonna get her some views. "Angels? Are we talking about angels?"

"I don't know."

"Sure, you do," his mother said. "They took you up a ladder, and you went up into the clouds and saw Grandpa."

"And then what happened?" the reporter asked. "Did you see God?"

Leading the witness, I thought. I disliked everyone in this video. The only person I had any empathy for was the squirming kid.

The boy swallowed hard.

"I know where your hamster is."

"I'm sorry?"

"He's in the backseat."

The video cut to the reporter outside the Gadzinskis' modest home, autumn leaves falling about her in a cameraman's wet dream.

"I had my doubts going into this story, but..."—she paused, and I sensed it wasn't for effect—"two days ago, I picked up a hamster for my little girl's birthday. Unfortunately, it somehow got out of its box." She held up a squirming rodent to the camera. "Well, I just found Hambone here hiding in the backseat of my car. Miracle or coincidence? I'll let you decide. I'm Kelly Wyndham reporting from Wayne, New Jer—"

I closed my laptop.

"Fuck me."

The reason these visions felt so unfamiliar, *tasted* so unfamiliar, was because they weren't mine; they were his. I was sneaking psychic scraps off JJ's plate.

I munched on the marshmallow bits and mulled this over. By the time I hit the last sip of sweet milk at the bottom of the bowl, I'd come to a conclusion that satisfied me: did it really matter who opened the door as long as I still got to see inside?

I showered and slipped into my favorite gray comfort sweats, their plethora of holes ventilating my thighs quite nicely. I got under the covers and flipped on the TV. The selection was limited, so I settled for reruns of *The Andy Griffith Show* simply because it was in black-and-white. Today's TV was too jarring—a monochrome palette was easier on the eye.

I dozed, elements of stories mixing together as the old sitcom's soporific pace lulled me to sleep. I dreamed of Sheriff Andy Taylor showing me around Mayberry, introducing me to Floyd the Barber, giving me a tour of his beloved police station.

"And this ol' boy here is Otis," Andy drawled, sticking his thumb toward a miserable sot sitting behind bars. "Otis has been a *bad* boy, ain't you, Otis?"

Otis looked up, his face drawn in all its bewhiskered, hungover glory, and it *wasn't* Otis, it was JJ Gadzinski; it was Chunky sitting on the cot, enormous backpack clinging to him like some symbiotic creature, and he was staring at me with a toothy grin plastered on his face.

"No worries!" he shouted. "You can stream it!" He hurled DVDs at the bars. One made it through and hit me on the boob. I reeled back, the impact like lightning.

I woke in a sweat. I leaped out of bed, dashed for the bathroom, and made it to the toilet just in time to sacrifice three bowls of cereal to the porcelain gods.

I sat back against the tub, legs splayed out in front of me, the cold tile floor chilling my butt. I yanked down the towel from the shower curtain rod where I'd left it to dry and buried my face in its still-damp coolness.

Whatever psychic contact high I'd gotten from hanging around JJ wasn't abating, and my inner self—my *spooky* self— had come a-knocking.

Suddenly there came a tapping, as of some one gently rapping, rapping at my chamber door...

"Shut up."

I took a deep breath and absorbed the cool calm of the room.

I've always found bathrooms comforting. Wrapped in their soap-scented embrace, a person can hide out for as long as necessary. They're little Faraday cages capable of blocking out radioactive reality.

I rose and locked the door.

Enough.

I leaned my head against the door and spoke the mantra aloud.

"Enough, enough, enough..."

The air in the room shifted, transitioned—I don't know how the hell to describe it, but it *changed*. The scent of body wash retreated, giving way to the sharp tang of disinfectant. The air grew heavy, and my armpits dampened.

I stepped to the sink, ran the cold water, and held the metal spigot until it turned icy. I filled my hands with water and submerged my face in the coolness.

Gasoline.

Gagging, I opened my fingers, spilling the foul-tasting stuff into the sink.

Fucking Chunky. What have you done to me?

I caught a glimpse of the door in the mirror behind me. A blue sign had appeared, plastered to the door's surface. Whipping around, I came face-to-face with it.

"Wash Your Hands Before Leaving This Room."

The sign wasn't there a moment ago.

This was no longer my bathroom.

This was nowhere that I wanted to be.

Still, I opened the door. The room beyond was white—walls and curtains made even more white by the overhead fluorescents.

Ahead of me sat a bed with rails on either side and in it, curled up like a pile of laundry, was my mother. She stared up at the lights, mouth agape as if bemoaning their brightness.

But nothing would annoy Rita anymore; Rita was dead.

A nurse with her hair pulled back in a bun entered the room from the hall, working hand sanitizer into every pore.

"Sorry, dear," she said, stationing herself at Mom's bedside. "She's been gone since three."

The clock radio I'd bought her so she could listen to her political shows sat on the nightstand. It read 3:08. She'd been dead less than ten minutes.

"My Uber driver got lost," I stammered.

The last hints of red faded from my mother's cheeks, entropy stealing her away and leaving behind a waxen double. Her eyes stared and her mouth hung lax, but the nurse made quick work of that. Coaxing mouth and eyelids shut, she closed Mom's face like a book.

I caught a whiff of something like an electrical outlet overloading, burning rubber and ozone, and tasted its foulness on my tongue, as noxious and thick as a cheap cigarette.

I should be able to hear her. I didn't understand. Mom lay before me, sprawled in her ill-fitting hospital gown, her body a battleground of bandages and tubes, but I couldn't hear a damn thing.

"Where'd you go?" I asked.

The nurse spoke perfunctory condolences. "Mama's gone to heaven. Sad day. Say goodbye, now—I have things I need to do for her."

I grabbed my mother by the shoulders and shook.

"Where are you?"

"No, no," the nurse said, grabbing my arm. "None of that."

I shrugged her off.

"Not fair!" was all I could manage. And it wasn't fair. Spirits had played soundtrack to my entire life, and now, when I had actual skin in the game, when the dearly departed was my own flesh and blood, I got the silent treatment.

I shook her again, my tears dampening her breast. The nurse was no longer passive. She had skin in the game now too.

"You mustn't!" she spat in a sharp staccato. "My patient!"

"*Your patient is dead*," I shot back, shocking myself with the finality of it. I stepped away from the bed, muscles twitching, adrenaline pulsing through my veins.

The nurse ordered me to sit, reaching for the call button as she did so, but I ignored her. Instead, I bolted for the bathroom, slamming and locking the door behind me.

The nurse pounded outside while I clenched my eyes shut, hands pressed to my ears.

Where did she go? Where did she go?

"Ellen?"

The lavender scent of hotel soap wafted over me as I caught my breath and slowly opened my eyes.

I was back.

"I tried calling your room," the voice continued, muffled but insistent. "Are you up? Ellen?"

I stepped out of the bathroom and peered through the peephole. JJ Gadzinski stood anxiously waiting in the hall. Undoing the deadbolt, I opened the door.

"You've got to come down to the lobby with me."

"Why?"

He flashed a toothy grin.

"Something's happening!"

4

I dragged JJ into the room and slammed him against the wall so hard he let out a wheeze.

"Ow!" he complained. "That hurt."

"What the hell did you do to me?"

"Huh?" The fact that he looked more bewildered than concerned made me even more cross.

"Eight years. Eight years and not a peep. Then *you* pop up, and suddenly, I can't shut it up."

"What are you talking about?" he asked, wriggling out of my grip. "You sound like you're still asleep."

"I haven't heard a thing since my mom died. Zip, zero, nada. The other side canceled my membership. You know what? Fine by me! Who needs dead babies crying you to sleep, dead perverts following you around campus—"

"Slow down."

"And then *you* show up and—"

JJ put a calming hand on my shoulder. "Are you done?"

"Yeah."

"Good. Because that was—"

"I know."

"That was a lot."

"Sorry." I shrugged off his hand. My face burned beneath his gaze.

"Look," he said, edging toward the door, "I obviously caught you at a...weird time. Why don't I catch up with you later?"

I had a startling revelation: I *did not* want to be alone. I grabbed his arm.

"You can't just knock on someone's door and say something's happening and not tell them what's happening. You just don't do that."

I was panicking. Any moment, it would be just me, this room, and whatever might care to crawl out the shadows.

"Sorry. I just thought you might get a kick out of what's going on downstairs."

I grabbed my shoes and slipped them on.

"Show me."

The lobby was oddly vacant, as if someone had performed a successful exorcism of the Meadowlands Conference Center. Gone were the barflies swarming the lounge and the goth couples swapping spit in the shadows.

"This way," JJ said, hustling me down a corridor branching off from the lobby.

"You gonna tell me where we're going?"

"Not yet!"

Why did people find surprises so much fun? They rarely lived up to the hype and were hardly ever enjoyable for the surprisee. But something had lit a fire under Chunky, and who was I to argue?

"Could you stop calling me that?" he said over his shoulder, rounding another corner.

"I didn't say anything."

He stopped short and turned back to me. "Chunky. You've been saying it all the time. Will you please cut it out?"

"I told you I didn't say—"

The realization hit us both at once. No discussion needed; we were cut from the same cursed cloth.

"Won't happen again," I promised.

We heard the crowd in Lecture Hall A before we saw them —a low rumble of conversation and anticipation. The sign out front announced a "Special Recording of the Dark Revels Podcast." JJ cracked open the door, and the scent of patchouli nearly knocked me to my knees.

The hall was packed. Every manner of paranormal fanatic was there, every Wednesday Addams, every Vampira, every wannabe Aleister Crowley. While the podcast crew fussed with their cords and equipment, the crowd batted about oversized beach balls from one side of the hall to the other.

I was embarrassed for the lot of them.

"No," I said.

"Come on," JJ insisted. "We don't have to stay for the whole thing."

"We're sitting in the back row."

"Fine."

A roomful of eyes glanced our way as we took our seats. I chalked it up to the fact I hadn't bothered to change out of my holey sweatpants.

"I take it we're not here for the ambiance."

JJ pointed to the banner hanging behind the recording setup: "Recording Preceded by a Midnight Challenge from our Sponsors."

"I think this crowd is challenged enough as is," I said, and when JJ didn't respond, I repeated it.

The sound system popped, and the attendees roared.

"Thanks for your patience," the MC said. He was rail thin with plastered-back hair and a skeleton vest. "I'll give our standard podcast etiquette spiel in a bit, but first...our special *Midnight Challenge*!"

The crowd erupted with applause.

"Here we go!" JJ squirmed in his seat like a puppy needing to pee.

A bearded keyboardist in steampunk regalia hammered out ominous chords, testing the limits of my eardrums. The mob responded with substance-induced hoots and hollers.

Great. I was at a rave.

The MC hushed the crowd. "And now, to present our challenge, I'd like to welcome to the stage the Mistress of the Meadowlands, the Tsarina of the Turnpike: the Halloween Queen!"

I turned to JJ. "This is *really* pushing it."

"Quiet!"

The Queen made a show of mounting the stage. She had swapped her convention garb for something more diaphanous with a neckline that plunged beyond reason. The keyboard player walked her on with the *Halloween* theme, dropping my estimation of him and this whole event to even lower depths.

"Thank you, thank you, my little devils!"

She drew a card from her sleeve and held it aloft.

"Our special sponsor—who wishes to remain anonymous —wanted me to read tonight's Midnight Challenge. And so, read it I shall."

The Queen continued, dropping her voice to a mysterious whisper:

"Deep in these halls
A true treasure is hid
Within a small box
With a latch to its lid."

"Puh-lease," I groaned.

A photo of a plain box with a brass latch appeared on the screen behind the Queen. The crowd replied with oohs and aahs.

"Cast your mind forth
And open your eyes
For the winner shall reap
An incredible prize."

"Who's this secret sponsor, Dr. Suess?"

JJ huffed. "Ellen, will you—"

"Okay, okay."

The Queen crossed, her spot following her.

"Somewhere at the Meadowlands complex, our sponsor has placed a wooden box containing a secret object," she whispered. "The rules of the challenge are simple: unleash your talents and search out the item contained within the box."

I groused silently to myself. I had no idea why JJ thought I might enjoy this display of hokum. This was yet more pseudo-psychic razzle-dazzle masquerading as serious inquiry, and it was giving me a headache.

"This could be fun," JJ enthused.

"I question your use of the word," I said, rubbing my temple as a shard of pain slipped behind my eye.

"Once you have the object clearly in mind, text your answer to this number." She flung her arms wide as the projector flashed five digits on the screen. "Only one text per person. Submissions will be accepted until the right answer is received. The person who solves the mystery shall receive"—she made a motion to the keyboard player, who supplied her with an atonal chord—"three thousand dollars and free admission to next year's Hooky Spooky!"

The room erupted in cheers. Phones lit up like fireflies.

Everyone was all abuzz, including JJ. He elbowed me in the side as he extracted his phone. "Aren't you going to save the number?"

"I left my phone in my room."

"I'll text it to you. What's your number?"

I didn't answer, stunned by how fast the migraine had hit.

"Don't you want me to text it to you? Three thousand dollars!"

I gave him my number, if only to quiet him. I focused on the stage through my steadily narrowing vision, hoping to stop the room from spinning. The Queen had morphed into a black-and-white blur surrounded by an ever-growing fractal aura. The shard in my skull burrowed deeper still.

"I gotta get outta here," I said, louder than I had expected. Jesus, I had to hold the seatback in front of me to keep from toppling into the aisle.

My abrupt exit caught the Queen's attention, and she incorporated the interruption into her schtick.

"Go forth, you 'sage-burning crystal-clutchers.' Go and prove the doubters wrong!"

With her voice still ringing in my ears, I bolted for the exit and fled down the hall.

5

I hit the lobby and made straight for the bar. Mama needed her medicine, stat.

"Shot of Fireball."

The bartender set down the shot glass with a sympathetic nod. "Looks like you need this."

"Don't go anywhere," I said, downing the liquid fire in a single gulp.

JJ materialized behind me.

"What happened to you?"

"Headache."

"I thought alcohol was bad for headaches—"

"JJ, shut up." I nodded to the bartender. "Another."

I threw back the second shot. You had to hand it to the folks at Fireball, their tagline nailed it: "Tastes like Heaven, Burns like Hell."

"Any interest in cracking this together?" He waggled his

phone in front of me, the challenge's number saved in a text file.

"Not in the slightest."

"Oh. Okay."

I waved off the bartender's offer of a third shot. "Look, I'm beat. I'm going to call it a night."

"Maybe we could circle back over breakfast. I really think I might have a shot at—"

I was already heading for the stairs. "Fine. Breakfast."

"Cool. How about seven?"

I threw him a quick thumbs-up and pushed open the door to the stairwell.

When I reached the fourth floor, the elevator doors opened, and—surprise, surprise—out stepped JJ.

"Why are you on my floor?"

"Because it's my floor, too," he said, more question than statement.

I shook my head and walked down the hall to my room. The pitter-pat of my new buddy's shoes fell in behind me. As I pressed my key card to the lock, JJ slipped past me and did the same at his door. I was Room 403; he was 405. Unbelievable.

I opened the door, and the room responded with a short bleep. The smoke detector probably needed a new battery, but for a moment, I could have sworn I'd just heard the electronic pulse of a heart monitor.

The thought was enough to make me pause in the doorway.

Enough.

"Hey, if you need anything, just knock on the wall."

I was about to shoot back with a sardonic rejoinder, but the concerned look on his face was so genuine, I swallowed my retort.

"'Night," I said.

"Good night, Ellen."

I went about the room and flicked on all the lights. I even left the bathroom's exhaust fan running as a makeshift white noise machine. I turned on the TV and settled for a documentary about 9/11. I'd been in middle school when the planes hit the towers. The screams reached me all the way in Iowa.

I kicked off my shoes and crawled into bed. My mouth tasted like cinnamon, but I had no interest in retrieving my toothbrush. The bathroom could go fuck itself, for all I cared.

Curling into a ball, I pulled the covers tight, cocooning myself against the outside world.

"I'm sorry I didn't make it there in time, Mom. Is that what you want to hear?" I asked the empty room.

The five hollow knocks that answered nearly made me piss myself before I recognized the pattern.

Shave and a haircut...

I rapped twice. Fucking Chunky.

Don't call me Chunky.

Sorry.

I burrowed deeper inside the comforter and wondered what infraction I had committed to be saddled with JJ Gadzinski. But as I surrendered to sleep, I was glad he was on the other side of the wall.

I woke to the jarring jangle of my phone. I squinted at the screen. Incoming call from the Sisters.

Shit, shit, shit.

I hadn't called them back. Damn it, I thought, what the hell time is it?

My phone was happy to oblige—it was 6:22.

Acknowledging that I'd have to pay the piper sooner or later, I touched the slider to connect the call and—

I left my phone turned off last night.

I was no longer in bed. Instead, I was sitting in the loveseat, next to the desk.

The Sisters' call screamed for my attention, and I quickly picked up.

"Sorry, I must have slept in."

"Are you seriously kidding me right now?" It was Jamie sans her sister-partner. "You're lucky I'm calling you and not Mika. This is a nightmare!"

"What did I do this time?" I was in no mood for guessing games. Besides, I was still trying to wrap my head around my nocturnal maneuvers.

"Very funny. I suppose you haven't read a single one of my texts—"

"Jamie," I cut in, "I just woke up. You're going to have to give me a minute—"

"Shit, Mika's calling. When I'm done with her, you and I are going to have a chat."

Click. Perfect. I'd been thinking my LinkedIn page was due for an update anyway. Where I'd wrangle next month's rent was anybody's guess, but playing the Sisters' piñata was getting old fast.

I flipped to my text messages and my jaw dropped. Between the two of them, the Sisters had sent me twenty-eight messages. Some had attachments. I clicked on the first, and enlightenment hit me like a nuclear blast.

The video was labelled, "Karen vs. The Queen: The Meltdown That Shocked The Con."

There I was, in all my glory, letting the Halloween Queen have it with both barrels.

"The internet is littered with your cosplay nonsense. If you ever came face-to-face with an honest-to-God ghost, you'd piss your pants."

Oh, no...

"We've got a shit-ton of your favorite crap over at Booth 38. One-stop shopping for gullible goons."

I scrolled through the rest of my messages. Yup, I'd gone viral. The Queen had blasted the video far and wide—I was on social media platforms I'd never even heard of before.

I came to the end of the Sisters' messages and found two more text threads awaiting me. The first was from JJ, sending me the number for the Midnight Challenge along with a gif of Mr. Monopoly tossing money in the air.

I opened the second and froze.

At 3:42 a.m., I had texted a single word to the number JJ had provided.

I had no memory of leaving bed or activating my phone. I'd never sleepwalked in my life, yet the evidence was clear—I'd been up and texting in the middle of the night.

I read my message over and over, trying to make heads or tails of it and failing miserably.

Hate.

6

I waited for JJ until seven thirty. When he didn't show, I
texted; when he didn't answer my texts, I gave up and
sought out breakfast. I didn't blame him for bailing on me—I
was the pariah of the paranormal conference. Who in their
right mind would deign to dine with me after that video made
the rounds?

The Meadowlands Buffet was a zoo. The place was a
glorified high school cafeteria complete with plastic trays and
juice machines offering something vaguely reminiscent of OJ.
After passing over the steaming trays of scrambled eggs and
stacks of stale waffles, I settled on two bowls of Froot Loops
and a plate of wilted bacon.

Every table contained groups comfortable in each other's
company. The thought of inserting myself into one of their
circles made me want to dash my breakfast into a bin and be
gone. Besides, my indecision had frozen me in place—I'd

become a beacon for those who had caught my little tirade. It felt like the whole room was staring.

A couple rose from a small table by the fogged-up windows overlooking the indoor pool. I sprang at the opportunity and claimed the table before they had completely abandoned it.

"Don't mind us," the man said, clearing the last of their dishes.

"Thanks," I said, uncertain if that was the correct response and past caring.

I nibbled on my bacon as I puzzled over my late-night text. I'd sent it; of that, there was no doubt. The proof was there in my phone. But why did I send it, and what did it mean?

Hate.

Was Dream Ellen angry? Awake Ellen was pissed, sure, but angry? No. Had watching the crowd lap up the Queen's drivel gotten under my skin to the point that Dream Ellen had to lash out? I didn't think so. The Halloween Queen was just a symptom of the rot spreading through the community.

"Anyone sitting here?"

The interruption broke my concentration, and I bit down on my tongue instead of the bacon. When I didn't answer, the young woman simply set down her overflowing tray and sat.

She was twentyish, with eyes that bulged just enough to be striking without suggesting insect. Her hair was a frazzle of red, and she sported an old leather jacket festooned with buttons of bands I'd never heard of. Beneath her perfume I detected a whiff of cigarettes and BO.

"What, are you trying to memorize me?"

"Excuse me?"

"You haven't blinked since I sat down." She eyed my plate. "Shit, I should've gotten bacon. You gonna finish that?"

My head shook of its own accord, and the interloper swiped two of the three strips.

"Zivy," she said, answering my unasked question. "You part of this circus?"

I nodded. My brain was misfiring. What sort of person just up and sits with you? Who does that?

"Interesting bunch," she said as she ripped open a carton of chocolate milk with her teeth. "Feels like Halloween back in grade school, you know? When everyone came to class in costume?"

Her tray was piled high with fruit and muffins. She threw back a gulp of milk and grinned.

"Not much of a talker, huh? No worries. I'll be out of your hair soon." She proceeded to squirrel a banana, an apple, and a couple bagels into her jacket pockets. "A rolling stone, you know?"

I didn't know. I didn't understand anything about this.

"I'm sitting here," I blurted, possibly a tad late.

"Ah. Definitely part of the circus."

I slammed the table with my fist, making the silverware jump. I hadn't meant to do it; I even surprised myself. It wasn't simply that my space had been invaded, it was Jamie's call and the fact that JJ hadn't shown up and—

"Whoa," Zivy said. "No need to get angry."

Angry. Anger. Danger. Hate!

"I don't know what's going on," I blustered.

"Chill."

"I can't chill! Why would I chill? Everything's turning sideways. 'Open your eyes,' she said. 'Think of the box,' she said. Why would that make me angry? I'm not angry. I'm *not* angry!"

She snorted. "Well, you sure fooled me."

"I can't...I can't..."

I was shaking—literally shaking—in the middle of the Meadowlands cafeteria. What was happening to me? I was becoming untethered, like one of those Thanksgiving Day balloons scooped up by the wind and carried off into the sky.

The gal with the red hair leaned in close.

"Jeez, you're really losing it, aren't you, chick? Would you like a mini muffin?"

"No...I...why would I want a muffin?"

She shrugged. "I don't know. Just trying to ease you off that ledge of yours. When in doubt, offer baked goods."

She waggled a tiny blueberry muffin, eyebrows raised. The image was so absurd I had to laugh.

"There she is," Zivy said, patting my hand. She popped the muffin in her mouth and chased it with some apple juice. "Not to play psychotherapist—I fucking hate those motherfuckers —but you seem to have a lot on your plate."

"Yes."

"Maybe you just need a little perspective."

"Yes!"

She leaned back, arms spread wide. "Well, you're looking at it."

"I don't understand."

"Me? I don't even belong here. I don't have a room, hell, I didn't pay for this food."

"No?" Whatever voodoo she was working was doing the trick. My pulse eased back to normal.

"Conventions like this? It's a lot easier to slip by the cashier in a crowd. Kind of like at IKEA. God, I love those meatballs. You been to IKEA?"

IKEA? My mind was still rebooting. What the hell was IKEA?

"Look, I've got thirty bucks in my pocket, a car in the parking lot with half a tank of gas, and zero, I mean *zero*, chance of getting up to Maine without having to suck someone's dick. How's *that* for perspective?"

I sat in stunned silence.

"Damn," she said. "I was sure the dick-sucking bit would get a laugh."

I'm sure I blushed. I know I felt better. It didn't make sense, but I did.

I tried to speak but was all out of words. I only managed a whispered, "Thanks."

She placed her hand over mine. "Hey, we weirdos gotta stick together, you know what I mean—"

A loud *crack!* rang out and Zivy jerked. I turned toward the source of the sound. A hapless gal with a mohawk stood over her dropped tray; scrambled eggs spread about her like an aura.

Zivy's fingers tightened on mine; cartilage clicked. She squeezed, her chipped nails digging into my palm.

Danger.

Her eyes...changed. Did they bulge even more? Did her

pupils dilate? I've wondered about that to this day. All I know is that something shifted beneath her gaze as her grip tightened.

"Cast your mind forth...you fuck!"

Her voice dropped lower than it had been. Raspier. And the grin I'd found so comforting twisted upward into a mockery of itself.

"And open your eyes...you bitch!"

She jerked back her hand, fingers twitching and clenching in the air. With great effort, she drew in all but her forefinger which shook accusatorially.

She stabbed downward with her finger, the tip making a sickening thwack as it hit the tabletop. *One-two-three-four*—she moved her finger in rhythm with her breath—*one-two-three-four*—her nail scratching the table beneath...

"Mama lies pale in the bed-bed-bed, not a single hair on her head-head-head, bald and reflecting the light-light-light..."

"Stop it."

"Mama's gonna die tonight-night-night!"

She pressed so hard her nail split, drawing blood. Still, she continued, smearing crimson across the table's surface.

I shouldn't have grabbed her wrist, but I did. Shouldn't have twisted, but I did. The result for her was instant and unpleasant.

Zivy yelped in pain and drew back her hand, nails raking my palm in the process. She leapt up, staring like a child waking from a nightmare, unsure if what they're seeing is real or part of the dream.

"I gotta go," she said, wiping the blood on her pants. She

dashed off, fruit falling from her jacket pockets, her hair a wildfire chasing her out the door.

For a long moment, I couldn't breathe; I simply sat there, listening to the blood roar in my ears, the strong smell of hospital antiseptic wafting about me.

Mama's gonna die tonight-night-night!

I released my breath with a *whumph*. My body's instinct was to give in to hyperventilation, but I curbed the impulse, choosing instead to take slow, measured breaths. Panic would lead back to the psychic pool where Mother awaited me—cold and dead and silent as the grave.

I stared at the image Zivy had scrawled on the table: a crude four-pointed shape. A diamond drawn in blood.

I sensed chess pieces moving into place but had no idea who or what was playing.

My phone chirped, an incoming text. A reminder from the conference that the morning vendor session would be beginning shortly. As much as I wanted to remain seated, remain *immobile,* I had to get up.

I cleared the table until I had a good view of the blood painting my new acquaintance had left. I switched on my camera and took a quick snapshot. Once captured, the red diamond stared back at me, daring me to delete it.

"Not a chance," I said.

7

It was five minutes before the East Room's doors opened, and the chintzy plastic payment square they'd sent me with wasn't connecting to the phone. I quickly rearranged the makeup of the table, putting the crystals up front where no one could ignore them—the front line of my merchandise.

I glanced around the room, hoping to catch a glimpse of Zivy's shock of red hair, but after the incident in the cafeteria, I was betting the girl in the leather jacket was gone with the wind. Probably smoking up a storm as she headed north to Maine.

Zivy's outburst had unnerved me. Had something latched onto her? Had I triggered her like JJ had triggered me? Or was she simply looney tunes? With my abilities playing hide and seek, I was left with a lot of questions and no answers.

In my distraction, I had rearranged the crystals into a diamond pattern. Like it or not, I had Zivy on the brain.

My phone chimed, and I picked up, hoping it was an

apologetic reply from JJ, but instead found a text from a familiar five-digit number.

Challenge complete. Thanks for participating.

That was fast. Some lucky SOB was three thousand dollars richer.

A follow-up message announced that Meredith Wohl, a hobbyist card reader, had clinched the prize. Her answer to the mystery box contents? An infant's skull, although the item in the box was revealed to be a resin replica.

A text went out to all participants with a photo of the winner and a gentle reminder to *stop* messaging answers. The challenge was definitely, positively, absolutely over.

The vendors showed less enthusiasm as we began Day Two. The Houdini energy drinks guy hadn't shown up at all; only a stack of leaflets atop his empty table commemorated his presence.

"What'd you guess?" Magic Feather Lady asked as I set up for day two of lackluster sales. "I chose a lighter. You know? An old-time cigarette lighter."

"I didn't play," I lied.

"A kid's skull." The woman shook her head. "That's messed up."

"Yup."

"I know it's the Hooky Spooky, but that's messed up."

I half expected the Sisters to phone the moment the doors opened to ensure I was at my post, but they were thankfully silent. That gave me time to text JJ.

Guess we lost. Where r u? Lunch at noon?

I waited for a reply or even those anticipation dots indicating he was considering texting back, but...tumbleweeds.

I flipped through my photo album and landed on Zivy's bloody diamond. By now, some poor cafeteria worker had probably bleached it away. Yet there it remained, trapped within my phone—red and ragged and full of rage.

One hour into the morning session, as I swapped out the tarot decks for sets of runes, a young man in a crisp shirt approached my booth. A red flag went up; his attention was on me, not my merchandise.

"Ms. Marx?"

"Who's asking?"

He lifted his convention ID and held it out. "I'm Jeff Long, one of the coordinators. Could I possibly speak with you outside?"

"I don't know, Jeff," I said, gesturing at the empty aisle before me. "Things are just starting to pick up."

"Only take a minute."

Magic Feather Lady, who'd been watching the encounter, dropped her gaze and gave a silent *ohhh*. She wasn't the only one who sensed I was being marched to the principal's office. But what for? Aiding and abetting the theft of cafeteria food? Dressing down one of their headliners? Had my run-in with the Halloween Queen become a black eye for the Hooky Spooky?

I scanned the crowd for JJ as I followed the man out the East Room doors, but JJ had ghosted me good and proper.

"Am I being taken to the woodshed?" I asked as my stiff-collared companion led me across the lobby floor.

"They told me to bring you to one of the conference rooms."

"Who's they, Jeff?"

"My manager."

Ah, so the word had come down from one of the Hooky Spooky managers, some gruff executive with a pointed hat and crystal ball. I supposed I'd learn my infraction soon enough.

After a few winding hallways, we reached Conference Room 6a. My escort opened the door for me.

"Wait inside, please."

I considered a quip about what might await me—witchy waterboarding or the like—and decided against it. Partly because Jeff didn't seem like someone who'd appreciate my attempt at humor, but mostly because, as I stepped into the room, I had to reassess my situation.

Sitting at the long conference table in the windowless room were JJ and William Quan.

"Hey, Ellen," JJ said as he gave a little wave.

"What is this?" I asked.

"I suspect we'll find out shortly," Quan answered, his tone dismissive, as if neither my question nor this meeting deserved his attention. Some people can't hide their smugness if they try.

I let the door close behind me and took a seat next to JJ. He drummed his fingers on the tabletop in excitement.

"Thanks for leaving me stranded at breakfast," I said. "Gave me the chance to meet some interesting people."

"Huh? Oh, sorry," he replied. "When they came to get me, I realized I'd left my phone in my room."

"You've been here this whole time?"

"They brought me snacks." He produced a half-eaten package of cheese and peanut butter crackers. "Want some?"

"I'm good."

The door opened and a tall man with a hefty over-the-shoulder bag entered. His attire was simple black and white, reminiscent of that of a limo driver's uniform. He wore the tired expression and five o'clock shadow of a college professor and sported round, academic glasses to boot. He closed the door with an apologetic grin.

"Sorry to keep you all waiting. With this many of you, we had to rejigger a bit."

He removed a leather binder from his bag. He set it on the table, unzipped it, and stared at its contents as his captive audience sat in silence. After a couple minutes of paper shuffling, Quan spoke up.

"I've got a book signing in twenty minutes."

The man with the binder didn't look up, just kept leafing through papers.

"Just a sec."

Quan rose. "I don't have a sec. How about you tell us why you've dragged us in so we can get back to work?"

His word choice struck me as funny. *Work?* Back in my heyday I was busy as all get-out, rooting out spirits, cleansing homes, chatting with dead loved ones and bringing closure. Not once during that time had I ever considered it *work*. It was just what I did.

"I'm glad you find this amusing," Quan said, staring me down. I must have chuckled aloud.

The man at the head of the table removed his glasses, tapping them against his lips.

"Right. Introductions," he said. "My name is Mr. Carter, and, if we got this right, you are Julian Gadzinski, William Quan, and Ellen Marx."

We all nodded. If Quan had wanted Mr. Carter to make it quick, it looked like he was going to be sorely disappointed.

I leaned over to JJ and whispered, "Julian?"

He shushed me.

"I apologize for the subterfuge, but we had to be certain we were making the right choice." He paused and, for the first time, made direct eye contact. "I trust you recognize this."

He reached into his bag, pulled out a small wooden box, and placed it in front of him.

Upon its appearance, I braced myself for the return of my headache. But it didn't come. Instead, a cool mist kissed my face, as if I had just stepped into fogbank. I touched my cheek, and my fingers came away wet. I was crying.

The Midnight Challenge hadn't ended after all.

Mr. Carter deftly unlatched the box, lifted its lid, and reached inside.

"I realize this might not be what you're expecting..."

He lifted out the object.

"But each of you, in your own way, was right on the money."

What he pulled from the box was not, in fact, a child's skull nor a replica of one. It was a shard of colored glass. Red. A broken section of a stained-glass window.

"You with me so far?"

I couldn't process it. It felt like a trick, like some switcheroo was taking place.

"Let me pass it around."

Mr. Carter handed the glass to Quan, who held it in both hands, seeming to absorb its meaning. Quan passed it to JJ, who gave a short *ahh* before giving it to me.

My fingers trembled as I gripped it. Not because it gave off any sinister vibe, but because I had fucking seen it before.

It was a fractured remnant of crimson glass, dark lead embracing its edges. Three sharp points remained while the uppermost corner was absent.

What I held in my hand was a diamond, fashioned of blood-red glass.

"We hid our test inside a fake one. The sponsor of the Midnight Challenge? That was us. The winner of the challenge?"

"Meredith Wohl," I whispered, gripping the glass.

"We picked a winner at random. Who knew plastic baby skulls were a thing? I had to send someone into the city to pick it up. Still, better than some of the other answers."

Cast your mind forth...you fuck!

I stared at the shard, seeing only Zivy's bloody version.

And open your eyes...you bitch!

"We weren't looking for a description of the object, just its essence. We would have accepted many different answers. Hate, rancor, rage. The texts we received from you three included anger..." He nodded toward JJ, who was excitedly nibbling crackers. "Wrath..." he continued, looking at Quan. "And hate."

His eyes had landed on me, but I didn't look up from the glass. It was dawning on me that this guy wasn't the one in charge; he was just another coordinator.

"You say 'we' an awful lot," I said. "Who's 'we'?"

Mr. Carter scratched the stubble on his cheek.

"That would be me and my boss. James Utter."

JJ gripped my leg beneath the table. Quan sat way back in his chair.

"Great," I said. "Who the hell is James Utter?"

8

JJ spat cracker crumbs. "James Utter. *The* James Utter." As if his emphasis should dispel any confusion.

"Oh, *the* James Utter," I said, brushing JJ's hand from my thigh. "That's a different story. Thanks for the clarification." I might have laid on the sarcasm a bit thick. Mother always said modulation wasn't my forte.

JJ shook his head in disbelief. "You've never heard of *The Wakefield Witches*? *The Unquiet Grave*?"

"Should I have?"

"They're only some of the most seminal books in horror history," Quan added.

JJ jumped back in. "He's up there with King and Barker and...well, he's way up there."

Fiction. That explained it. I had no time for fiction, never had. Why read something someone made up? The last fiction I touched was back in high school before discovering the wonder of CliffsNotes. *Of Mice and Men*. A grim story that only got grimmer. Give me the good old *Malleus Maleficarum* any day.

"May I continue?" Mr. Carter said with no small hint of annoyance.

He held out a hand, presuming I'd pass back the glass. But I didn't. I was mesmerized by it.

Carter continued, unabated. "As I said, we're in new territory here. I was tasked with bringing back someone who might be of assistance to my employer. You see, he has a... predicament that requires your special gifts."

I turned the shard in my hand. Had it grown warmer? The leaded framework remained cool to the touch, but the glass radiated a low heat that excited my fingers. Any warmer and I might be able to bend it.

"Here's the proposition: one week of your time in exchange for twenty-five thousand dollars."

JJ whistled; Quan sat stoically silent.

"If you agree, you'll accompany me to Utter Hall where food and lodging will be provided. If you have merchandise that needs storing or flights that need changing, we will handle it. I understand I haven't given you much time to process this, but as your answers came in, we had to move. Time is something Mr. Utter does not have in abundance."

"What's this predicament?" Quan asked.

"It's a haunting, right?" JJ asked. "I mean, it's got to be."

"That's not for me to say. Mr. Utter—"

"What about my team?" Quan asked. "My consultations require a team."

"Mr. Utter wants only you. We hoped the three of you

might work together to suss out the situation. Any other questions?"

Quan had tons. Could he bring his equipment? Could he film inside the house? Was there any sort of bonus situation for the one who solved the mystery?

His voice faded into the background as I stared into the glass. Its ruby waves enticed, urging me to take the plunge. Through the red rippled surface, a figure appeared, amorphous, like a swimmer returning from the depths. It was a woman—her outline was undeniable. The longer I stared, the more she came into focus.

The glass grew hotter as I traced its broken edge, knife-sharp, bisecting my fingerprint. No blood yet, but if I only pressed harder—

"Ms. Marx?"

Mr. Carter's voice yanked me back. He was brandishing a document. Quan and JJ were already signing theirs.

"The liability waiver and an NDA," Mr. Carter said. "Do you have a problem with either?"

I stood and rounded the table, ignoring the papers in the man's outstretched hand. The glass was my only concern.

"May I have that back, please?" Carter asked.

No, you may not.

I bounded out the door and, with Carter's and JJ's voices behind me, took off down the hall, glass upraised, following the figure trapped inside. For the woman was walking away, and I was determined to follow.

"Ellen!" JJ or Mr. Carter? Didn't know, didn't care. I

wasn't letting them take it away from me. I'd already lost so much.

A door presented itself halfway down the next hallway, and luckily, as I tried the knob, it opened. For the woman had turned, you see? I had no choice.

Upon entering the room, the lights switched on automatically. Another bathroom—wouldn't you know. A service restroom, judging from its spartan appearance. It would do. I locked the door a second before the pounding began.

I gazed deep into the glass and the woman moved toward me, backing me into the stall. I sat on the toilet, and still she came—a vision cloaked in swirling darkness.

Once again, tears rose. I didn't know what I was seeing. Didn't care. Because if I could see *this*, I could still see *her*.

I'm sorry, Mom. I'm sorry I stopped coming to the hospital.

The metal stall began to hum.

I'm sorry we fought. I'm sorry you couldn't love me.

The vibration filled my chest.

I'm sorry I didn't say goodbye.

Something burst. For a moment, I was certain the glass had shattered, the woman on the other forcing her way through. Only when JJ forced open the stall door did I realize the rupture was happening inside me.

I had to go to Utter Hall.

"It's okay." JJ spoke soft and low. "You can just sit there as long as you like."

Mr. Carter appeared behind him. "I'd rather know now if she's in or out—"

JJ whirled on the man. "If she needs a minute, she gets a

minute. If you've got a problem with that, then you can go pound sand."

Chunky. I didn't know he had it in him.

Shaking his head, Carter disappeared into the hall. JJ met my eyes, and for once, I didn't feel the urge to look away.

"You don't have to go. Neither of us do."

"I want to," I said. "But—"

"But what?"

Did I dare risk it?

"I'm afraid." The words tumbled out before I knew the true weight behind them. And now that I'd said it aloud, "afraid" didn't quite cut it. "Terrified" was more like it.

JJ took my hand and held it—not pressing any further, not doing anything other than *being* there.

"Did you watch my DVD?" he asked.

"Some of it," I admitted.

JJ smacked his lips. "Well, you needn't have bothered. It's all a bunch of hooey."

"Really? So you didn't...die?"

"Oh, I did," he said, rocking nervously on his heels. "For five minutes or so, I was gone."

"And the angels? Heaven?"

"Mom always had a vivid imagination. And I always wanted to please."

I didn't quite know how to respond, so as before, I let my mouth do the talking.

"My gifts are on the fritz. Put me in the most haunted spot on earth, and there's a good chance I wouldn't hear a peep."

JJ chortled. I liked his laugh—it bubbled with goodwill.

"Well, maybe we can both fake it until we make it."

"Maybe so," I said.

He helped me to my feet. I stood there with quivering knees.

"Who were you calling out to?"

I hadn't realized I'd spoken aloud earlier. I could have deflected, but what the fuck would be the point?

"Mom," was all I could say.

JJ nodded. He led me out of the bathroom and back to the conference room where Mr. Carter stood waiting like a man about to miss the last train. I sat without a word and signed his damned document.

"The glass?" he asked.

I set the piece on the conference table. As he took it, I opened my phone's photo album and placed it before him. Zivy's bloody red diamond stared up at him.

"You're missing someone."

9

After a heated back and forth—me insisting on Zivy's inclusion in our little team, Mr. Carter remaining steadfast in his opinion that he had too many people already—Carter texted the photo to his boss.

"If he goes for four, we may need to readjust the budget."

"Are you serious?" Quan asked.

A call came in, and Carter took it.

Quan gave me a look. "I'm not taking a reduced fee because you want your friend to tag along."

"She's not my friend," I pushed back, realizing even as I said it that it wasn't quite true. Before the blood, before her jarring shift, I'd actually been enjoying her company. That spoke volumes for someone who cherished their solitude. "And if I need to, I'll split my portion in half."

"You'd give her half your cut?" Quan laughed.

"Why not?" I didn't like the idea, but anything to settle this argument and shut Mr. Quan up. He was getting on my nerves.

"No need," Mr. Carter said, hanging up. "Mr. Utter is happy for the extra help. The more the merrier was his basic message. Of course, I'll have to meet this woman first. Where can I find her?"

Oh, shit.

―――――――――――

It was no use asking the front desk for any help in locating Zivy; she'd been flying under the radar, an undocumented guest of the Meadowlands Conference Center.

"You didn't get a picture of her, did you?" JJ asked, as always eager to assist.

"Nope. Just this." I showed him the photo of the bloodied tabletop.

"That doesn't help much."

"No shit, Sherlock."

The two of us sat in the lobby watching scores of non-Zivys walk by. Quan had already moved on to alerting his team of his departure. Mr. Carter, in the meantime, busied himself taking care of our room charges, making arrangements to pack up our booths, etc.

"The van will be out front by three thirty," he'd said. "I'd prefer it if we could leave on time."

"Are you sure we need her?" JJ asked. He'd been checking the time on his phone.

Mama lies pale in the bed-bed-bed...

"Yes, I'm sure."

"Okay. Well, how do we find her? And in the next twenty minutes?"

"You're as much a Midnight Challenge winner as I am," I said. "Why don't you lend a hand and turn on your psychic sniffer."

"It doesn't work like that."

"No? How *does* it work?"

"You had breakfast with her, not me."

We were getting nowhere, and on top of that, we'd started bickering like an old married couple. I rose and headed for the exit, something Zivy had said tickling my mind.

"Where are you going?" JJ asked, padding along behind.

"The parking lot."

Once I knew where to look, it wasn't difficult locating Zivy's car. It was the only one from which cigarette smoke wafted.

I motioned JJ to stay put as I approached the battered blue Honda.

"Zivy!" I called out.

I caught sight of her behind the wheel the second before she hit the ignition. Blue exhaust poured out the back, adding even more fumes to the New Jersey air.

She was making a run for it.

I scanned the parking lot, pinpointing her only possible escape route. Heart pounding, I lunged between the vehicles and planted myself firmly in her way.

I really thought she was going to stop.

The Honda must have been going ten miles an hour plus when it hit me. The impact rattled my bones and sent me flying backward. My head met asphalt, and my teeth clamped shut. One false move and I'd be missing a good chunk of tongue.

"Ellen?" JJ shrieked.

"Jesus!" Zivy called out. "You came outta nowhere. Are you okay? Jesus!"

Hands lifted me to my feet. I was flanked by the pair of them—JJ, his face red with concern; Zivy, choking on smoke and adrenaline.

I shrugged them off and turned to JJ. "Give us a sec." It wasn't a question.

JJ grudgingly stepped away, leaving me to face my scarlet assailant.

"I'm so sorry. I really didn't see—"

"What's *that* all about?" I asked.

The young woman in front of me was momentarily confused, but when she saw my eyes directed at her bare arms, I sensed shields going up. With her coat in the car, she was exposed. She hugged herself tight, doing her best to hide the fresh cut on her forearm.

"It's nothing."

"Nothing? Seriously?"

She grimaced. "Look, I'm sorry I hit you. If you're looking to squeeze a little cheddar out of me, you should know I got no insurance."

"I'm sure that'll go over great with the highway patrol."

"I'll be fine." Penitent Zivy vanished as her belligerence resurfaced.

I was tempted to let her go, but instinct told me to cool my jets. It was vital to have the person who drew that bloody diamond along for the ride. And so, as I pondered how to break through to her, I settled for the first thing that popped into my mind.

"Aren't you tired of running?"

Bullseye.

Her face reddened, the impulse to lash out apparent. Then, tears rolled down her cheeks, betraying her. Her guard slipped away, and she fixed me with a look both raw and pleading.

"What do you got in mind, chick?"

10

After giving Zivy the preliminaries, I ushered her to the commuter van and handed her off to Mr. Carter to fill in the details.

Back in my room, I stuffed my belongings into my luggage, ditching my Weird Sisters sweatshirt and a few other items that had magically fit when I'd packed my suitcase. I dropped a few bucks for the cleaning crew, gave one last look around the room, and headed back down to the lobby.

JJ stood waiting for me just inside the main lobby doors. He had one backpack slung over his shoulders and held another by his side.

"What? I pack light. You ready for this?"

"Not yet," I said, setting my luggage next to him and heading for the East Room.

"They're going to pack up your booth for you!" he called after me, but it wasn't the Sisters' merchandise I was worried about—it was what I had stashed under the table.

As I approached my spot, I saw that Quan's booth now sported a sign which read, "Due to Circumstances Beyond Our Control..." I didn't bother reading the rest.

I scrawled some quick instructions for whoever was going to pack this shit up—crystals in bubble wrap, tinctures kept right-side up—and set them in the middle of the table, using the vial containing the grasshopper as a paperweight.

Magic Feather Lady was in the middle of making a sale. Good for her, I thought as I rummaged through the boxes stashed beneath the table.

"You getting the hell outta Dodge?" she asked, taking her customer's credit card.

"Something like that."

I finally found what I was looking for buried under a plastic bin filled with black candles: the rest of my books. I wasn't about to let them get lost in the mix.

As if on cue, Jeff, the same young coordinator who'd accompanied me to the conference room appeared on the scene.

"We'll get that sorted for you, ma'am."

Ma'am? I gotta get outta here.

"Just finishing up," I said.

"Oh, I think you're finished." I recognized the voice before I saw the face. It was none other than her Royal Pompousness, the Halloween Queen.

"Hey, Lauren," Jeff said.

Miffed by his informality, the Queen smirked. "I take it this is a result of my complaint?"

"Excuse me?"

"The formal complaint I filed against this...vendor." She said "vendor" with such venom I thought I might snort.

"You think this is funny? I don't think publicly disparaging me and this convention is the least bit funny."

I guess I actually *did* laugh.

"Don't worry, Lauren," I said, gathering up the last of my books. "I'll be out of your ridiculous hair soon enough."

This hit home, and she spluttered, "Jeff!"

JJ appeared in the doorway. He threw up his hands—*what gives?*

My phone vibrated in my pocket. Anything to get me out of this conversation.

It was the Sisters. Out of the frying pan and all that.

I raised a finger to the Queen. "I have to take this."

It was Mika, the Scarecrow.

She launched into me immediately. "Do you have any idea what kind of damage control we're having to do back here? Every person who walks through the doors has seen your little temper tantrum, and boy, have they let us know about it!"

"Listen, Mika—"

"No, you listen to me!"

Her rant continued unabated as the Queen insisted I get off the call and face her. Me? I simply stared down at the poor grasshopper. With curses and complaints raining down hard, I placed my attention on the vialed insect. And the more I watched, the more certain I was that he had twitched.

"Is that your boss? I'd like to talk to her."

"Who is that? Is it that Queen bitch?"

A familiar buzz filled my head. The grasshopper's antennae flicked.

Before Mika could blurt out any more chardonnayed invectives, I threw her on speaker and announced, "I quit."

I handed the phone to Lauren.

"Queen, meet the Scarecrow; Scarecrow, here's the Queen. Have a nice chat."

I reached for the vial, but it had broken in two. The grasshopper was nowhere to be seen, just a small pool of alcohol dampening my note. I left the warring parties to do battle and headed for the exit where an impatient JJ still stood.

"Finally," he said, exasperated.

"Damn straight," I replied.

I followed him to where Mr. Carter and the others sat waiting in the van.

"Thanks for joining us," Mr. Carter said, ever the prick.

"Wouldn't miss it."

I slid open the door and crawled to the back, past Quan, who was fiddling with a piece of recording equipment, and past Zivy, who had stretched out, arms folded, leather jacket standing in for a pillow.

When I reached the last seat and settled in, luggage piled up in the space behind me, JJ crawled over next to me.

"Exciting, huh?" he whispered.

As we pulled away from the conference center, leaving the Hooky Spooky and its denizens behind, I couldn't help but feel a page turning. Whether that would prove exciting remained to be seen.

"Buckle up," Mr. Carter called from the front.

Buckle up, indeed.

11

We headed north on I-95, a stretch of highway where laying on the horn was mandatory; following speed limits, not so much. Once we hit the Palisades Parkway, the congestion eased and the woods closed in on either side, reminding me of the more isolated stretches of the Midwest. Autumn leaves gave way to gray-fingered branches. Destination: Cold Spring, New York.

Mr. Carter, we soon learned, was little on small talk, instead preferring to listen to classical music. After peppering him with questions for the first half hour, to little avail, Quan gave up and stuck in his earbuds.

Zivy roused a few times, once even long enough to give me a quick nod, which I took as a good sign. I might have rushed her entrance into this odd excursion, but I'm glad I did. Having her in the mix felt good, balanced.

A light autumn rain pattered on the van's roof, and I

instantly regretted leaving my windbreaker behind. I'd have to pick something up in town.

"We're going to swing by the mercantile before we head up to the house," Carter had said. "You should be able to find any toiletries you might need."

JJ, who'd allowed himself a catnap, came to with a snort. "We close?"

"Just passed into New York State."

He peered through the rain-streaked window and nodded. "We still have to cross the bridge to get to Cold Spring. Hungry?" He held up a full pack of the peanut butter crackers.

"Not even if you paid me."

"So, how'd you guess the secret password?" Zivy asked Quan, nudging him with her foot.

"What's that?" Quan asked, removing an earbud.

"She asked how you figured out what was in the box," JJ explained.

"Simple," Quan said. "My brothers told me."

"Brothers?"

Quan removed a second earbud with a sigh. "You've never read any of my books, I take it?"

Blank stares all around.

"I'm a triplet. The only one who survived." Quan spoke in measured tones. "Sometimes my brothers tell me things."

"That's dark." Zivy frowned. "What sort of things do they tell you?"

Quan offered her a smarmy grin. "Buy my book and you'll find out."

"Thanks a lot, dingus." She turned to JJ. "How about you?"

"Me? I peeked."

"You cheated?"

"No, no, no..." JJ was at a loss. "After my accident, I found I could see stuff I had no right seeing. Nothing special—just a little trick."

"Cool." Zivy trained her gaze on me. "How about you?"

I balked. I hadn't a clue how I'd stumbled upon the answer to Utter's riddle. I'd always considered myself a psychic mutt—clairvoyance, mediumship, with a dash of super-tuned intuition thrown in for good measure. All of which had been on the fritz for longer than I cared to admit. And so, instead of being straight with her, I chose the mysterious route.

"Some things can't be expressed in words."

Quan chuckled and replaced his earbuds. As he did so, I thought I caught him say "bullshit" under his breath.

"Excuse me?"

"Nothing."

The Bear Mountain Bridge was intimidating, all cables and concrete, suspended between cliffs that looked like they belonged in a Nordic tourism brochure. I'm not afraid of heights, but if I were, I would have been freaking out the moment the van started up the bridge's incline.

The view made for a perfect photo op, but my company phone was long gone, no doubt dumped in a wastebasket by the Halloween Queen.

"Is the temp still good for everyone?" Mr. Carter called back. We assured him it was, and I thought he might follow up with a historic rundown on the bridge—it was built in such-and-such a year by that famous Mr. So-and-So—but playing tour guide apparently wasn't part of his duties.

Being in such tight quarters with the others, their gifts nudged against mine causing interference not unlike putting a phone too close to a speaker. The resulting *click-click-click*? Imagine that, but spread out over every inch of your skin. Little thoughts, flashes of insight popped into my head like flies hitting a bug zapper.

Which is why I wasn't surprised when I saw all the people standing on the railing.

"Go ahead and jump already," Zivy said, her voice muffled by her jacket-pillow. "It's not like you haven't done it a thousand times already."

"What are you talking about?" JJ asked.

"Never mind."

When JJ caught me staring out the window, he turned his attention to me. "What is it?"

"Can't you see them?" I asked.

JJ followed my gaze. "No."

It dawned on me that the four of us in the van were very different people with very different abilities.

"People," I said. "Dozens of them. Waiting to jump."

Some of the figures were contemporary, like the man in the Carhartt jacket. Others had been hanging around since the twenties or forties—women in pillbox hats, a grande dame in a long fur coat. The bridge had been collecting jumpers since it was opened, from the looks of it, and they were all here for a reunion.

The man in the jacket was the first to take the plunge. The moment he stepped over the edge, he vanished like breath on glass.

"And we have a winner," Zivy announced, turning over in her seat to a more comfortable position.

One by one, the spirits reenacted their demise; one by one, they dissolved in the air. They were just shadows of the past sketched in mist, but with each leap, my stomach dropped.

By the time we reached the bridge's apex, the vision began to fade. Possibly because the rain was letting up and the sun had returned. Or because their audience had moved on.

Upon reaching the eastern side, we turned north. The Hudson flowed far below, parallel to us as we navigated the serpentine two-lane highway weaving through wooded neighborhoods. I caught town names like Manitou and Garrison as we passed stately homes and private schools partially hidden from view—all the better to keep out the riffraff.

I caught myself the moment the thought invaded my head. *Keep out the riffraff.* Those words weren't mine—they were Mom's. A bit of vitriol she kept in the chamber, ready to fire off at a moment's notice. Don't mess with narcissists; they always come fully armed. I made a mental note to strike the saying from my repertoire.

We reached Cold Spring about five thirty. It was surprising how the scenery changed in a mere ninety minutes. We'd traded the stench of refineries for the scent of autumn leaves, urban decay for small town charm. It was Norman Rockwell as shit. Even I, who could take or leave any setting, fell instantly for Cold Spring.

"Let's try to keep this stop to a minimum, folks," Carter said as he pulled into a parking space in front of a white, clapboard building. The weather-aged sign identified the place as Ebb's Mercantile. "And if you could wait until everyone's ready to check out, that'd be great. I've got this covered." He waggled a credit card at us to drive home the point.

Funny how it was *we* until it came to taking credit for buying our necessaries. If I'd met Mr. Carter under other circumstances, I bet I'd like him just as little as I did now.

A small bell rang as I opened the door. Of course it did. Ebb's was a sprawl of a store with high ceilings, stocking everything you ever needed and even more of what you didn't. The floor was made of wide warped planks that sagged underfoot, and the walls were adorned with antique photos and metal signs.

The toiletries aisle was a Martha Stewart version of Walgreens—artisanal toothpastes, craft deodorants, and stacks of lotions made with goat's milk.

"Oooh!" JJ cooed. "Anise mouthwash."

I spotted the only item I needed in the joint hanging along a wall above a display of books and candles: sweatshirts and jackets. One step outside the heated van, and I'd realized how Cold Spring had got its name.

"Can I help you find anything?"

I turned to find a wiry woman with white hair pulled into a tight bun standing at my elbow. Her handmade vest screamed homespun hospitality.

"May I see that hoodie?" I asked, pointing at a rack of Cold Spring sweatshirts.

"Let me get the hook," she said, tottering off.

As I awaited her return, I perused the mercantile's collection of new and used books. Many explored local cooking —*Casseroles with Kimmy* featured hot dishes aplenty—and local history, but the book that caught my eye was buried in a stack of used mass paperbacks.

I quivered with delight, like I'd found the missing piece of a jigsaw puzzle.

I pulled the book from its place in the pile and studied it. A woman in black. A fog-shrouded cliff. The author's name, unknown to me until that day.

Sorrow's Leap by James Utter.

I flipped it open and read:

Justice was the glimmering gem of Manhattan society, dancing until dawn, courting suitors galore, orchestrating all manner of mischief that women thought scandalous and men found irresistible.

"He's a local, you know," the woman with the vest said as she returned with a long wooden rod with a brass hook on the end. She proceeded to fish at the sweatshirt's hanger with all the grace of a toddler with a stick.

"What's it about?"

She grunted in her effort to snag the sweatshirt. "Ghosts, haunted houses, creepy crawlies. His usual stuff. Although, if you ask me, I think he was onto something with this one. Felt fresh."

The hook caught the hanger, and the woman lowered the garment. Only when she had it in hand did I realize what I'd done: I'd just picked out my first black piece of clothing in years.

"Cold Spring," it read. "Established 1846."

"We used to carry his books, back when he was still writing. Even had a signing here, once. Hot apple cider, pumpkin cookies. I had a photo from that night hanging on the wall for the longest time."

"I'd love to see it," I said.

"It's buried in a box somewhere. Someone knocked it off the wall. Not sure where it is now. Doesn't matter. From what I hear, he's retired."

I flipped through the pages, landing on the "About the Author" section at the back.

There he was. James Utter. A photo of the man sat above his bio, staring at me with practiced solemnity. He sported a dark Van Dyke beard...or was it a goatee? In any case, the rest of his hair was white, worn long, and he was wearing a wool sweater with a high, rounded collar. He looked like a James Utter, all right.

"How much for the book?" I asked.

"You buying the hoodie?"

I nodded.

"I'll throw it in for a buck. Let me ring you up."

In my excitement, I paid for the items myself, remembering as the woman handed me my receipt that Mr. Carter was footing the bill. No matter. I wrapped the book in the sweatshirt and headed back to the van, leaving the others to their shopping. *Sorrow's Leap* would be my little secret.

I had to wait for Mr. Carter to unlock the van. The air was getting nippy, so I slipped on the hoodie and stuffed the book in the middle pouch.

"New sweatshirt?" Mr. Carter asked as he returned to the van, the rest of the group falling in behind with their paper bags of goods.

"Like it?"

"I can't reimburse you," he said. "We all checked out together."

"No worries," I said, offering him a big grin.

We all climbed back into the vehicle, each returning to their favored spot. Quan had one measly bag that probably contained nothing but dental floss. Zivy had quite the haul; from what I could see, she'd cleaned Ebb's out of small batch potato chips as well as a bright Hudson Livin' T-shirt. I hadn't noticed if the mercantile sold cigarettes, but if they did, Zivy had got 'em.

"I can't wait to try it," JJ said much too excitedly, pulling the anise-flavored mouthwash from his bag.

"I'm happy for you," I said. I stuffed my hands in my pouch, letting my fingers run along the book's spine. Sometime soon, I hoped, when I was alone, I could scan *Sorrow's Leap* in private.

JJ threw back a mouthful of the licorice swill and gargled heartily.

"Where you going to spit that, buddy?" Zivy asked.

JJ looked perplexed, then alarmed, then resigned. He swallowed.

"Yikes. That was...bracing."

Yup, a little privacy couldn't come soon enough.

After our brief sojourn, we continued northeast out of Cold Spring, this time taking a less traveled route. The trees along this road curled overhead, interlacing their branches like prayerful hands.

We passed an abandoned gas station with soaped windows and absent pumps, weed-choked drives leading into the woods, and faded road signs peppered with buckshot. Cue the banjo music.

Soon, the pavement gave way to gravel, and the van lurched every time we hit a dip in the road.

Quan, who had been an island unto himself the whole trip, turned back to the rest of us and mouthed, "Where are we going?"

At that moment, we came to the edge of the woods. A wide vista of dead grasses awaited us. Beyond the field, a rocky, treeless promontory rose toward the sky. Atop it perched a massive house—cathedral-like in its splendor, somewhere between Gothic Revival and Victorian in design. Its stern stone edifice glared down at our approach. A lone corner turret stood at attention, and windows gaped like dark and hungry mouths.

Mr. Carter turned down a drive choked by milkweed and bittersweet. He hadn't bothered announcing our arrival. It didn't take a psychic to realize we were in the presence of Utter Hall.

12

My first impression of Utter Hall did not prepare me for what awaited us up top. After several minutes climbing the rocky hill, Mr. Carter hitting every bump and hole along the way, the van finally crested the rise.

We turned onto the circular drive that led to the building's main entrance. Someone had abandoned the job of replacing the pavers, stopping halfway through. The result was a main drive that looked in bad need of a dentist—peppered with gaps where stones had either been removed or never replaced. The rough terrain caused the van's tires to murmur a mournful *whum-whum-whum* as we slowed in front of the entryway.

"If you wouldn't mind toting your own luggage, I would appreciate it," Mr. Carter said, getting out of the van and allowing himself a stretch.

"Sheesh, would you look at that?" JJ gushed as we tumbled out into the drive. At first, I thought he must be talking about Utter Hall, which loomed over us like the set of some forgotten horror film—Andrew Carnegie Meets Frankenstein. But, no, he stood staring over the hill's edge, past the sea of brown grass below us, to the Hudson River beyond—a sparkling ribbon running through the landscape.

A lone halogen lamp flickered to life, its sickly light casting distorted shadows across the drive.

"October's so depressing," Zivy said, pulling a pack of generic cigarettes.

"No smoking inside the house," Mr. Carter warned.

"Got it, chief," Zivy replied, lighting up.

"I thought we were all required to love October," Quan said. I couldn't tell if he was making a jab or not.

Zivy took a deep puff. "Try living in your car in the fall. Raining one day, snowing the next, mud everywhere. If you can find something to love in that, more power to you."

JJ piped up. "I like October."

"Good for you, sunshine."

"Let's go inside, shall we?" Mr. Carter grabbed his bag from the van and herded us toward the massive front doors.

The entryway was a stark departure from the house's exterior. What had seemed a well-preserved specimen of Gilded Age decadence gave way to dust and disorder. Utter Hall had been caught in mid-renovation. The foyer's ornate tiled floor was partially obscured by planks of plywood. Oak paneling stripped from the walls lay in stacks, revealing the stonework beneath. New electrical wiring hung loose and unattended, like so much silly string.

"Jeez," JJ whispered, summing up our collective surprise at the state of the place.

A single staircase curved upward, its steps worn by decades of use. To our right, a large empty room that might have been a formal parlor stood waiting its turn for a makeover. Until that time came, it had to endure the humiliation of acting as storage room for building materials.

"Mind your step," Mr. Carter said, making his way past us to take the point. "We're in the throes of renovation at Utter Hall, as you can see. I've given the space a once over, but you still may find the occasional screw."

Zivy snorted.

"A quick introduction of the house, yes?" Carter continued. "It was built in the 1880s by Walter Thackery, owner of Mid-Central Railways, as a summer retreat. Although he never deemed it necessary to give it a name, locals took to calling it Thackery Castle. After Mr. Thackery's death, it passed to his son, who let both his father's company and house fall into decline. After sitting vacant for many decades, Mr. Utter—through no small effort, I might add—acquired the funds needed to bring the old girl back to life."

If Utter Hall was an old girl, we'd caught her in a state of undress.

"I trust none of you have any problem with stairs?" Mr. Carter asked.

I instantly thought of Chunky. It was the type of staircase that made you understand why people used to die of consumption. The wooden steps groaned beneath our feet as if sick. Halfway up, the stairs took a sharp turn, past a small stone statue of an owl, then doubled back as they continued upward.

By the time we'd reached the second floor, JJ was breathing hard.

The second-floor landing offered an even more commanding view of the river through a cluster of Gothic windows, tall and curving to points. Mr. Carter positioned himself in front of these windows, effectively becoming a silhouette.

"Your rooms are to your right."

We followed dutifully, though my instinct to snoop had kicked in big time. I wanted to put my ear to the wall, listen to the pipes gurgling within, run my fingers across the dark wainscoting, pick at the torn edges of the wallpaper—

"Ellen?"

JJ had hung back and was now waving me forward. The group was already well down the north hall. How long had I been mesmerized?

Mr. Carter opened the first door. The room was plain but clean. What it lacked in décor it made up in view. Its west-facing windows made sure of that.

"Mr. Quan?" Mr. Carter said, holding the door. Quan, weighted down by multiple bags, shuffled into the room and set down his luggage. "Ms. Marx next, I believe."

My room had less of a view due to a scraggly tree that stood guard outside, yet I still managed to pick out West Point in the light of the setting sun. My room was appointed similarly to Quan's: a twin bed, a standing lamp, a card table with folding chair. What it didn't have was...

"Where's the bathroom?" I asked.

"All in good time," Mr. Carter said. "Let me get the others settled first, okay?"

Rebuked, I set my bags down on the bed and waited for him to show JJ and Zivy their quarters. I pulled *Sorrow's Leap* from my hoodie pocket and stashed it beneath the pillow.

Mr. Carter returned, a faux apologetic look on his face.

"Someone mentioned restrooms," he said.

Me. It was me, you prick.

"With the remodel standing where it does, we have one working restroom on this floor. I'm afraid you'll have to take turns. But our boiler has just been replaced, so I think you'll find you have hot water to spare."

The guy actually smirked when he said this, and a thought that had been niggling in the back of my head wormed its way to the front.

He doesn't want us here.

"Hey," Zivy said, sporting her new T-shirt. "Beats pissing in the bushes."

"Let's return to the ground floor, and I'll show you our kitchen."

As Mr. Carter started toward the stairs, I asked, "What's upstairs?"

He turned and smiled. "Just some rooms the workers haven't gotten to yet. Old servants' quarters. I'd say it's off limits, but I'm not here twenty-four seven. Remember the waivers you signed. Utter Hall is not responsible for anyone who wanders off and gets themselves hurt."

The dining room was in a similar state as the rest of the house, yet a long, polished table with matching highbacked chairs sat dead center, ready and willing to accept diners.

Passing first through the butler's pantry, we emerged into the kitchen. Half expecting a collection of butter churns and flour sifters, I was pleasantly surprised to find a modern setup awaiting us. A K-Cup station, a microwave, a central rolling island, a Viking stove—much more Airbnb than the rest of the house's D&D vibe.

Mr. Carter opened an industrial-sized refrigerator. "We're stocked with fruit, veggies, yogurts, sandwich meats, the makings for pizza, etc. If there's anything in particular you'd like during your stay—"

"A nice juicy ribeye?" Zivy asked.

"Just ask." Mr. Carter closed the fridge door.

"Thought I just did," Zivy whispered in my ear.

After pointing out the plates and silverware and showing us how to work the pizza oven, Mr. Carter ran out of patter.

"Any questions?" he asked.

"Just two," Quan said, all business. "What's our job and when do we meet Mr. Utter?"

Mr. Carter spread his hands. "Now, *that's* a perfect transition, I must say. As to your first question, I'll let the boss answer that. As for your second...follow me."

From the kitchen we proceeded back to the foyer, headed down the north hallway, through a series of arches. At the end of the hall, we turned left into a large room seemingly untouched as of yet by the renovations—a stubborn holdout of the past.

It was the library. And it was devoid of books. Its ornate built-ins, once home to countless volumes, sat empty.

And hungry?

"Please don't," Mr. Carter snapped.

I turned to find JJ looking sheepish, his hand on the handle of a door set into one of the empty bookcases.

"Sorry," JJ said, stepping back quickly.

Mr. Carter stalked over to the door and tested the knob. Locked.

"This door leads to the South Wing, and the South Wing is off limits. I trust you'll not try it again?"

"Yeah, you can trust that," JJ stammered. "For sure."

"Why is it off limits?" Zivy pressed.

Mr. Carter smiled. "Let's get to it, shall we?"

He directed our attention to an enormous TV mounted on the wall behind us. He picked up a remote from a side table and gave it a quick tap.

The screen flickered, and an image appeared—a study not unlike the library in style, and at its center, a green leather chair. A fireplace roared in the background.

"Sir?" Mr. Carter said.

A strange, curdled sourness filled my mouth. I smacked my lips, willing the foul flavor away.

A gentleman stepped into frame and eased himself into the chair with a sigh.

"Welcome to my home, my friends," the man said. "I'm James Utter."

13

The face staring from the TV screen was the same gracing the back of *Sorrow's Leap*, if the owner of the latter had suddenly aged twenty years. James Utter certainly looked the part of reclusive writer, in his silk robe and slippers. His beard had whitened over the years, yet still came to a sharp point, a mirror version of those Gothic windows. His hair was long and wild, a style he'd stolen from Walt Whitman.

"I apologize for the state of things around here," Utter said, "We had expected renovations to be complete a couple years ago, and yet, as you can see, the end is nowhere in sight."

Mr. Carter stepped forward, flashing a smile he must have kept in his back pocket for meetings with the boss. "They're all settled in. Would you mind if I garaged the van, sir?"

"That's fine, Carter. Leave the box, if you would."

Not Mr. Carter—just Carter, like a butler in an old mystery movie.

Carter removed the box from his bag and set it on a small

table to the side of the screen. Then, he excused himself, leaving us alone with the man on the screen.

A burning log crackled in the fireplace behind Mr. Utter as he regarded us through the glass.

"Mr. Quan, Mr. Gadzinski, Ms. Marx, Ms. Wilde," he said, calling roll.

Wilde? Fits Zivy to a tee.

"If you're feeling a bit in the dark about your current situation, well...that's by design." Utter's voice was refined, if rough, with just enough of the boroughs hidden in there to make me wonder—Brooklyn? Queens? "I instructed Carter to keep the flow of information to a minimum so I can speak to you directly. There's no use pussyfooting around it, so let's dive in, shall we? I fear Utter Hall is haunted."

"I knew it," JJ gloated, master of the obvious.

"For the past few years, there's been a growing antagonism between the past and present. Something seems to have taken umbrage at my attempt to revive this house. I'm afraid whatever walks these halls sees me as an interloper to be dealt with."

He shifted in his chair. Four pairs of eyes watched him with rapt attention.

"My health is not good. This is a direct result of the haunting, I'm sure of that. Just as Utter Hall is stuck between versions of itself, so am I. Before work commenced, I was fit. You noticed the climb it took to reach the house from the road? That was once a daily walk for me. Now?"

He raised his arms as if to illustrate his decrepitude. To my eyes, James Utter still had a lot of pep in him.

"And so, my plan. Locate a practitioner—or practitioners —with certain sensibilities, a certain openness, to stay here with me and report their findings back. It's my hope that, together, we can root out the reason for the disturbance and put it to rest. It's been a long time since I've felt welcome in my own home, and I'm ready to do whatever is necessary to reclaim it. Are we on the same page?"

We offered a collective nod.

"Good. Any questions?"

Before I could launch into my litany of inquiries, Zivy jumped in.

"Why the Zoom call?"

"As I mentioned, my experiences here have left me quite ill. As a matter of fact, you may see a member of my medical team pay me a visit during your stay. My physician thinks it wise for me to remain secluded for the time being. And as I have a dread of hospitals, I've opted to sequester myself here."

"Where's here?" Zivy pressed.

"The South Wing. I trust you'll afford me my privacy. Anything else?"

Quan, who had pulled a pad and was furiously writing notes, tried to get in the next question, but I beat him to it.

"Yeah. Why'd you go slumming at a con to find your 'practitioners?' Seems like you'd have a whole internet of options at your fingertips."

"Back in my publishing heyday, I spent quite a bit of time at conventions," Utter replied. "People with the sort of skills I require tend to gravitate toward such events. People such as yourselves"

Quan jumped in. "Despite being absurdly prolific, I find it difficult to believe that royalties paid for all this." He gestured at the house in general. "Magnates own mansions, not horror writers."

Our guest waggled a finger in mock reproach. "You're a sneaky one, Mr. Quan. While it's true I've had my fair share of bestsellers, it's also true that I come from a family of privilege. My mother's inheritance allowed me to build my literary empire, such as it is. Still, it didn't hurt that the good people up in Albany offered up a wide variety of grants. I paid for the renovations, the State provided historic funds, and the grants got us over the finish line."

"So...you don't own it?" Quan puzzled.

"Oh, I do. Every brick and stone. Part of being a man of means is knowing when to let others foot the bill." He winked as if letting us in on the ultimate secret of life. "Once the project is complete, I will be sharing this hall as a writers retreat and lecture space, as well as opening the not insignificant grounds to the public as a nature sanctuary."

He said this with all the good nature of a used car salesman attempting to convince us his Geo Metro was a vintage treasure.

I was about to probe further, but JJ blurted out, "What's the deal with the stained glass?"

All eyes flitted to the box.

Mr. Utter turned solemn. "Whatever resides here carries a burden of great anger. It's undermined my renovations, driven away workers, attacked me physically." He pulled back his sleeve to reveal a series of thin white scars along his forearm. "These are just the marks that show."

My ears perked up. Physical manifestations were rare— most hauntings stuck to moving furniture and cold spots. But actual wounds? That suggested something more than your average ghost with a grudge.

"You've felt it, no doubt. Or at least...you will. It's soaked into every pore of this place. I figured if I offered up a piece of Utter Hall for examination, the right people would answer my call." He clapped his hands. "It is now...six thirty. Why don't we meet back here tomorrow. Same time, same place. I look forward to your first report."

"Hold on," I said. "I'd like to go over the hall's history, if you don't mind—"

Utter gave a phlegmy cough. "Mr. Carter will provide you with a brief overview of previous residents and whatnot. As for questions, let's save the rest for tomorrow, eh? Even this short conversation has left me winded. Besides"—here he leaned in, almost, I thought, with no small measure of pleasure—"you may find many of your questions answered during the night."

With that, Utter disappeared, leaving four astonished psychics standing in the library.

"Damn," Zivy said. "I should have asked if there was any booze in the joint."

"I wonder what's wrong with him," JJ said, grabbing a Coke from the fridge.

"You should have asked," Quan replied. He had rolled the center island beneath the overhead light to better illuminate his notes—an army general laying out his war plan.

"Wouldn't that have been rude?"

"You don't get answers to questions you don't ask."

As Mr. Carter had yet to return—and since our stomachs were doing backflips—we'd retired to the kitchen to take advantage of the free grub and compare notes.

"So, we're just supposed to hang out and...what? Wait for a ghost to show up?" Zivy asked, rifling through the cupboards.

"That's pretty much the job," Quan said.

I suddenly realized who Quan reminded me of: Mr. Kelly, my high school biology teacher. He was younger than the rest of the faculty by far and wore his sense of entitlement like a badge. Mr. Kelly was all eye rolls and sarcasm and condescension. He was slumming it at school and made sure everyone knew.

"How many investigations have you been a part of?" Quan continued.

"Zip," Zivy said, flashing a big zero with her fingers.

"You're kidding me."

"I think we all earned our place here," JJ offered. "Right?" He threw his last thought to me.

"I suppose," I said, though the more I thought about it— with my abilities only putting in cameos—I was lucky to be included at all.

"We need a solid plan if we want to do this right," Quan said, leafing through his notepad. "We need to observe, detect, discern, and disperse."

"Is that from one of your books?" I asked.

"Yes, as a matter of fact, it is."

JJ held up a loaf of bread. "PBJs anyone?"

"Aha!" Zivy squealed, pulling a bottle from a cabinet. "Vodka ain't really my thing, but it still wets the whistle."

"Hey," Quan said, looking up from his planning session. "Your nose."

A small trickle of blood trailed from one of Zivy's nostrils. "Must be all the dust," she said, wiping it away quickly, more embarrassed than surprised.

Mr. Carter popped into the room, startling me and making JJ shriek. He held four file folders in his hand.

"I have the histories Mr. Utter promised."

We descended on the man and gave the pages within a quick scan.

Utter Hall: An Historical Brief.

It was only five pages long, and from the looks of it, gave only a cursory timeline from the hall's construction to the present day. Names and dates, but nothing you could sink your teeth into. The *Historical Brief* certainly lived up to its name.

"By the way," Carter said over the sound of turning pages. "You're missing it."

"Missing what, chief?" Zivy asked.

"Why, the first appearance of the evening, of course."

14

We stood in the entryway, gathered around Mr. Carter, Quan with a recording app at the ready. All I sensed were the chill flowing in from under the door and the damp stone scent in the air.

JJ was the first to break the silence.

"Where did you—"

"Hush," Mr. Carter hissed.

And then we heard it, the first tentative footstep on the stairs. Skin on wood. First one, then another. Small bare feet picking their way down toward us. As if curious at our presence.

Zivy nudged me. "You see anything?"

I shook my head. Footsteps pattered toward us, and the stairs creaked, but I didn't see so much as a shadow on the wall.

"They're early," Carter said.

"They?" I asked. Utter had called what roamed the halls *it,* singular. Had we just been sold a bill of goods? "But Mr. Utter said—"

"Mr. Utter says a lot of things."

Then, as if provoked, the invisible horde descended as one, feet slapping against cold tile as they reached the main floor, circling us, picking up speed. Zivy batted at the air as JJ spun around, trying to get a bead on the little intruders. Quan calmly trained his phone's mic toward the sound.

And me? I took a deep breath and closed my eyes. There was a thing I used to do to sharpen my senses, to home in on disturbances and bring them into focus. I raised my right hand, my "seeing" hand, and allowed the rest of the world to fall away. Goodbye Carter, goodbye Zivy, goodbye JJ and Quan. I let myself melt into the vibrating essence of Utter Hall, into its—

"Fuck!"

I stumbled backward and quickly withdrew my hand. Three thin lines, like paper cuts, now graced my skin.

"You okay, Ellen?" Zivy asked.

"One of the little shits scratched me!"

Bare feet slapped gleefully against tile.

Why didn't you visit?

No...no...no...

"Ellen?"

I was in so much paa-aain...

"Leave me be!"

Why did you leave me there—

"Shut up!" I shouted.

The sound of phantom feet fell silent. So did Zivy and the rest. They were all staring at me, startled by my outburst.

They hadn't heard her. Of course, they hadn't. It was the damn scratch, opening old wounds. It was the *fucking* scratch!

"Just when we were getting somewhere," Quan sighed as he shut down his recording.

"Give her a break." Zivy came to my side and took my hand in hers. "Does it hurt?"

I was in so much paa-aain...

I shook my head, stifling a scream. "It's fine."

Eager to make his exit, Mr. Carter stepped to the door. "Anyway, there's your appetizer. More courses coming." He rapped on the wall next to the doorframe, revealing a small compartment containing an old Bakelite phone. "Pick this up, and you get me. I'll give you a buzz around nine just to see how things are going. Make sure someone's around to pick up."

"Hold up," JJ said. "You're not staying?"

"Of course I'm staying. Just not with you."

"Why not?"

The man opened the door. "Because I live in the carriage house. Now, if you'll excuse me, I'm going to whip up some dinner. I suggest you do the same."

With that, our man Carter was gone. The door closed behind him with the deep thud of a coffin lid.

Quan whirled on me. "The first step I suggested was to observe, not go batshit crazy at the first sign of—"

Zivy didn't let him finish. "Back...the fuck...off."

"Not batshit," I stammered, unable to come up with

anything more cogent. Little nails raked my mind as Carter cried, "*More courses coming! More courses coming!*"

"Hey, chick," Zivy said, giving my hand a squeeze. "Let's go get you cleaned up."

———

Zivy chaperoned me to second floor. I was appreciative, but I was ready to be alone and told her so.

"You sure? You really blew a fuse down there. I don't mind staying."

"Look like *you* blew a fuse too," I replied, motioning for her to wipe her nose where a thin line of blood had dried.

"It's nothing. I just bubbled over a little bit."

"You...or what's inside you?"

She regarded me in earnest, and for a moment, I thought she was about to spill the beans. Instead, she drew me close and whispered in my ear.

"You asked me if I was tired of running. Maybe it's time for me to ask you the same thing. Now, wash that hand. Who knows if those little spooks had their shots." She gave me a peck on the cheek before bounding down the hall. "Hands off the vodka, boys. Finders keepers and all that."

I stared at my hand. The wounds, if you could even call them that, were shallow. But it wasn't the scratches that caused my head to throb; it was the voice that had awakened inside.

Why did you leave me there?

"Hush..."

I sat on the bed and pushed pause. Tending to the scratches

would have to wait. I was untethered. The world was slipping through my fingers. That voice. The people downstairs and their potpourri of personalities. It was too much. I needed a distraction. I needed to withdraw.

I pulled the tattered paperback from under the pillow and flipped through its pages...

Ah, Justice. Such evenings became her: champagne hoisted high and often, silk gowns twirled in playful abandon, and everywhere the music of youthful laughter echoing through staid and sober halls. Yet time has a way of transforming even the brightest star into something altogether dim and unrecognizable.

Pure dreck.

I read on, but it was going to take a miracle to get me through it.

The thin, red lines on my hand began to itch. I rifled through my toiletries, not expecting to find any Band-Aids, but still looking, nonetheless.

"Damn."

I picked my way down the hall, past the landing, and down into the unexplored south end of the second floor. The farthest end of the hall was blocked by hanging plastic sheets, but before that lay the lone lavatory.

Switching on the light and closing the door behind me, I found the bathroom to be quite large. The wall behind the sink sported a large rectangular hole where a medicine cabinet no doubt once sat. Looking about, I saw there wasn't a mirror in the place. Fine with me. Vanity was one of the seven deadly sins that had never taken root in Ellen Marx.

I soaped up my hand and held it under the faucet until the water scalded my skin. Then, I tore length of toilet paper from the roll and dabbed at the scratches. It stung, but there was no blood on the tissue. It had just been a warning shot.

Nature suddenly called, and I dropped my drawers. As I peed, I took inventory of the room: a clawfoot tub with a retrofitted showerhead and curtain, a single buzzing overhead light, a bent towel rack. A spartan space; one that would have usually brought me comfort. And yet, at any moment, I half expected a knock at door.

Are you done in there yet?

I gotta go.

You've been in there fifteen minutes.

I finished my business and washed my hands yet again. They were trembling.

Easy, Ellen. Eyes on the prize.

And what was the prize exactly? It certainly wasn't the fame Quan sought, or the money Utter offered. I felt like a monkey on an escalator asking, *Why the hell did I get on this damn thing?*

With no mirror to reflect my thoughts back at me, I looked inward to find the thread I'd been following ever since I'd bumped into JJ in the East Room.

You asked me if I was tired of running. Maybe it's time for me to ask you the same thing.

I wasn't running from anything. What the hell did Zivy know? I hated it when people spoke in riddles.

What are you, deaf, Ellen?

What purpose did vagaries serve but to bung you up?

I'll teach you to ignore me.

"Stop."

I'll teach you!

"Stop!"

The memory struck me like an openhanded slap.

The waiting room. The hacking patients. The coffee table littered with outdated magazines.

"Ellen!"

My mother in the chair next to mine, digging her elbow into my side.

"Earth to Ellen, Earth to Ellen!" she jeered.

"Fuck!" I said, shoving her elbow. "That hurt." Her little outburst was going to leave a bruise. Her outbursts often did.

"That hurts!" Mom mocked. "Don't talk to me about pain. You know *nothing* about pain."

She held a hand to her temple and moaned under her breath. A stern gentleman across the room glanced up from his *Field & Stream* and shook his head at me in admonition. What an uncaring daughter.

"You're right, you're right," I replied, doing my best to play nice. "I'll make sure the doctor ups your meds."

"Oh, you'd like that wouldn't you?" she spat. "You're not going to be happy until I'm drugged to the gills like *that* poor thing!"

She nodded toward an ancient woman sitting in a wheelchair next to her equally ancient husband. A line of drool ran from her lower lip to her lap.

"That's not true."

"It is and you *know* it is!"

She was getting unruly, and when Rita got unruly, the world had better hide.

Her elbow shot out once again, this time catching me in the ribs. I grabbed her wrist and held it firm.

"Cut it out!"

At the contact of skin on skin, my mind filled with a brilliant flash. The source of the light? Deep within my mother's skull. A throbbing mass gnawing away, swallowing her thoughts, eating her—

Her untended nails raked across the back of my hand, digging into flesh, forcing me to lose my grip.

"We're leaving!" she screamed, struggling to her feet.

"Mom, please."

"I'm your mother, and I will *not* be ignored!"

She hauled back her hand, and...

The blow never came. The only hand in the picture was my own, the thin, red lines on the back burning like fire.

The truth hit me like a hangover on Sunday morning.

I hadn't lost my gift—I'd buried it.

Why?

Because I didn't want to let her hurt me anymore.

I'd wrapped my abilities up nice and neat and shoved them in the darkest corner of my mind, right next to all those missed hospital visits and one-sided arguments.

But now? The people downstairs were like psychic lightning rods, and every time one of them sparked, another brick fell from the wall.

I pressed my fingers against the cool marble of the sink, letting the chill ground me. Reluctant tears fell, and I caught myself almost smirking at the irony. I'd given my gift the same treatment I gave everything else that hurt too much—I'd ghosted it.

The question was: would it come back willingly?

Time to stop whining, time to open the floodgates and let every ghost, ghoul, and dead civil servant come pouring in. Because somewhere in that tsunami of voices, maybe—just fucking maybe—I'd hear the one voice I'd slammed the door on and put her to rest.

I had to make sense out of the psychic jigsaw puzzle inside me. It was time to start piecing myself back together. And I knew exactly which piece to start with.

15

The others were having a heated discussion in the kitchen as I returned to the first floor, although I couldn't pick up on its theme. They were either jockeying for position in this investigation or arguing over what toppings to put on the pizza. Whatever the case, with my companions engrossed in conversation, slipping into the library unnoticed was a breeze.

The room seemed even more empty than it had when we'd gathered for our chat with Utter. The empty shelves gave me the willies, as if, denied their volumes, they'd just as happily accept me into their collection.

The box containing the glass remained where Mr. Carter had left it, which meant crossing in front of the TV to retrieve it. The screen was dark. Did that mean the video stream from the library to the author's study had been severed? Or was there a chance ol' Utter might still have eyes on this room? It was a chance I'd have to take.

I attempted to walk casually across the library floor, probably amplifying my guilt rather than disguising it. I was shit at subterfuge.

Upon reaching the box, a floorboard behind me creaked. I whirled about. Nothing.

Are you going to let every little noise send you into a panic?

I shed all pretense of stealth, flipped open the lid, removed the glass, and slipped it into my front pocket, my Cold Spring hoodie reaping dividends once again.

The TV popped.

Just a single, electronic burst, but enough to make me freeze.

He *was* watching, wasn't he?

Not waiting to find out, I put my head down and quickstepped it out the way I'd come.

First stop: the parlor. I held the stained glass in front of me like a compass, hoping for some twitch or quiver that might direct me toward something, anything that might be of interest. But the shard remained stubbornly silent.

I held the glass in front of my eyes, turning the piles of building materials and abandoned power tools red. All quiet.

I hadn't expected to find anything in the parlor—its windows, where they hadn't been replaced by plywood sheets, were clear glass. In fact, I was realizing, I had yet to see a single pane of stained glass anywhere.

Slipping from the parlor and past the dining room—I'd

check out the dining room last, lest my fellow guests might suddenly appear from the kitchen—I returned to the site of our first encounter: the entryway.

Despite its earlier activity, the tiled entry was still. If I'd expected some little spirit to appear and try to steal away the shard, I would have been sorely disappointed. But once again, the space was as devoid of demons as the parlor had been.

Up the stairs, then.

As I hit the switchback hallway up the staircase, the glass grew warm in my hand. Mind you, I'd been clutching it most firmly and had no doubt infused it with nervous body warmth. But the heat seemed to be coming from inside the glass.

"Getting warmer, eh?" I asked the stone owl. He just stared back at me with cold and indifferent eyes.

And so, I proceeded upward.

I considered making a sweep of the second floor, then thought better of it. Mr. Carter had known exploring the floor above would be tempting even as he warned against it. Hell, he was probably setting us up—dangling the apple, daring us to pick it. Make the third floor off-limits, figuring we'd disobey, and sit back and enjoy the screams as we stumbled upon ghoulies and ghosties.

As I ascended the stairs, I began to reassess. The number of steps that had been replaced by wooden planks made me wonder if Carter had been warning of practical rather than paranormal issues. The railing swayed under my touch, its balusters as loose as rotten teeth. By the time I reached the top, I had already begun dreading the trip back down.

The second floor had been five-star accommodations

compared with the third. Here, no effort had been made to coax the space into livability. The ceiling was water-damaged and crumbling, the walls were pockmarked with holes from which wires sprouted, and everywhere, the scent of mold and decay followed me. Whoever had been working on this level had left in a rush, leaving tools and jackets behind to gather dust.

The third floor existed in concept only. Like the floor below, plywood sheets lay upon a crisscross of supporting beams. One misstep, and I'd plummet through the second floor's ceiling.

The shard's temperature had not increased any further; however, I sensed a slight vibration coming from its surface. Back in college, I'd owned a used toaster oven purchased from Goodwill. It did the job, but if you ran your fingers across its metal surface, you could pick up a dull, electric hum, due no doubt to faulty wiring. I was picking up the same unpleasant sensation from the glass.

I stepped from one plywood sheet to another, making my way north, reenacting the childhood game of "the floor is lava." The wood beneath my feet warped under my weight, threatening to snap in two, but it held, allowing me passage down the darkened hallway. No bedrooms here, spartan or otherwise. The rooms I encountered resembled rats' nests, corners littered with shredded drywall and burger wrappers.

Yup, the workers had definitely made a hasty exit. In the middle of the floor of the final room I entered sat a man's wallet, complete with credit cards, an expired driver's license, and an ancient condom.

For all my skulking about, I had yet to discover a match to the piece of stained glass. My mind flitted back to the stairs. The steps had continued upward. Dare I follow?

I returned to the stairwell and stopped short.

You're not really searching, are you?

That damn niggling voice was right. Sure, I'd covered a lot of ground, but that was only on the outside. It was time to start unlocking my interior doors.

I closed my eyes, took a deep breath, and let it out in an invitation. If there was anything here that had anything to say, I was all ears. I took another breath, and this time said aloud, "Let's go."

The vibration began in my feet, as it always had. There were steps to warming up the engine, psychically speaking, and the onset of vibrations was the first indication that the process had begun. Next would come the pounding in my veins followed by a chill in the sinuses. Whatever these indicators actually indicated, I had no earthly idea. It had always been this way, I thought, ever since I was a little thing trying desperately to keep my curious ventures into the beyond from my mother. She'd made me feel dirty about my abilities. Told me it was cheating, slapped me across the head if she found me exercising my gift. But what did she know other than how to make a ten-year-old girl cry?

Nothing.

All that build-up and nothing was taking the bait.

Maybe I needed to go deeper. And by deeper, I mean higher.

A single bare bulb glowed overhead. I put my foot on the

first step of the final flight of stairs, and the wood didn't groan so much as squealed. Was it worth it? The others, no doubt, would be missing me soon. Time to keep moving.

With a speed that surprised even me, I mounted the stairs in a burst of adrenaline, only stopping once I'd reached the top. The landing was small, no bigger than a king-sized mattress, and a lone door stood directly to my left. My heart began fluttering like a bird in a cage, and a trickle of sweat ran from my armpits. I considered casting my mind toward the room beyond the door but thought better of it. A quick turn of the doorknob, and I'd know everything there was to know about this abbreviated fourth floor.

The latch clicked, and I pushed open the door.

There was no room beyond the doorway. Instead, what greeted me was a spiral staircase, its wood lacquered and dark. I fumbled around on the wall for a switch and found none. There was no way I was going to go stumbling up those stairs without a shred of light to help me find my way—

My hand hit a metal box. Two buttons protruded from within—one was depressed. My thumb found the other and pushed.

High overhead, a bulb flickered to life. The light it gave off was sickly yellow—warm but without warmth. The staircase circled around the point of light in herky-jerky angles, growing smaller as they ascended. I was a lighthouse keeper visiting her new home for the first time.

I am not *going up there.*

But of course, I was. It was time to push back against the

frightened voices that had taken up residence where resolve once had been.

Bits of stone had dislodged themselves from the walls, and I wedged one of the larger chunks under the door as a stop before mounting the first step.

Just as I had with the last flight of stairs, I gritted my teeth and plowed upward. The rhythm of my ascent was as jarring as the stairs' construction. *Three steps...angle...three steps...angle.* I caught myself humming "Pop Goes the Weasel" as I climbed.

The air smelled different here, damp and slightly rotten. I had the unnerving feeling I was clambering up the house's decaying windpipe.

When I reached the top, the madhouse layout suddenly made sense. I'd just ascended Utter Hall's lone turret. An octagonal floor encompassed the stairs, and windows afforded me a 360-degree view of the grounds. I could see Carter's little carriage house, the flicker of a TV dancing across curtained windows. Opposite, at the rear of the house, the level ground abruptly fell away, nothing but darkness beyond its edge.

I paused my sightseeing. The view was not a true 360... more like 330.

One pane of glass held not shrouded scenery, but nothing at all. At first, I thought some worker must have swapped out a plywood plank for shattered plate of glass, but as I ran my fingers over its surface, it wasn't rough as I'd expected but smooth. The glass remained; it was the view that was missing.

I pressed my nose against the glass and stared. As my eyes adjusted to the absence of light, I began to see small flickers, sparks floating in space. Embers, maybe. Red and darting through a starless sky.

I glanced right and left to make sure I was seeing what I was seeing. Through the other windows, dim but clear, the grounds were still visible. Straight ahead? A void.

The light in the cramped room dipped.

No. No, no, no...

How the hell was I going to get down in the dark?

The light dimmed again, and I could swear the bulb's wiry workings *hissed*.

I grasped the railing.

A moment later, the lightbulb winked out. Darkness swallowed me whole.

One thing I need to tell you about myself: I don't have the best sense of balance. So, when I say my anxiety rocketed skyward the moment the lights went out, I mean my anxiety *rocketed*.

Paused between immobility and a tumble down the stairs, I weighed my options. I could close my eyes and proceed with a caution usually reserved for bomb defusers, or I could sit on my rump and butt-hop my way down, one step at a time.

Being balance blind, I chose the latter.

Slide-thump-slide-thump. My glutes bore the brunt of my descent, although my tailbone seemed eager to get in on the action—every so often, my old coccyx met wood, sending shockwaves up my spine as I dropped from one step to the next.

Low light from the fourth-floor landing came into view

when I was halfway down, buoying my spirits. But as I took my next *slide-thump*, I heard a sound that filled me with dread.

The stone I'd employed as a doorstop skittered across the floor and struck the wall. The light from the doorway dimmed as the door swung shut.

I was in darkness once more. But I was not alone.

The first step groaned.

Something was coming up the stairs.

16

S *hit.*
    I briefly considered scrambling back up the stairs, but to what end? All that awaited me above were windows from which to jump.

Still, what lay below didn't promise to be any picnic either.

A second step groaned.

I allowed myself an investigative *slide-thump.*

A third step groaned.

Great. I guess we're playing chicken.

I was on a collision course with the very type of phenomenon I'd been avoiding for years. They say reengaging in activities you've put aside is "just like riding a bike." They say all you've got to do is "get back on the horse." My parents never bought me a bike, and the only horse I'd ever seen up close bit my finger, mistaking it for a carrot.

I was hoping whatever was on the stairs didn't bite.

If there were ever a time to shake the mothballs out of the old telepathy, this was it. I relaxed my body as best I could and reached out toward the darkness below.

Let me pass.

No reply.

I put a little muscle behind it.

I'm coming down. Let me—

The thing took two stairs in rapid succession.

I'd dealt with aggressive spirits before. Usually they backed down if you flicked on the lights, lit a bit of sage, or incanted a few words from a dusty text. Unfortunately, I had no light or sage, and the only words that popped into my whirling head were those I'd been thinking of earlier...

All around the Mulberry Bush,
The monkey chased the weasel.
The monkey stopped to pull up his sock,
Pop—

The thing in the darkness claimed two more steps.

Any second, the location of our encounter would no longer be my decision. If I was going to move, by God, I'd better do it quick. And I wasn't going to meet my fate on my butt.

I rose and placed my foot on the lower step.

Cree-eee!

The thing below took a step.

Craa-aaa!

With nothing left to do but hoof it down the stairs, I bolted. My heel misjudged the next step, and I nearly tumbled headlong into the unwelcome visitor. I didn't bother to listen for my companion's footfalls—I was too busy getting the fuck out of there.

As I neared the bottom, I plowed straight into a cold pocket of air. It slowed my descent momentarily—it was like pushing through heavy curtains. A flare of rage seared my skin, and my teeth rattled in my head.

And then I was through. I hit the bottom step, grabbed for the doorknob, swung the door wide.

The sound of fabric whipping about told me my escape was not yet complete. Without so much as a glance backward, I tore down the stairs to the third floor, taking them two at a time. As I started down the next flight, frost chilled my neck as a voice whispered, "Pop! Goes the weasel..."

I'd held it together until then rather nicely, I must say. But at the breathy vocalization, my legs gave out, and I tumbled down the stairs. I rolled forward, the shard in my front pocket poking me badly, the steps playing whack-a-mole with my head. I hit the wall at the halfway point between third and second floors at full speed. Bones clicked, and I bit the side of my mouth, a veritable fireworks display of pain.

Now stopped, I turned my head to face the way I'd come. There was nothing on the stairs—nothing, not even the hint of a shadow.

I'd escaped.

I took a deep breath and prepared to test out my sore body.

That's when the stone statue of the owl slipped from its place on the ledge above me and came crashing down on my head.

I didn't black out, but I must admit my recollection of the next fifteen minutes or so are still sketchy.

I recall JJ and Quan lifting me to my feet, Zivy peppering me with the same questions one would ask a stroke victim, and bits of shattered owl crunching underfoot.

By the time I had my wits about me, I'd downed half a can of ginger ale. And I *hate* ginger ale.

The kitchen smelled like burnt toast, and I spied the source of the stink: a haphazardly assembled pizza sitting on the island.

Quan stood in front of me, my interrogator.

"Rule number one of paranormal investigation: no one goes it alone." If it wasn't for the look of genuine concern on his face, I might have decked him.

"He's right, Ellen," JJ said, taking the unwanted ginger ale from me. "Solo is a no-go."

Zivy, who had perched atop a counter sipping her vodka on ice, gave a snort of disapproval.

"You think this is funny?" Quan asked.

"No. I think *you're* funny. In fact, I think this whole thing is fucking hilarious."

"How do you mean?"

Zivy hopped off the counter and approached. She held out her glass, and I took it willingly, taking more than just a sip.

"Got a little restless, huh?" she asked. "I could tell you're a curious one by nature. What are you, a Gemini?"

"Not enough…" I began talking but my tongue felt heavy in my mouth. Perhaps another gulp.

"Not enough what?" Quan was determined to get to the truth about my little sojourn.

"Answers," I said. Even though my neck remained chilled by my encounter, the vodka was doing a yeoman's job of warming me up. "Too many questions and not enough answers."

"I get that," JJ agreed.

Quan gave a little laugh, turning his attention to JJ. "So, what are you saying? Now you think she's justified in poking around on her own?"

"No. I'm just saying that I understand where she's coming from—"

"You know what kind of damage she might have caused, besides breaking Mr. Utter's owl? Do you have any idea how many investigations have gone south because someone decided that protocol didn't apply to them?"

"Give it a rest, will you?" Zivy said, swiping back her drink. "Jesus, chick, I didn't think anyone could down vodka faster than me." Quan tried to get a word in edgewise, but Zivy wasn't having it. "Do you think we should *maybe* ask her if she found anything before we read her the riot act?"

All three heads turned my way.

"Well?" JJ asked. "Did you see anything?"

"No," I lied. "Nothing. I just tripped. I'm clumsy that way. I tripped."

At that, I felt a stirring near my belly. The shard in my marsupial pocket twitched. I placed my hand over my stomach, but the shard slipped free. It shot upward in a crimson streak, glinting in the light before striking the ceiling. The glass exploded into a million fragments, spreading out across the ceiling tiles in a red spray.

"You were saying?" Quan asked.

Gravity regained control, and the scores of tiny bits of glass rained down on us.

17

After picking bits of glass from our hair, JJ dumped the shard-peppered pizza in the trash, and we got to work.

I rectified my less-than-truthful account of my upstairs activities and clued the crew in on what I'd found on the staircase...or rather, what had found me. Armed with my admission and this new information, Quan seized control.

"We're going to do this by the book or not at all."

Zivy put up a protest, but JJ was uncharacteristically quiet. He kept looking at me like I'd grown a tail. What was up with him?

Quan's plan was simple: we pair up, choose two hotspots to station ourselves, and wait. He retrieved a silver hard case from his luggage and introduced us to the equipment inside. It looked like someone had merged a mini-DJ setup with an HVAC system—it was all dials and displays and vents.

"This is a prototype of the kit my group will be selling in the near future. It's a portable detector system that doubles as a lure. It aerosolizes a number of liquids to attract spirits. This particular vial contains a mixture of artificial sweat and lavender..."

"Gross," JJ said.

"It's been proven that sweat, an indicator of stress in humans, makes great bait."

"And the lavender?" I asked. "I'd always heard it was a repellant."

"Then you heard wrong."

It went on like that for some time. Quan had his audience, and he was going to make a meal out of flaunting his expertise. Long and the short of it, his device—soon to be available for purchase at the low, low price of fifteen hundred dollars (sweat cartridges sold separately)—emitted sounds and scents designed to coax the undead from the shadows.

When Quan finished his presentation, he grinned like an expectant tech bro, eager for us to bow down in praise. Zivy offered him a wet raspberry instead.

"Sorry, but I'm not buying it," she said. "Not literally, not figuratively."

"Can't you call on your brothers?" JJ asked. "You know... your spirit brothers? Wouldn't they be more helpful than a machine that squirts sweat?"

"No," Quan said, turning stern. "They're not always... reliable. My device will do the trick. Unless one of you has a better plan, I'm setting it up in the foyer."

I could have made a stink, said that the only way I'd ever managed to "lure" a ghost was through sheer stupidity—such as my most recent escapade on the spiral stairs—but I figured he and his machine had stupidity sewn up pretty tight. Besides, my stomach had started to rumble.

Somewhere between the conclusion of Quan's dog and pony show and my miraculous find of an assortment of mini-cereal boxes—no milk, unfortunately—the "pairing up" our new leader had wanted happened naturally. Zivy remained with Quan as he set up his equipment, firing off question after question as JJ appeared at the kitchen door, catching me munching on dry Froot Loops directly from the box.

"Why'd you lie?"

"Excuse me?" I asked.

"You said you didn't see anything."

"And then I said I did, so what?"

There was that look again, like he was reassessing my value. It unnerved me more than it should have.

"Don't you trust me?"

"Trust has nothing to do with it. I work alone," I said. "Always have, always will."

"And how has that been working out for you?"

I wanted to throw the empty cereal box at him. Not because he was wrong, but because he was fucking right.

"What do you want? An apology?"

He shrugged. "Wouldn't hurt."

I chewed the last mouthful of Froot Loops and forced it down. "I'm sorry. All right? I'm sorry."

JJ looked down at the floor.

"What?" I asked. "Not good enough?"

"I'm not sure you meant it."

That got me heated. "Look, Mr. I-Died-And-Went-To-Heaven, you're one to talk."

"You're right."

"If I've learned anything in this life, it's that everyone lies."

Quit complaining, Ellen. I'll be back in time to tuck you in. Jesus, don't moms get to go out and have a bit of fun?

The memory startled me, not so much for its abrupt arrival as for its total lack of truth. My mother never tucked me in—not once.

"Everyone lies," I repeated.

"Okay," JJ said. "Let's drop it."

"Fine."

He'd been hanging back until then, but now he fully entered the kitchen and leaned against the island. Quan hadn't locked down its wheels when he'd moved it, and it shifted under JJ's weight. He caught himself none too gracefully and opted for a stool instead.

"What was it like?"

He meant the thing I'd encountered, but I wasn't going to make it easy on him. "What was *what* like?"

"You know...the ghost?"

"I already told you."

"Tell me again."

I sighed and grabbed a box of Rice Krispies. "I didn't *see* anything."

"What did you feel?"

"Cold. Anger. Usual ghost stuff."

Now it was his turn to sigh. "Anything else?"

"Nothing that I can remember—"

I stopped short. There *was* something I'd left out in my description of my experience to the group. And not only to them; I'd kept it from myself as well.

"Ellen?"

When I'd slipped past—or *through*—the thing on the stairs, I'd felt something else. Something apart from the chill and the rage.

Fear.

"It was afraid."

Zivy appeared in the doorway.

"The ghostbuster in the other room would like to have a word."

***

Quan stood waiting for us in the entryway, looking like a proud papa.

"Let me show you the setup, shall I?" His phone was mounted to a selfie stick, and he spoke as much to it as he did to us.

Quan's contraption sat atop a worktable pilfered from the parlor, an altar to techno-foolishness. Three GoPro-sized cameras mounted to spindly tripods had been positioned equidistant from the device. Little red lights atop the cameras blinked on and off.

"It's simple, really," Quan said, turning to get the rest of us in frame. "Each camera is equipped with an EMF detector. The device emits both scent and sound. I find infrasound to be most effective."

"Okay, I'll bite," I said. "Infrasound?"

"Tones below the level of human hearing."

"Ah, of course."

Quan lowered the selfie stick. "Have you finished scoffing or may I go on?"

I bit my tongue and let Quan proceed. The scent/sound combo was meant to lure ghosts into the center of the circle where their presence would be picked up by the EMF units, setting off the cameras and alerting Quan via an app.

"It's all proprietary," he crowed.

It's preposterous, I thought.

"Our first visitors traveled down these stairs," he explained to his imaginary viewers. "Zivy and I will station ourselves on the second-floor landing: the point of origin. You two hang here.

"If something triggers the device, we'll reconnoiter with you."

"Yes, Drill Sergeant," I said.

"What?"

"Nothing."

"Let's do one-hour shifts," Quan said. "We've got all night —no reason to get blurry." And then, to his phone. "Ghosts don't sleep, and neither will we."

I rolled my eyes. I couldn't help it.

Quan bounded up the stairs. Zivy followed reluctantly, mouthing "help me" as she did so.

JJ circled about Quan's device, careful not to upset the tripoded cameras.

"What do you think?"

"About?"

He waved his hand at the setup. "All this?"

"Not much."

The device gave a little fart, and floral sweat filled the air.

"Why don't I get us some chairs," JJ said.

"Sounds good."

We sat silent vigil for twenty minutes before JJ broke the silence.

"What's the scariest thing you've ever experienced?"

"Why do you ask?"

He shrugged. "Maybe I'm trying to prepare for the worst. You know? Like psyching yourself up before riding a roller coaster?"

"I've never been on a roller coaster."

"Not my point. You've had a lot more practice with this sort of stuff. I guess I'm trying to figure out what I've gotten myself into."

I nodded. It made sense. A little bit of control over a situation went a long way.

"So, you want to know..."

"The scariest thing you've seen."

I checked my mental inventory. I'd seen ghosts aplenty in my life, some wistful and mournful, others angry and vengeful. The most disturbing had been the floating torso of a cyclist who'd tangled with a freight train. His mouth hung slack, and he cried low as he circled the place of his death, dragging his entrails behind him. With every pass, he'd lock eyes with me as if to ask, *Why me? Why me?*

But...scary?

"There was a woman who used to hang out next to the bus station in Iowa City," I said. "She had a kid, must have been around one year old. One day, I stopped to give her a buck. No little kid. I asked her where he was. She held up his little shirt. It had all these little holes in it. 'The rats got him,' she said. That shirt was the scariest thing I've ever seen. You?"

JJ leaned back in his chair. "Jesus, Ellen. I thought you were going to tell me about some spooky ghost shit, but *this?* Jesus."

We settled back in silence. I hadn't expected JJ's reaction. After all, *he* was the one who asked the question. What was I going to do, lie? I considered telling him the story had a semi-happy ending: the next time I saw the woman, she had her kid back. They were both spirits, of course, but they had each other. Probably best to drop it.

A piercing scream echoed from upstairs.

JJ's chair toppled over, spilling him onto the floor.

I guess the game's afoot.

I rose. Had the pattering footsteps returned? Was it my friend from the turret? Or the spirit of Jacob Marley announcing the arrival of three ghosts?

Turned out I was wrong on all counts.

"Something's wrong with her!" Quan cried as he led Zivy down the stairs.

In the darkness, the blood that covered Zivy's Hudson Livin' T-shirt appeared black. But as she approached the foyer's glowing warmth, the gore flowing down her front transitioned to vibrant red.

"She just started gushing," Quan said.

I grabbed my chair and set it to the side of the stairs. "Sit her down."

"We should call Mr. Carter," JJ said.

Zivy sat with a plop. This was no nosebleed—blood trickled from her mouth, down her chin, and over her chest.

"Zivy, can you hear me? What's going on? Talk to me."

She raised a hand as if to shush me, red blood blisters on her fingertips.

"Something's coming," Zivy rasped.

"What's coming."

"He says it's something *nasty*."

"He?" Quan asked. "He who?"

The blisters on her fingertips burst, and crimson tendrils emerged, growing like arterial branches.

"Why, me, of course."

She wiped her fingers across her mouth, painting her smile red.

"Her little bird..."

18

It wasn't just Zivy's voice that had changed; it was her face. Muscles usually reserved for screaming were in full use. And the blood—it trickled from the corners of her mouth like tributaries.

It was her *hands* that disturbed me the most. She stared down at them in amusement, watching as blood-red branches grew from her fingers, from her wrists. It must have been excruciating, yet all she did was grin.

"What the fuck?" JJ whispered.

Zivy's eyes flew open.

"Language," the voice warned.

"Zivy, can you hear me?" I leaned in as close as I dared.

"She can't hear nuttin', honey."

To prove his point—for I would have bet the farm I was talking to a *he*—blood trickled from Zivy's ears.

Zivy squeezed her eyes shut.

"He's scared."

Her other voice objected. "The hell I am."

Zivy raised her hands. Red tears welled up in her eyes.

"You only hurt me when you're scared."

"I am *not* scared!"

"Who the hell are you talking to?" Quan insisted.

She looked up at him. Or at least, someone did.

"Wouldn't you like to know, sweetheart..."

Quan took a step back, unnerved by being addressed directly. Still, he wasn't going to back down. Not on video, he wasn't.

"She's been infected by some sort of...blood demon. Don't worry. I've studied this sort of thing."

"Have you? Have you now?" The thing inside Zivy chortled with glee and stared down the barrel of Quan's phone. "Bet he hasn't studied anything like *this!*"

Zivy's "companion" hauled back and spat a mouthful of blood into Quan's face. He spiraled back, dropping his phone, hands clawing at his face.

"What the hell!" Quan wiped away blood with his shirt sleeve.

"That's enough of that," I said. I was over this thing, whatever it was.

He turned Zivy's head toward me.

"If it isn't Frumpty Dumpty."

"Shut up. I want to talk to Zivy."

"Sorry. She can't come to the phone right now—"

The slap I delivered surprised even me.

It did the trick.

Zivy was back.

"Byrd!" she snarled. "His name is Byrd."

Her pronouncement immediately staunched the flow of blood.

"Our secret! Our ss-ssecret!"

"D. Ellis Byrd!" She spoke the name like an incantation, and the result was immediate.

Blood rolled down her cheeks in a final, angry torrent before ceasing altogether. She slumped in the chair.

I placed a hand on her shoulder. "Zivy?"

"Just let me sit a bit."

"What was that?" Quan said. His selfie stick was back in action. "What's inside you?"

"Leave her alone."

"I think we deserve to know."

"You mean your fucking *audience* deserves to know!"

Zivy waved me off. "It's okay. I'm okay. He just caught me off guard, that's all. He can be...rude."

"Rude?" Quan laughed incredulously, wiping a bit of red from his cheek. "That's the understatement of the year."

Ignoring him, I kneeled before her. "He's the one who drew the diamond, isn't he?"

"That's him. My little bird."

"You better hope your 'little bird' doesn't have any diseases, that's all I can say."

I grabbed Quan's selfie stick and bent it over my knee.

"What the fuck?"

I tossed it back to him. "We didn't agree to be part of the William Quan Comedy Hour."

"What the hell's that supposed to mean?"

"Guys..."

"It means you can take that stick and shove it up your—"

"Guys!" JJ whispered. "Something's happening."

The house groaned like a ship at sea.

The entryway walls bent and distorted as if folding in on themselves. But, no...that wasn't right. The walls stood perfectly still. It was the *shadows*. The room was alive with them.

And they were on the move.

19

The shadows emerged from every corner, sliding down walls and across the tiled floor like ethereal fish. They glided aimlessly, floating about the room as if directed by invisible currents.

"This is freakin' wild," Quan said, extracting his phone from his ruined selfie stick. "This is good stuff."

One of the shadows brushed past my ankle. It was cold and rough. It circled back, making another pass, like a cat rubbing against its human's leg. I gave it a little kick and it moved on.

"We have apparitions, people," Quan said.

"Give it a rest, will you?" I begged.

Quan ignored me, opting instead to have a little chat with his invisible audience.

"What you're witnessing is a full-on paranormal event here at Utter Hall...or should I say utter hell?"

Groan.

"Our first encounter was auditory only, but now? We have

eyes on the prize. See how the shadows move? Independently and yet with little intent. Like they're searching for something. What that might be, I haven't a clue. But I have a feeling we'll have our answer soon enough."

"Hey!" JJ squealed in pain. "One of them just bit me."

"Impossible," Quan said. "These are just shades. They're just low-energy manifestations. In my experience...whoa!"

He jumped back, clutching his hip.

"See?" JJ cried. "I told you!"

"I've just been attacked," Quan announced. "This is serious business, folks. I may have been mistaken in my initial evaluation of our circumstances, but no matter. I shall proceed with protocol..."

I'd had enough of Quan's blathering. He *was* right about one thing: this sort of manifestation never interacted, let alone *bit*. I had to hand it to Utter Hall—it was certainly performing some new tricks.

I took a leap and reached out to the shadows. I'd done similar many times before. It was a good way to "taste" the room, so to speak. No harm in it. Just a little peek.

The moment I opened myself to the shadows, blackness flooded my mind. It was as if a spigot turned on in my brain, pouring in liquid darkness, leaving me gasping for breath.

I had to pull back before I drowned.

"Ellen?" JJ asked. "You okay?"

I spat, trying to rid myself of the shadows' filth. My spittle was black.

"I'm good," I lied.

A dark squadron formed around Zivy's chair. Shadows

circled, their circle growing, forcing us back. That rough coldness touched my skin again.

Teeth bit down on my wrist...

"Fuck!"

...forcing me to retreat.

"They're not triggering the cameras." Quan stared at his setup, perplexed. "Goddamn it!" He squealed again, shadows nipping at him, forcing him into a corner.

The attacks kept coming—*nip-nip-bite-bite!* Separating us. Containing us. Only stopping once they'd maneuvered us to four corners of the room: Quan and Zivy flanking the stairs, JJ pressed up against the front door, me trapped in the transition between the entryway and the parlor.

"What do we do?" JJ asked, wincing each time a shadow whispered past.

"Stay still," I said.

Quan ignored my advice and took a bite to the chin as punishment.

"Don't move. Don't breathe a word. Let's pause and see how this plays out."

Everyone froze—red-light-green-light style—save for Zivy, who followed the shades as they swirled past.

"I think they're rabid," the other-Zivy voice sang.

"Shh!" I hissed.

"Raa-aabid!"

The Bakelite phone on the wall rang, only inches from JJ's head.

"Jesus!" JJ said. "What should I do?"

"Answer it," Quan ordered.

"Don't move!" I countered.

"But..." JJ stammered, "it's gotta be Mr. Carter. He'd said he was going to call—"

"Don't. Move."

"Answer it!"

"Yes, answer it, answer it, ANSWER IT!" Zivy shook with terrible glee.

JJ reached for the phone.

Invisible teeth did their job. *Nip-nip!* Bite marks bloomed on the back of JJ's hand. He quickly pulled back, nursing his wounds as the phone continued to ring.

Why doesn't anyone ever listen to me?

"Damn!" Another nip for Quan. "Have you ever come across something like this?" He'd lowered his phone and his guard—was that nervousness seeping into his voice?

"Nope," I said, stiffening as a particularly dense shadow slithered past my face.

"I feel sick to my stomach," JJ moaned.

Come to think of it, so did I. The moment the shadows began their dance, I'd felt a rising nausea. The things messed with my head. Made me dizzy. I had to concentrate to remain steady, knowing that the slightest stumble on my part would earn me a toothy reminder to stay in place.

I took a deep breath, and my restless belly eased ever so slightly.

Quan wasn't so lucky. He lost his lunch in a nervous splat.

"Seriously?" JJ asked, turning away as his stomach lurched.

Forcing us apart seemed the shadows' only intention. Like

pawns executing a move. And if that was the case...where was their queen?

It was Quan who announced her arrival.

"Wh-what's that?"

I turned my attention from the ringing phone to the staircase where Quan stood encircled by his own swarming shadows. He was staring up at the second-floor landing.

Where was the queen?

Why, she was coming down the stairs.

20

The dark woman descended the stairs like death itself.

No need for an introduction. We'd already met in the turret.

"Oh, Jesus," JJ wailed. "Oh, God."

She was young and ancient at the same time. Her mourning garments billowed about her as if submerged. Her skin was like tallow, her dress ink black, a beaded vulcanite necklace about her neck. She glared down on us in loathing. Miss Havisham at midnight.

"Late 1800s, if I were to guess." I spoke aloud despite my rising fear and the palpable gloom filling the room. "Her clothes speak wealth and privilege. A former resident, no doubt."

JJ tried to break away, but the shadows corralled him. He wept openly, howling like a frightened child. "Our Father, who art in Heaven..."

I had two choices available to me: give in to dread or do my job.

"Late twenties/early thirties—"

"I want to go home," JJ cried.

"Quiet, Chunky." I had no time to handhold. "She's dressed in mourning clothes. But who is she mourning?"

The dark woman took another step. It was difficult to look at her—it was like staring into the sun but in reverse. Her very essence was *darkness*. A negation. And what would happen should she train those empty eyes at me?

Zivy's demeanor changed as she neared. Her skin reddened as if her blood would be free of her.

"No! Go! Away! No!"

The woman took another step. One more and she'd be down the stairs and among us. Why was it so hard to look at her?

"I'll speak to it," Quan said, still finding the wherewithal to film.

"I don't recommend that," I warned, knowing I spoke in vain.

"Listen to Ellen!" Faithful JJ.

And yet...

"Who are you, and what unfinished business do you have?"

I thought the shadows were bad, with their sharp coldness and toothy attacks. But nothing prepared me for what happened next.

The Dark Lady—for that was what she was, after all—swooped in on Quan like a bird of prey and grasped his head in her pale hands. She held him firmly, head tilting in curiosity, staring deep into his ever-widening eyes.

"Oh God, please don't."

The Dark Lady snaked her fingers into the young man's hair, gripping him tight. Quan struggled but couldn't turn away—a fly mesmerized by a spider.

I'd heard stories about investigators' hair going white with fear, but I'd never seen it. Not until that night. Quan let out a slight *ahh* as the Dark Lady drew the color from him, leaving his hair as white as chalk.

"Quan? You okay, dude? Quan!" JJ's voice rose in panic.

Quan was beyond answering. He stood slack-jawed and dumb. He remained standing, I was certain, only because the Dark Lady wasn't finished with him yet.

It was time to ignore my own advice.

"Hey, lady." My voice was strangled, and I cleared my throat. "Lady!"

She released Quan, who promptly crumpled to the floor, and turned my way. Slowly, like a tide shifting.

"That's right, over here! You got a problem? Take it up with me!"

The woman glided toward me as if she skated on ice. Black ice.

Those eyes!

They latched onto mine with fierce intensity, and I discovered I *could* look back. But at what a price! If sorrow had an electrical charge, this bitch was on overload. It poured into me, lighting up terrible memories and shame and guilt. Her gaze was fire, my mind, the fuel.

She approached, hands outstretched, and now I could see her face. Before, I had only a vague notion of it, but as she drew nearer, it came into focus.

It was the Halloween Queen's face. She'd stolen it along with the Queen's trademark black and white hairstyle.

"Looky here!" the fake Queen cried. "If it isn't Booth 38."

I had hated that face from the moment I saw it, and now that the Dark Lady was wearing it, I hated it all the more.

"Where are your trinkets? Where are your charms? Where is your little gra-a-asshopper pal?"

"Ellen!"

JJ's voice was miles away—blood pounded in my ears, blocking it out. My world had reduced to the spirit's gaze and my heartbeat. If this went on any longer, I knew which would win.

Faux Queen laced her fingers in my hair.

"Miss us?" she crooned.

I blinked. She was no longer the insidious influencer but the Weird Sisters, swapping their faces back and forth, ghostly flesh rending at each transformation, both sisters vying to press forward.

"You gotta push the crystals, Ellen. You gotta puu-uu-uush!" There was no emotion behind the voice, simply hollow mimicry. "Puu-uush!"

A scream rose in my throat, and I tried unsuccessfully to swallow it down. The Dark Lady screamed with me, her horrific shrieks mixing with mine, creating a deranged duet.

Had JJ asked me his earlier question now, I would have

responded that this, *this* was the scariest thing I had ever experienced.

"Do you trust me?"

Who'd said that?

"Ellen," JJ shouted. His voice was closer. "Do you trust me?"

The thing in front of me raged. "Trust me, Ellen! Trust mee-ee!"

Undeterred by the wailing woman, JJ said for a third time, "Do you trust—"

"Yes!" I screamed, squeezing my eyes shut. "I fucking trust you!"

A hand grasped mine, the fingers in my hair dissolved, and I heard the Dark Lady cry out.

"Noo-oo!"

Then, she fell silent.

JJ released his grip.

A cold breeze whipped my cheeks as the scent of gasoline hit my nose.

I slowly opened my eyes.

A green sedan lay upside-down before me, its wheels still spinning, headlights illuminating the gently falling snow. The car's turn signal flashed as if its driver wanted desperately to turn right-right-right...

But there was no driver behind the wheel. No one riding shotgun, either.

A small hand reached from the backseat window through shattered glass. I took a step forward in the slush and snow, and I spotted the object of the child's attention.

Sitting on the pavement, soaking up gas from the car's split and spilling tank, was a battered stuffed animal.

JJ's dog, Jersey.

21

"Who's there?" A child's voice.

I tried to answer but only croaked, my mouth dry as a bone. *Where the hell was I?* The scene was self-explanatory—a flipped car, a trapped passenger, an icy stretch of highway—and yet it was incomplete. Aside from the car and the shoulder on which it lay, I could make out an overturned semi, the car's headlights splashed across its side, and a road sign that read, "Exit 46," and...that was it. The rest of this place was nothing more than a sketch. The more I looked, the less I saw. Like an illustration out of a kid's book—detailed where it mattered, vague where it didn't.

Gone was any trace of Utter Hall, the Dark Lady, and her shadows.

"Hello?"

The voice pulled me from my fog, and I picked up the dog. It was damp with gas.

"Are you okay?" I asked as I approached the car.

"My leg's stuck."

"Does it hurt?"

"No...but it feels funny."

I knelt at the broken window and looked inside, slush soaking my knees. I tried the boy's door, but it might as well have been welded shut.

"You found him!" the boy in the backseat cried. He reached out for his toy, his trapped leg forgotten.

I handed him the dog.

"He stinks."

"Sorry about that." I scanned the interior of the car, not finding what I was looking for. "Where are your parents?"

The boy wrinkled his brow in confusion, doing an amazing if youthful impression of JJ, right down to the thick glasses.

"I don't know."

"Who was driving?"

"Dad."

"Was Mom with you?"

The boy didn't answer. He scanned the car as well before his eyes landed on me.

"We crashed."

"Looks like it."

"We slid on the ice. Dad was screaming. Mom was screaming."

A rogue wind whipped up, the snow it kicked up temporarily blinding me. I was trapped in this moment as surely as the boy was trapped in the car. There was nothing I could do about my own situation, but perhaps...

"Give me your hand," I said, brushing ice from my eyes.

The boy considered me warily.

"Are you an angel?"

"Hardly," I said. "I'm Ellen. And you, I take it, are JJ?"

"Julian," the boy said. He had begun to shiver; either from the cold or the onset of shock, I had no idea. "But I like JJ. That's a cool name."

Shit. Had I rechristened the kid *Back to the Future*-style? No time to worry about that.

"Okay, JJ, I'm going to get you out of there."

"Okay."

"You just have to give me your hand."

He offered his right, carefully holding tight to Jersey with his left. I gripped his forearm and pulled.

It was no use. The boy was stuck but good.

"I'm going to try coming in through the front," I told him.

But both front doors and the rear opposite the boy were immovable, the metal crushed under the car's weight.

I returned to the boy's window, and wriggled partway in, feeling the ragged edge of the broken window nipping my chest.

Nip-nip-bite-bite.

A blast from the past. A shockingly clear memory of the shadows swarming me. Or were they swarming me *right now?* My mind flitted back to my previous question: *Where the hell was I?* Was I here with the boy or was I fighting off spirits? Which *here* was really *here?*

The radio let loose a squeal of static and sparks flew. I smelled ozone over the gasoline, and suddenly, an orange glow rose from the front seat. I stared in disbelief, only regaining my senses when the smoke hit my nostrils.

The car is on fire.

The boy is trapped, and the car is on fire.

The boy coughed. "Smoke."

"I know, I know," I said, quickly weighing my options. I didn't have many. When the first flame licked upward, I made my move, pulling myself all the way into the backseat.

Great, Ellen. Now you're both trapped.

"Shut up," I told myself.

"What?"

"Nothing." The smoke was growing thicker and had a decidedly burned plastic stench. Before long, I was coughing along with the boy.

I snaked my hands down the kid's leg. Part of the car's roof had folded in on itself, creating a metal trap encasing his right foot. I kicked at the roof, hoping against hope I had the strength to loosen its grip.

From the boy's cries, I gathered I was only making matters worse.

Sweat dripped from my brow. Waves of heat rolled through the interior as the smoke turned black as pitch.

As black as the Dark Lady...

The boy stared at me with wild eyes, his dog pressed against his chest in a rib-crushing hug.

"Go," young JJ whispered.

"No."

"I'm stuck."

"Yeah, and I'm going to get you unstuck," I said, choking on the blackened air.

I pulled on the boy's leg. I pulled and pulled, but it was no use. Either we both burned or...

"Go!" he screamed, kicking at me with his free leg.

"I said, no!"

The heel of his foot connected with my nose, and I felt it click. Blood trickled down the back of my throat. When he kicked again, I caught his foot and held it tight.

"Stop that."

The fire took hold of the carpeted flooring, spreading overhead, forcing me down to eye-level with the kid.

"Go," the boy pleaded. "Go now."

"You'll burn if I go."

He shook his head frantically. "I'll burn if you *stay.*"

Self-preservation is one of the most basic instincts, one that's near impossible to overcome. I saw it in my mom as she forced her chest to rise and fall, rise and fall despite the cancer's tight grip. Every cell in my body begged me to move, to obey the kid, and *go!*

But I wasn't about to leave him to the flames.

And so, I took his hand in mine.

"I'm not going anywhere."

Immolation, it was.

"Ellen..."

The voice tried to reach me through the rising smoke.

The flames rose and the upholstery hissed, and I smiled at little JJ, insisting he return my gaze, even as the smoke obscured him from view. The heat flared and my heart raced, but I wasn't leaving his side. Not now, not ever. Not—

"Ellen, look..."

And now I recognized the voice. It was JJ. Not Julian, not the trapped boy, but JJ from the elevator, from Utter Hall, from—

"Look!"

Despite the fact the boy hadn't said a word, he stretched out his hand and pointed. Past me, past the licking flames, out into the dark beyond the car.

The headlights. The way they lit up the side of the semi... no, *danced* along its side. Like a projected movie.

I saw myself painted in light, saw the entryway and JJ standing over me. I saw the Dark Lady splashed across the side of the truck as she turned from my crumpled form toward Zivy.

"Time to go!"

"Go," a small voice next to me reiterated.

"Or he'll burn."

Loath as I was to do so, I turned my back on the boy. Plastic burned with a crackle, and fresh waves of heat licked my back as I crawled out the window, my hands feeling the bite of countless bits of glass.

Once outside, I rose, not daring to look back, and walked stunned toward the overturned semi. Standing in the headlight beams, casting a shadow over the projected scene.

Go. Or he'll burn.

There was nothing else to do.

The boy screamed—or had I—and I took a running leap at the flickering image.

There was a moment of stillness as I passed into the light, feeling my heart squeeze tight, feeling my whole essence contract as if I were attempting to pass through the eye of a needle.

And then I was through.

Back to Utter Hall.

22

I tumbled into the entryway, landing hard against JJ.

"Oof!"

I quickly rolled to the side and sat up.

As I'd seen projected, the spirit had moved on from me—JJ's little trick had reduced me to an empty shell, after all—turning its interest toward Zivy, who was still glued to the chair.

"I couldn't save him," I breathed.

"It's okay," JJ said, getting to his feet.

"He's going to burn."

"No, he won't."

"I let him burn!"

JJ dragged me to my feet. "I didn't burn. Not then, not now. Can you *please* drop it and help me stop her?"

The dark apparition circled Zivy as her shadows had done, evaluating, taking note. Zivy and her "bird" were at odds as to how to react.

"Sit still."

"Must run!"

"Sit!"

"Run!"

The inner battle was taking a toll on her, physically. Every time D. Ellis Byrd would take charge, he would struggle to be free. Every time Zivy clawed her way back, she pulled in the opposite direction. I could only imagine what sort of damage muscles might incur straining both ways at once.

I caught sight of Quan and knew at a glance he was of no use in this fight. He lay curled at the foot of the stairs, stroking his newly whitened hair as if doing so gave him a degree of comfort from the silent screams emitting from his mouth.

We stood side by side, JJ and I, facing down the horror at the heart of the house.

"What do we do?" JJ asked, his voice quavering.

I had nothing.

The phone rang again.

This time, I was able to answer it before the shadowy onslaught. The caller might be a prick, but he was our only lifeline.

"Mr. Carter!" I shouted into the mouthpiece. "She's here. The Dark Lady's here!"

The ghost looked up at the sound of my voice and snarled. Her shadows swirled up about her like smoke-black wings, turning her into a dark and avenging angel.

I let go of the phone, the voice on the other end a distant babble.

The pale woman's interest in Zivy fell away. All her rage, all her venom was directed at me. I was the one who had answered the phone, after all.

I wasn't able to save the boy, but maybe I could save the man.

"Sorry, Chunky," I said, and shoved JJ aside with all the strength I had left.

He stumbled over his own feet and toppled into one of Quan's tripods, an echo of his unfortunate tumble that day in the East Room. He went down hard, rolling clear.

I summoned the last of my courage and raised my arms, making myself a bigger target.

"I'm not afraid of you."

I was.

"I know who you are."

I didn't.

"So, if you want to play, I'm your best bet..."

Don't say it, don't say it...

"You bitch."

The Dark Lady's shriek was so loud, so piercing it drove icicles into my brain.

The staircase behind her shifted, widening, growing a blood-red carpet runner. An amber chandelier swayed overhead in time with her screams. The windows at the upper landing blazed to life, as if illuminated by a crimson spotlight. The individual panes of stained glass stood out like angry teeth —diamonds of every shade of red. And as she approached, growing in stature, filling my vision, she became silhouetted in the scarlet glow.

A single thought came to mind as she neared, her shadows in tow: *the Queen of Diamonds knows I'm bluffing.*

My back up against the door, there was nothing left to do but...

JJ said it for me. "Run!"

Good idea.

I turned, grabbed the doorknob, and bolted out the door into the October night.

I didn't look back. I knew she was following me. The same way I knew every time I walked down a darkened hallway and felt that familiar electric tickle on the back of my neck that I wasn't alone. But as I dashed across the patchwork drive under the moonlit night, it wasn't a tickle I felt—it was a raging electrical storm.

The edge of the promontory was fast approaching, but there was no letting up now. I'd have to time it right or the leap would be my own. My foot caught a divot, my ankle twisted, but I kept on going. Pain was nothing compared to what followed on my heels.

I was twenty feet to the edge...ten...cold breath tickled my neck, and she whispered my name.

"Ellen..."

Still running at full speed, I dropped, skidding across the ground, gravel cutting into my palms, my cheek. I slid within inches of the drop, rolling as I did so. Watching the dark thing blot out the moon as it passed overhead.

And then, silence.

I'm alone with the night...

A flashlight beam hit my eyes.

...at least for the moment.

Mr. Carter called out, "Hold on!"

I stared up at the moon's familiar face as Utter's man raced forward and dropped to his knees beside me.

An hour later, we were gathered in the kitchen—Zivy, JJ, and me along with a frazzled Mr. Carter. Mr. Utter's physician, Dr. West, was examining Quan in the parlor while the rest of us twiddled our thumbs.

"Has anything like this ever happened before?" JJ asked.

Mr. Carter sighed, and I thought I detected scotch on his breath. "This is a new one."

"That sounds like a bullshit answer." Zivy had changed out of her bloodied T-shirt and was mixing herself a potent vodka drink.

"Look, it's late. Once the doctor's finished, I can take you back down to Cold Spring, put you up for the night or I could drive you back to the Meadowlands. Your choice."

"We're not going anywhere," I stated flatly.

"You're not?"

"We're not?" JJ chimed in.

Zivy sipped her drink, watching how this was going to play out.

"I just assumed—"

"You assumed wrong." With Quan out of the mix, expressing myself was easier. I'd never been run off an investigation before, and I wasn't about to let that happen now. Especially with so many questions left unanswered.

Mr. Carter looked at the three of us with bloodshot eyes. "Are you all on the same page?"

I wanted to answer for Zivy and JJ and tell him, "Yeah, of course we are. We're going to finish what we started." But speaking for others had gotten me into trouble in the past. An old therapist had told me, "As much as you'd like to believe you're the center of the world, Ellen, the fact is *you're not.*" Even though I ditched him after that session, I still carried his words with me.

JJ looked first at me, then at Zivy, obviously feeling put on the spot. "I...I'm not sure."

Zivy downed the last of her drink in one gulp. "What the hell, I'm in."

"Fuck," JJ said, gritting his teeth. "If they're staying, I'm staying."

Carter nodded slowly. "I'm sure Mr. Utter will be pleased to hear that."

Dr. West stepped into the room.

"His vitals are fine. I'd feel a lot better if he spent a night at St. Luke's, but he's informed me he has no intention of going. I'm sure Mr. Utter won't be pleased to hear that." This last bit she directed at Carter—a remonstration.

Quan appeared at the door. Despite having seen the change occur up close and personal, his white hair was still shocking.

"I'll gather your things," Carter said.

"No." Quan's reply was slow and deliberate, as if even uttering the simplest of words was a chore.

"But, your equipment—"

"Leave it." He stood staring at me, all his bluster gone.

"All right," Mr. Carter said. "Let's go."

The entryway was a clutter of tripod, chairs, and drying blood. I took note that Zivy avoided the spot where it had spilled. Other than that, the room had returned to its original state. The staircase had shrunk, no longer rising to meet stained glass, its stairs devoid of their red runner.

All was as it had been before the Dark Lady's arrival.

Dr. West opened the door for Quan, who paused in the threshold. Without looking back at us, he said, "Ghost..."

"Yeah, you got that right," JJ said, laughing nervously.

Quan turned back. Again, he looked to me.

"Ghost..." he stammered, having difficulty getting out words. "Ghu...Gho..."

Dr. West ushered Quan out the door, Carter following behind. The door closed with a solemn *thud*, and our little team was alone once more.

Where there were four, now there are three.

Zivy broke the silence.

"I don't know about you, but I'm famished."

She made a beeline toward the kitchen, JJ and I following her lead.

"This is a bad idea, isn't it?" JJ asked.

"Could be."

"Listen, about the kid in the car—"

"Later, huh?" I said. "Right now, I could sure use some cereal."

"Yeah. That sounds good."

Lights played across the entryway floor as Dr. West's and Mr. Carter's vehicles departed the hall, the illumination of headlights creating a mirror image of the biting shadows.

We stepped into the kitchen and proceeded to gorge ourselves. Not a word passed between us about the events of the evening. That would come later. Until then, it was time to bury our fear in Froot Loops and Fig Newtons.

23

It was just before midnight when, overstuffed and overtired, the three of us gathered up Quan's equipment and set it neatly at the door. Whatever he'd said in the moment, I was going to make sure he got his belongings back. He deserved that much.

Our task complete, we gathered at the foot of the stairs, each waiting for the other to take the first step, like kids at the edge of a frozen lake.

"Together?" JJ asked.

"Lions and tigers and bears..." Zivy sang.

"Huh?"

"Forget it."

We ascended as one—Zivy on JJ's right, me on his left—passing the site of the stone owl's demise and continuing to our floor.

We took turns using the bathroom. Zivy chose to leave the

door open, and JJ and I followed suit. No need to tempt whatever might crawl up the drain.

We said our good nights and dispersed to our individual rooms. Someone watching from afar might ask, "What the fuck's wrong with you? Why not leave with Quan and Carter and the good doctor?" I'm not sure I have a good answer for that other than to say I *knew* nothing else was going to happen that night. My inner radio transmitted nothing but white noise.

As a child, I used to love thunderstorms. I'd lie awake at night after Mom went to bed, my nose pressed up against the screen, sniffing the air for the scent of rain and watching the horizon for the first flash of lightning. Then, it was all howling wind and rolling thunder. Chaos incarnate. But as the storm passed—as all storms must—the air turned sweet, and the lightning faded. The melancholy of a tempest spent.

That's the way Utter Hall felt after the Dark Lady's departure. The storm had passed, and all three of us felt it—I know we did. The barometer would drop again tomorrow, no doubt, bringing with it fresh horrors, but for now...it was time for sleep.

At least that's what I told myself. After lying awake for over half an hour, I switched on the light and pulled *Sorrow's Leap* from beneath the pillow.

I flitted through the book's three hundred plus pages, trying to get a sense of it without actually doing the work of reading the damn thing. The story's heroine, Justice Hardy, appeared to get in all sorts of scrapes. I detected an inordinate amount of boudoir scenes evidenced by pages wrinkled by multiple readings.

At this point, I nearly chucked the book out the window. Utter's hall might be terrifying, but his dialogue was downright ghastly. The book was doing its trick. Not ten minutes after perusing its pages, my eyelids began to flutter.

That is, until I came across page 157...

The woman appeared at the landing, a figure dark in both demeanor and dress. She wore the night about her like a wrap, as if the darkness were a jealous lover.

I sat bolt upright in bed.

A host of spirits held court about her, their forms suggesting limbs and faces before sinking back into her orbit with the rustle of fabric and the chitter of teeth.

Holy fuck.

There was a knock at the door, and my heart nearly leaped from my chest.

"Ellen?" JJ called. "You still up?"

"What the...get in here!"

The doorknob turned and JJ appeared.

"Sorry," he said, "I couldn't sleep."

I was about to lay into him for his untimely interruption when I saw he carried his childhood dog in his arms. The night must have done quite a number on him to allow himself to be seen clutching Jersey.

"No problem," I said.

"Mind if I hang out a bit?"

I offered him the floor and my extra blanket. He took me up on both.

"I see you've brought your friend."

He glanced self-consciously at his stuffed dog, its felt tongue lolling to the side. "He's more a lucky charm than anything else." He gave the pup's ears a tender scratch and looked at me sheepishly. "What happened downstairs? That was...a lot."

I nodded. Even for someone who'd come face-to-face with all manner of spooks, shades, and gibbering things, the phantom in Utter Hall's foyer was, as JJ said, a lot.

I wriggled down in bed to perch on the edge. JJ's fingers were worrying the dog's ear in a spot where the fur was frayed down to cloth. I don't think he even knew he was doing it.

"You sure you want to stay?" I asked. "After what happened to Quan?"

"Why?" he asked quickly. "Are you having second thoughts?"

"No."

"Then neither am I."

It was settled then. No need to revisit.

"Are we going to talk about your little party trick?" I asked.

JJ gave a pained sigh. "Yeah, about that..."

His words hung in the air so long I thought he'd abandoned his train of thought. But then...

"I never was 'The Boy Who Went to Heaven.' I died, that much was true. But heaven? I wouldn't know it if I saw it."

I nodded, encouraging him to continue.

"Five minutes," he said, holding up five fingers. "That's how long my heart stopped beating. Five long minutes. I was out; I was gone. If they hadn't shocked me, maybe I really would have seen some angels."

"So, when you asked me to trust you—"

"I pulled you into those five minutes."

I let loose a snort—Jesus, the supernatural was certainly making up for lost time.

"Did you know it would work?"

Now it was JJ's turn to snort. "Nope! But I had to do something. Usually, if I need to...you know, take a peek behind the curtain, I just pop in, find out what I need to know, and pop back out. I've never brought anyone *with* me."

"What happens if you stay longer than five minutes?"

He shrugged. "I don't know. I guess I burn."

"You or the kid?"

"Is there a difference?"

I was eager to dig further. His was one of the most unique gifts I'd ever come across. I was about to ask if he'd be willing to take a peek behind Utter Hall's curtain when another visitor came a-knocking.

"Having a slumber party without me, are you?" Zivy asked. "That's downright rude."

She wore a throw around her shoulders and had stripped down to her T-shirt and boy shorts. JJ's cheeks turned red, which tickled Zivy to no end.

"Eyes up here, buddy," she teased.

"I..." he stammered. "You're welcome to join us. Isn't she, Ellen?"

"A long as her 'little bird' minds his manners," I said.

Zivy shifted in the doorway, as awkward as JJ had been when I'd mentioned his stuffed animal.

"I think he's had enough for tonight."

"I think we all have," JJ agreed.

Zivy scanned the room. "Hold on." She disappeared back into the hall only to reappear a moment later, comforter in tow. *"Now* it's a slumber party."

She flopped down at the foot of my bed and settled in. JJ shifted, self-conscious at her close proximity, and pulled his own covers tightly around himself, cocooning.

"So, what's first?" Zivy asked. "Ghost stories?"

"Haven't we had enough of those for one night?" JJ visibly shivered. "I think we should debrief."

"JJ!" Zivy cried, hand to her chest. "We barely know each other."

"No...I meant..." His cheeks flushed anew.

"Anyone up for a little light reading?" I held up my ragged copy of *Sorrow's Leap.*

"That's one of Utter's," he said, staring at the cover art of the woman on the cliff.

I proceeded to read aloud the passage I'd found about the woman on the landing surrounded by spirits. By the time I'd finished, the two of them were speechless.

"What the hell?" JJ whispered.

"What else is he hiding in those pages?" Zivy asked.

"Why don't we find out?" I flipped to about a third of the way in and ripped out a chunk of book, tossing it to JJ. I divided the remaining pages in two and ripped again.

We settled in, each of us with our portion of *Sorrow's Leap*, and soon slumber was the last thing on our minds.

24

By the time we'd finished our respective chunks of the book—Zivy finishing in a blur; JJ reading as slowly and methodically as a monk—sleep was whispering in my ear.

The story of *Sorrow's Leap* was far from original. Justice, the main character, moves to her new husband's mansion in the Hudson River valley only to find herself plagued by the series of hauntings: a dark woman, her shadowy entourage, spirit children. Turns out, the ghost in question was her husband's first wife—a woman who bore him numerous stillborn sons and daughters before going mad. The husband throws her from a cliff, he remarries, his dead wife commences haunting—yada yada, yada.

The only standout aspect of the story was that we were living it.

"So...which came first?" Zivy asked. "The haunting or the book?"

"If I was a betting man," JJ said, "I'd say Utter was doing what authors do—writing about what he knew."

"Author gets haunted, author writes about the haunting, author rakes in the big bucks?"

"Something like that."

Zivy furrowed her brow. "You think he killed his wife?"

"Utter never married," JJ said.

"How do you know?"

"It's called Google. You should try it."

I was getting tired, and their back and forth was making it difficult to think. There was something we were missing, but I was either too exhausted or out of practice to see what it was. I picked up my third of *Sorrow's Leap* and buried myself in Utter's words.

"Are we boring you?" Zivy asked.

"Huh?"

I glanced down at the two people sharing my room. They stared back at me expectantly.

"You have any thoughts?" JJ asked.

"No. Not yet," I said.

"What do you think we should do next?"

Wasn't that obvious?

"I think we should read it again."

The two of them sighed.

"I don't know about you two, but I'm done for the night." Zivy pulled her comforter about herself. "Catch you in the morning."

JJ looked up at me, his eyes as bleary as mine felt. "We do need to sleep."

"Go ahead," I said, turning the page.

JJ paused, unsure of his next move. For a moment, I thought he was going to stay up with me, but judging people's next move was not a skill I possessed. He shot me an apologetic shrug, removed his glasses, and curled up next to Zivy, careful to leave a modest space between them.

I was actually a bit relieved. Now it was just me, the book, and the night.

Three pages in, a low groan echoed through the house, as if it were suffering a bad dream.

JJ's head popped up, his eyes no longer so bleary.

"Sheesh," he said, rolling into sitting. "I guess that's that."

He picked up his glasses and his section of book and dove back in.

"Fuck it." Zivy wriggled out of the confines of her blanket and grabbed up her pages.

Utter Hall remained silent for the rest of the night, the only sound issuing from inside its walls the papery swish of turning pages.

JJ succumbed first, halfway through his second read. I thought I'd outlast Zivy, but somewhere around Justice's arrival at Sorrow's Leap, my batteries dipped, and the words blurred. Try as I might to stay awake, consciousness slipped through my fingers like sand, and soon I was tumbling into darkness.

I came to face down on the floor, cheek pressed against a cool and mildewed carpet.

Where the hell was I?

I rose slowly, as one does in a dream. The carpet's pattern was familiar to me—geometric patterns and swirls designed to hide any stains. Like that in an airport or casino or...the Meadowlands Conference Center.

I was back at the Hooky Spooky Convention.

The cavernous room was empty, save for the rows of merch-stacked tables. Instead of music, the loudspeakers gave off a reptilian hiss of static. The overhead lights flickered cinematically, warning me that this was not going to be some childhood dream filled with sunshine and butterflies. No, this outing in the midnight realm promised to be anything but peaceful.

Did I say the conference room was empty? It was not—not quite. Another trick of the dream.

A young man sat at a table piled high with books, head down, locked in on the volume he was signing.

It was Quan. Of course it was Quan.

Dream logic placed me suddenly before him, where I stood like one of his groupies eager for him to add their name next to his. He scribbled ferociously, finishing one book before frantically cracking open another.

"Quan," I gurgled as if underwater. Fuck, dreams can be the worst.

He looked up at me. His mouth hung loose in dumb silence, his eyes as milky white as his hair.

"Ghooo..." he moaned.

I glanced down at the book he was signing and wasn't a bit surprised to find that it was *Sorrow's Leap*.

"Ghooo..." he repeated, returning to his task.

The book was blank, save for his handwriting. "Ghooooooo..." he had scrawled, the *O*'s filling the page like a howl.

"What are you trying to tell me?" My words came out thick and gummy, as if I were trying to speak while chewing taffy.

Clunk.

A bank of overhead lights switched off.

Clunk-clunk.

Two more. As if someone were tripping breakers.

Clunk. Clunk-clunk. Clunk.

The visible room was shrinking, chunks of it swallowed up by black nothingness.

"I think we better get out of here," I whispered, but Quan was way ahead of me. He'd pulled a fast one and disappeared, leaving me alone in the ever-darkening room.

Clunk.

Only one narrow channel of light remained, with me at its center, at one end the double doors to the hotel proper, at the other end...

Why is it that some dreams are so sketchy? No flavor, no details. Just a gray watercolor blur of memory and emotion. And why were some filled with minutiae? An itching palm, a trickle of sweat. Or, as was the case this time, the mouth going instantly dry.

For at the other end of the room stood the Dark Lady, regarding me with predatory awareness.

Shit.

As during our first encounter, it was difficult to focus on her face. Whose would she be wearing this time? Zivy's? My mother's? The Barefoot Contessa's?

No.

For this special occasion, she had pilfered mine.

Dark Ellen.

Staring at me from across the room.

The final three banks of lights dimmed in rapid succession, first plunging the spectral woman into darkness, then me, then the double doors—my only means of escape.

All was blackness.

The rustle of fabric informed me of her approach, and I turned and dashed toward the exit.

Seeing as I was dimly aware of the dream logic at play, I should have anticipated the obstacles that would eagerly bar my way to the doors.

I ran full force into a table that had no business cluttering up the aisle, falling to my knees. The pain was all too real.

Swish. The sound of spectral silk.

I clambered to my feet, wresting free of the toppled table's multitudinous legs which meant to hold me down like a centipede's prey. Once in the clear, I stumbled forward in what I hoped was the direction of the lobby. Again, the dream was determined to undercut me. My foot came down on an uneven surface, and I slipped, finding myself once more on the floor.

The static from the loudspeakers had been replaced by heavy breathing. The scent of snuffed candles filled the air. The darkness pulsed, and my eyes filled with pressure. Where was an alarm clock when you needed one?

I felt around and found the DVD case I'd slipped on. The floor was covered with them. It didn't take a genius to know each and every one was a copy of *JJ Gadzinski: The Boy Who Went to Heaven.*

I struggled to my feet once more, and in so doing, my hand brushed against a metal handle. I was up against the doors. Mere inches from freedom.

I grabbed the handle and yanked.

No use.

I yanked harder.

The hinges complained, but the door stood firm.

"Wake up, you idiot!" I shouted at myself.

A cool hand caressed my cheek.

"No," the Dark Lady said, her voice hollow as a skull. "Sleep. Sleep with me."

I leaped out of bed, ready to do battle. Only there was no one to do battle with—just JJ curled up on his side of the mattress snoring his ass off.

The other side was empty, save for an oval bloodstain where Zivy's head had lain.

Where the hell is she?

25

"JJ!" I whispered.

He rolled over, cutting short his nocturnal snorts.

"Whassit?" he mumbled.

"Zivy's gone."

He smacked his lips. "I'm gonna keep the pickle."

"Huh?"

"Get your own."

I gave him a kick. He merely farted.

"I'm gonna keep it..."

And resumed snoring.

I was on my own.

I scrambled out of bed and slipped out of the room. Upon entering the hallway, I promptly stepped in blood. Zivy had quite the gusher going. I wiped the sole of my foot on the wooden floor and moved on, following the drops of red dotting the way.

I stopped at the stairs.

I should go back and get JJ.

But I'd come this far alone already, and so far, no sign of the Dark Lady or her cadre of critters. My mind flitted back to the Halloween Queen and her followers. God, was that only yesterday?

I followed the crimson trail down the stairs, careful to sidestep the sticky droplets gathering on each tread. Each step cried out in anguish, as if I were descending the scale on some terrible keyboard.

This place does not *want us here.*

Zivy sat amongst the abandoned building supplies and tools in the darkened parlor. She was perched atop a stack of unpacked floor tiles, legs bared and bleeding. She held a bloodied box cutter in a tightened fist.

"Drop it," I insisted.

The figure in the T-shirt and boy shorts flicked blood my way from the tip of the reddened blade.

"Zivy?" I said, knowing that Zivy was far, far away.

"Zivy's takin' a little time-out."

"What did you do to her?"

"Wasn't me. This is her handiwork," motioning toward the slices in her thighs. "She thinks it keeps me quiet."

I shuddered. His voice, while still containing elements of my new friend, was guttural and snide.

My eyes adjusted to the makeshift lighting, and I spotted pages of *Sorrow's Leap* littering the floor—some ripped to shreds, others crumpled and smeared red.

"What made you wake up?"

"Just didn't want to miss the party."

"Really? Because it seems like earlier, you were ready to run away with your tail between your legs."

"That's a lie."

"If I didn't know any better, I'd say you were scared out of your fucking mind."

"That's a lie!"

Byrd pressed the blade against Zivy's thigh, threatening to add another bloody hashmark.

"Careful," Byrd snarled. "Me? I don't feel a thing. But poor Miss Zivy?"

He drew the blade ever so slowly across her skin. Blood appeared in angry beads.

"That's enough," I said, stopping short. "Let me talk to Zivy."

"Oh, she and I have already chatted. When she wakes up, she's going walk those pretty legs of hers right out that door."

"And why would she do that?"

Byrd raised the box cutter to Zivy's neck.

"Because she knows how messy I can be."

I laughed. Not because D. Ellis Byrd was the least bit funny, but because I'd learned early on the best way to respond to threats was with laughter. It took all the air out of the person doing the threatening. It had certainly worked with my mother.

"Stop laughing!"

And it was working with Byrd.

"I'm sorry," I said, circling the figure on the stacked tiles, "but I was just picturing what you'd be without her."

"I'd be free."

"You'd be a puddle of goo."

Byrd pressed the blade against Zivy's throat.

"How about you stop being cute and drop the box cutter? We both know you need her *a lot more* than she needs you."

It was Byrd's turn to laugh. He let loose a low croaking sound, like a complaining crow. He flipped the box cutter my way—its blade embedded itself in the floor between my feet. He smiled, pleased with his aim.

I quickly retrieved the box cutter, holding it tight to still my shaking hand.

"Better?" he asked.

"Yes. Now, how about you and I have a little chat?"

"Please," he replied with a mocking flourish of the hand.

Byrd was gently kicking Zivy's bloodied legs back and forth, like a child on a swing.

I approached him head-on, like a TV prosecutor.

"How about you tell me why the woman on the stairs rattled you so much?"

"Rattled? Ha!" he chuckled. "You're a slippery one, aren't you?" He eyed me up and down, making a show of licking his lips. "Almost my type, but not quite. You'd have to hit the gym a bit more to catch ol' Byrd's attention."

"Don't you talk about her like that!"

I whirled about at the sound of the voice, blade raised, and ready to defend myself.

JJ shrieked at the sight of the knife.

"What the hell, Chunky?!?"

His hand flew to his chest, and rightly so—someone with quicker reflexes than me would have plunged the blade into his sternum. The shock of finding him standing right behind me caused me to lose my grip, dropping the box cutter to the floor with a clatter.

"Sorry," JJ said, retrieving the knife. "I woke up and everyone was gone."

"Listen, kids. I haven't got all night."

I turned back to Byrd.

"Are you going to answer my question or are you just going to keep jerking off?" I asked, doing my best to push his buttons. "What scared—I mean, *rattled* you?"

Byrd scowled, turning Zivy's natural beauty into an unnatural nightmare.

"Nothing rattled me."

"Then why are you hiding here in the dark?"

Byrd waggled a finger at me. "Because my mama didn't raise no idiot."

"Meaning?"

Byrd gave a big, dramatic sigh, and just when I thought our conversation had come to an end, he surprised me.

"There's something not right about that lady on the stairs."

"That says a lot coming from a disembodied voice."

"You're funny," he snorted. "Maybe you are my type after all."

My patience was growing thin.

"Aside from being dead, what was 'not right' about her?"

"I'd rather not say."

"Answer her," JJ growled. Apparently, his patience had grown thin as well.

"Wittle JJ speaks!" Byrd spat.

"Answer her!"

Byrd giggled furiously. "Wittle JJ took a ride, hit the ice and almost died. No use screaming, no way back—Wittle JJ's burning black!"

JJ's legs almost gave out.

This was getting out of control.

"Must I compel you to answer?" I asked.

Byrd turned his venom on me.

"Mama lies pale in the bed-bed-bed, not a single hair on her head-head-head..."

"I repeat, must I compel—"

Byrd let loose another corvine caw. "Compel me? Who do you think you are, Max von Sydow?" He stood atop the tiles and screeched at the top of Zivy's lungs, "The power of Christ compels you! The power of Christ compels you!"

"Screw it," I said before igniting my gift and latching on with everything I had.

"Stop that. No fair! STOP THAT!"

But there was no stopping now. I was *in*.

The room disappeared. Wailing wind whipped my hair, and I got my first taste of what it must be like to be D. Ellis Byrd. He was hanging on in the middle of a storm.

"What's happening?"

Nothing but mist swirled about me. Heat and rot hit my nose, making me gag. His world was a prison filled with secondhand smoke, and I sensed his desperate need to get *out*.

"Tell me what was so odd about the woman on the stairs, or I'll pluck it out of you!" To back up my threat, I wrenched a random memory from his mind.

I caught my first glimpse of D. Ellis Byrd. He must have been ten years old. The boy gripped a carving mallet in his hand and was beating a squirrel to death with it. No...into obliteration.

My stomach churned. Byrd exuded joy, laughing with every downward *thwap*.

"No fa-aa-air!" he howled.

A whiskered gentleman in a sawdust-covered apron lit upon the scene, beating Byrd down with hands and curses. The old fellow grabbed the mallet and turned it on the boy, bringing it down—*crack!*—on his collarbone—*crack!*—again and again.

"Fuck you!" he screamed. "That's private!"

"Will you tell me what I want to know?"

"Yes!"

"No tricks?"

"Yes! I mean...NO!"

"All right then."

I released his memory. It felt good to be rid of it; its nastiness left emotional residue.

"Tell me about the woman. Why did she scare you so much?"

"Because..."

"Shall I root around inside your memories again?"

"Because she...wasn't!"

With that, some supernatural vent opened, and the vile vapor dissipated. A moment later, I was standing once more in the parlor before the girl with the bloodied legs.

"Fuck," Zivy whispered.

I helped her climb down from the stack of tiles while JJ stood apart from us, his phone/flashlight in one hand, the box cutter poised and ready in the other.

Zivy was shivering. I glanced around the room, finding nothing but discarded painter's tarp. I grabbed it and threw it over her shoulders.

"I'm...I'm..." she said through chattering teeth.

"Cold. Yeah, I bet." I gave JJ a nod. "Let's get something warm into her."

Minutes later in the kitchen, JJ pulled a steaming hot mug of water from the microwave and plopped a bag of herbal tea into it.

"Do you want sugar in it?" he asked.

"I'd prefer whiskey." Her cheeks were reddening up as she sat at the island under the paint-speckled fabric.

JJ set the mug in front of her and nodded for me to join him in the corner. He'd picked up the box cutter after setting down the tea.

"Look, I'm all for staying," he said, glancing nervously back at Zivy, "but maybe she shouldn't."

"Meaning?"

"Meaning I'd rather not wake up with a knife in my neck! Ghosts are one thing. *That*..." He stuck his thumb at Zivy. "That is something else entirely."

I regarded him intently. We'd already lost Quan, and now JJ was suggesting we shrink our numbers even further.

I was about to try to reassure him when Zivy spoke up.

"Maybe you'd feel better if I gave you my confession. Or rather, his." She took a tentative sip of the tea and promptly spat it back into the mug. "But if I'm doing this, I'm going to need something a lot stronger."

"You killed the last of the booze," JJ said.

Zivy grinned wryly. "I think I know where we can find some."

26

The three of us got dressed and slipped out into the moonlit night. The cloud cover was thick, turning the sky a sickly yellow, and the threat of rain hung in the air.

We made a quick survey of the grounds. Carter's van was nowhere to be seen.

Zivy led the way across the drive toward the carriage house, a lone structure surrounded by dead weeds. "Just a quick in and out."

"That's what she said," JJ said. His joke was met with crickets. "Sorry."

The small structure Carter called home was built of the same stone as its larger neighbor and wore the same dead ivy. A tall arched doorway led into the heart of the structure where horses once rested for the night—replaced, in time, by slumbering cars. Lights still burned in Carter's little upstairs apartment. A sloping slate roof with numerous missing shingles capped it all off. The carriage house was in as much need of renovation as the rest of the place.

"Locked," Zivy said, tugging at the massive doors.

"Well," JJ sighed, "I guess that's that."

"Hardly," she scoffed.

Zivy stepped around to the side of the house and, grabbing a fistful of ivy, proceeded to climb her way, hand over hand, up the stone exterior.

About five feet up, she discovered the folly of her method. The ivy was too brittle to hold her—hell, it was probably too fragile to hold the squirrel Byrd had smashed with the mallet—and she slipped back to earth, landing with a *whumph*.

"I don't want to hear it," she said, her finger in JJ's face.

"I didn't say anything!"

"You were about to."

I circled the house and found a second set of double doors opposite those facing inward toward the drive. I tested the handle. Both swung open wide without so much as a creak.

"Guys," I called.

"Well, shit," Zivy said upon finding me at the open entrance. "I still think I could have made up the outside wall."

"Right," JJ muttered.

"Shall we?" I asked.

I half expected to be greeted by the scent of hay and manure, but the day of equine aromas was long past. Various pieces of maintenance equipment sat idle in the stalls: a snowblower, a push mower, a collection of rakes and shovels.

A fresh oil stain decorated the cement floor. Next time I saw him, I'd tell Carter to get the van to a mechanic, stat.

Uneven stairs led up to a door set in the ceiling. They rose at an alarming angle—most definitely *not* up to code. I pictured Mr. Carter returning home after a night on the town, slipping and breaking his leg on the rickety stairs. With Utter fully ensconced in the South Wing, I bet ol' Carter might dangle there for days before anyone found him.

"We really going up there?" JJ sounded as nervous as I'd ever heard him. "We don't know when he might be coming back—"

Zivy gave an annoyed moan. "If he's driving Quan back to the Meadowlands, it's an hour there and an hour back, minimum. Plenty of time for a little larceny."

"But at this hour there won't be any traffic—"

Ignoring him, Zivy clambered up the stairs. Upon reaching the door in the ceiling, she gave it a little knock.

"You home, Mr. Carter? No? Well, I guess you won't mind if we check out your liquor cabinet."

She pushed on the door. It opened easily, a shaft of light hitting us at the bottom of the stairs.

"Last one up's a rotten egg!"

Zivy disappeared through the door.

JJ turned to me. "After you."

The stairs were even more precarious than I'd imagined, visibly swaying as I mounted them. Why Carter hadn't secured them was a mystery to me. Maybe it was deterrent to keep folks like us from doing what we were doing.

Cresting the top, I pulled myself up into Carter's abode. A pungent odor hit my nose. Hay and horse droppings had nothing on the musty decay awaiting us inside the little studio apartment.

"Yeesh," Zivy said, wrinkling her nose. "I guess our man Carter's the real rotten egg."

The cramped apartment had an extra low ceiling. If he were any taller, the place would have forced Mr. Carter into a permanent hunch. The walls were lined with books. Instead of cabinets, the kitchenette had multiple shelves stocked with a minimum of cookware and a maximum of Trader Joe's Mac 'n Cheese.

If it weren't for the clutter, the space would be a cozy hideaway, the kind of place I'd kill for. Every nook held new secrets: a taxidermy rabbit, a green convex mirror, fat candles that must pull double duty as light sources and air fresheners.

The miniature sink was stacked high with dirty dishes— hence the stink—and wadded up socks were scattered across the floor like billiard balls.

"What died up here?" JJ asked as he climbed through the door in the floor.

"Carter's hopes and dreams, from the smell of it," Zivy said, already beginning her search for a spare bottle.

Along the wall opposite the sink sat a heavy wooden desk from the 1950s. Sitting next to an ancient phone were stacks and stacks of manila folders, loose papers, and, oddly enough, a porcelain phrenology bust, its hollow eyes watching us with admonition. Another of Carter's quirky knickknacks.

"Let's make this quick," JJ said, no longer hiding his unease.

"If I were a secret tippler, which I am," Zivy hummed, "where would I stash the good stuff?"

I approached the desk, drawn forward by the wealth of documents despite the watchful eyes of the bust with the diagrammed dome. Careful not to displace a single sheet, I gently rummaged through the pages.

"Don't just stand there looking handsome, JJ," Zivy chided. "Help me look."

Sticking out from one of the manila folders was a familiar face. A printed copy of the homepage from a website.

My website.

The one I'd left active "just in case."

A younger version of myself stared back at me along with the promise of "thorough spiritual investigations."

What a joke.

I flipped to the next folder. Inside was a receipt for the rental of *JJ Gadzinski: The Boy Who Went to Heaven.*

He was tracking us. He knew we'd be at the Hooky Spooky and had already done his research.

Leafing through the next few folders, I spotted a number of other familiar faces, people I'd seen at the Meadowlands. But each of their folders had red checkmarks on the front.

"Ah ha!" From the sound of it, Zivy had hit the jackpot.

No longer concerned with keeping any semblance of order, I dug deeper into the pile, coming up with a copy of a news article about a Pennsylvania psychic named Paul Rodriguez, the headshot of a TV personality named Lucy Bosch (the Boston Seer), and a transcript of a podcast from a show called *Unliving Proof.*

We weren't the first to visit Utter Hall. Far from it.

"What's that?" JJ asked.

Too shocked to explain, I handed him a few of the files. His eyes bugged out as he took in their meaning.

"What happened to them all?"

I shrugged. "Your guess is as good as mine."

I turned at the sound of a cork stopper popping.

"Whiskey anyone?"

Zivy stood proudly holding up a semi-drained bottle of Jameson.

JJ nodded vigorously. "Please."

"And since I don't trust a single glass in this place..." She proceeded to down a healthy swig before offering it to JJ, adding in an abysmal Irish brogue, "To your health, boyo!"

JJ gave the bottle a sniff and looked to me, as if to ask permission. When I didn't reply, he took a sip.

"Fuck," JJ whispered, eyes shut tight.

Zivy laughed. "Was that a good fuck or a bad fuck?"

He took another, longer sip. "Fuu-uuck."

"Sounds like a good fuck to me!"

I arranged the folders in some semblance of their original order, but judging by the surrounding mess, I probably needn't have bothered.

Zivy grabbed the bottle.

"If we're doing this, then we're doing this," she said.

She took another gulp of liquid fire, throwing back her head to force it down, that wild red hair of hers threatening to set the place on fire.

"I met Byrd when I was thirteen," she said, reveling in the

whiskey's burn. "It was the year Jamie Weimer shot up my school."

27

"It was a cool September day for North Carolina. Why is it awful things always happen in September? That's been my experience, anyway."

Zivy spun one of Carter's two dining chairs around and straddled it, hugging the backrest.

"I'd done okay in school up until then. Neither good nor bad, keeping my distance from As and Fs. I had a few friends, not too many. Tom Deaver was my bestie. We just kind of slid by, Tom and I, flying under the radar."

It was odd, but I could swear her voice got younger as she spoke. Not just the tone but the size of it. I'm sure if I were recording her story, there wouldn't be any discernible difference when I played it back, but still...it *changed*.

"Anyway, I was at my locker before the day started. It was just after the band kids got out of practice. See, they had to come in early and work with Mr. Reese before school, and a couple of them had just hit the lockers to put away their flutes or horns or whatever. The speaker system squawked, and this kid named Guy got on the mic and started singing, *'Suck my balls! Suck my balls!'* like a real jackass, and you could hear Mrs. Penn trying to get the microphone away from him—"

"Ziv?" JJ said in the smallest of voices.

"Yeah?"

"I think you're stalling."

Zivy took a breath and offered him a thumbs up.

"The first bell rang," she continued. "Tommy Mason ran up to my locker, all excited to tell me about some stupid movie he'd just seen, and *crack!* Half his head disappeared.

"Jesus," JJ moaned.

"I saw this shadow or...no...what's the word I'm looking for? Oh, yeah—silhouette. I saw the silhouette of someone standing just inside the side entrance. It was Jamie Wiemer, a sophomore transfer. Kids used to call him Veiny Wiener. He had a gun...a rifle, I mean. He had one and he was...anyway, I felt something hit me hard, and then I was falling."

"You got hit?" JJ asked.

Zivy rose slightly in her chair and lifted her shirt to her chest. Just below her right breast sat a star-shaped scar.

"Two inches to the left and..." She rolled up her eyes and lolled her tongue.

"That's not funny," JJ huffed.

"You're right." She sat back into her seat and gripped the backrest with both hands. "I don't remember much before the hospital. Maybe the sound of the ambulance? Someone screaming? I don't know. Doesn't matter. By the time I came to in my hospital room, it was already done."

"What was already done?"

Zivy allowed herself a deep sigh.

"The transfusion."

She held out a hand for the bottle, and when I passed it back, she drained a good third of the remaining whiskey. When she came up for air, tears flowed down her cheeks.

"It's okay," JJ said, soothing her. He looked at me as if I'd missed my cue.

"Yeah," I said. "It's okay."

"No, it sure as fuck is *not*," Zivy hissed. "Because on top of being a universal donor, D. Ellis Byrd was a serial kidnapper. I'd lost a lot of blood, and it was ol' Byrd's that made its way into my veins." She laughed ruefully. "Imagine getting fucked over by two guys in the same day."

"I don't understand." Something wasn't adding up. "How'd he...get inside you?"

Zivy shook her head. "He didn't, at first. Not until he was spread across I-95 by a drunk driver. After that, he got real chatty. Some nights, he'd keep me up late talking about all the girls he'd picked up, all the things he'd done to them. I could feel him growing. Like a cancer. Like..."

Headlights panned across the windows, the porcelain bust casting a looming shadow across Zivy's face.

The van.

"Shit," JJ whispered. "Carter's back."

You could feel the temp in the room drop as a collective shudder passed through us.

Zivy made a move toward the door.

"Stop," I said, holding up a warning finger.

She paused, her hand on the door handle.

I listened intently, trying to drown out my racing heartbeat. There...the sound of a car door slamming shut—or rather a *van* door—followed by the crunch of shoes on gravel. A second later, the high arched doors wobbling open.

JJ let out a squeaking fart, and it was all I could do to keep from giggling. That was the function of laughter in my life. Never connected to jokes and always appearing under pressure.

The floor rumbled beneath us as the van pulled in, and the smell of exhaust fumes rose, obliterating the stench from the sink. Soon would come the sound of footsteps and the slow creak of the door as it swung open, exposing our guilt.

We were toast.

"We gotta bolt!" JJ whispered.

He crept to the window next to the sink and ever so quietly slid it open. It would be a tight fit, but it was our only escape route. Unfortunately, it entailed a ten-foot drop to the drive below.

"You can't be serious," I said. "You wanna break your neck?"

"It beats letting Carter catch us up here. You saw those files. Who knows what he might do to us."

Carter didn't strike me as the strong-arm type, but JJ's fight-or-flight response had been activated. And he damn well didn't look ready to fight.

"Come on," JJ insisted, grabbing Zivy's chair and setting it beneath the open window.

Zivy went first. She was out the window as the van's engine sputtered to a stop.

"You're next," JJ said, reaching out a hand.

"No thanks."

A single creak. Carter was mounting the stairs.

"Suit yourself."

Wasting no time, JJ took the plunge, disappearing from view. He landed with a *whumph* and whimper, and Carter paused mid-ascent. For a moment, I feared he might retrace his steps, investigate the commotion, but no. His footsteps quickened, confirming I had no way of making it out the window in time. Resigned to my fate, I grabbed the Jameson and tossed back a burning mouthful, steeling myself against what was to come.

The door rose, and Carter peered inside. I raised the bottle in salute.

"You got me, Sheriff," I said.

Carter, still half-in, half-out of the room, furrowed his brow.

"That's too bad," he replied. "Now I'll have to kill you."

28

C arter's ominous proclamation turned my mouth to dust.

"Uh..." I croaked.

The man sticking up through the opening in the floor like some giant prairie dog yawned. He pulled himself up until he was standing between me and the exit.

Not the only *exit. There's still the window...*

Mr. Carter reached out a hand, and I flinched.

"Ellen? The Jameson?"

I braved a few steps forward and offered him the bottle. He gave it a swirl, watching the remaining liquid circle the green glass.

"You put quite a dent in this," he said, downing the last of it.

"What can I say? Irish whiskey is my jam," I lied.

His eyes flitted to the open window.

"You had a little help, I see." He walked to the sink, set the empty bottle in the sink amongst the dirty dishes, and peered out the window. "Your partners in crime seem to have abandoned you."

I considered using the phrenology bust as a weapon until Carter gave a tired chuckle.

"Relax, Ms. Marx. I suppose I'd be disappointed if you hadn't taken advantage of my absence to do a little snooping."

"We aren't the first people you've brought here."

"No, you're not."

"There have been dozens of others."

"Dozens and dozens."

He wasn't even making the slightest effort to hide it, which was remarkably confusing. I crossed to the desk, grabbed up a handful of file folders, and waved them in his face.

"What happened to them?"

Carter looked from the folders to me and offered a wistful expression I couldn't quite identify.

"Most of those people left after spending only a few hours in Utter Hall. Some held on overnight only to bolt the next morning. And the rest..." He let that bit hang in the air. "You know what happened to your friend, Mr. Quan?"

How could I forget? The image of him struggling in the grip of the Dark Lady would no doubt be a recurring feature of my dreams.

"Let's just say he wasn't the first investigator to require medical attention."

Carter turned his back and began rooting through the shelves, no doubt in search of a replacement for his Jameson.

"Where is he?"

"Down in Cold Spring. He didn't trust me to drive him to Secaucus," Carter said, landing upon a full bottle of schnapps. "He thought I was too impaired." He cracked the top off the bottle and took a swig.

"You just left him down there?"

He sighed. "I got him a room for the night. The night clerk at the Riverview Hotel hooked me up—we go way back."

I quickly did the math in my head. If that was the case, Carter should have returned over an hour ago.

He must have picked up on my mental calculations. "Once I made sure he was comfy, I grabbed a little nightcap at the hotel bar. Or two. Yeah, yeah...it was after, *after* hours, but like I said, the night clerk and I go way back. Quan will catch the first Metro North into the city tomorrow...*this* morning. He said his next gig was at Chelsea Piers anyway, so..."

He turned his back to me again, attacking the schnapps. If he planned on drinking himself to sleep, now was time to make my exit.

But I had one question, first. And a demand.

"What's haunting Utter Hall?"

He didn't turn to answer, and I was glad of that. Making eye contact with the inebriated was a special kind of hell.

"You mean the woman in black?"

Dark Lady, woman in black, same thing.

"Yes."

"I fucking wish I knew."

Had his back not been to me, I might have missed it—the intermingling of truth and lies. He knew more than he was letting on while knowing less than he wanted.

Now for the demand.

"We want to talk to Utter again."

"No problem. I'll have the video stream set up again around six tonight—"

"We want to talk to him now."

At this, Carter perked up. He set down the bottle and turned to stare at me.

"Now?"

"Yes, now. Or the three of us are walking ourselves down the hill." I was never good at bluffing, but damned if I didn't nail it.

"Mr. Utter is a sick man."

"I know."

"He's sick," Carter repeated, as if unsure he'd spoken aloud the first time.

"That's our demand. Take it or leave it." I felt odd speaking for the other two, especially since only a third of our current crew was making the demand, but as they'd flown the coop, leaving me to clean up the mess, I wasn't going to lose any sleep over it.

Carter shook his head.

"That's not going to happen—"

The phone on his desk rang. We stared at it, both of us frozen in place.

Carter stepped past me and answered it.

"Yes?"

I strained to hear the other side of the conversation but to no avail. One thing you can say about old-timey phones—they offered a hell of a lot more privacy than today's gadgets.

"Yes, sir. I'll tell her."

He replaced the receiver in the cradle.

"You've got your meeting. Give me thirty minutes to set up the call."

I expected to find my companions waiting for me, but alas, they must have retreated to Utter Hall.

I stood in the middle of the drive and stared up at the monstrosity of stone and secrets, searching its façade for some semblance of sanity and finding none. Even the foliage encircling the place kept its distance. Was it wise to remain or should I take a hint from the hedges that shrank from the mansion like onlookers awaiting some horrible event?

I allowed myself a brief sojourn to the cliff's edge and breathed in the moonlit night—the decay of fallen leaves and the musk of rotting vegetation. Aside from that, the air was crisp as an apple. I kicked rocks over the precipice, listening to them clatter far, far below.

Sorrow's Leap.

I rolled the name around in my head, feeling the weight of it, the poetic poignancy.

But whose sorrow and whose leap?

I found JJ and Zivy back in the kitchen. Even though there was not a single cigarette in sight, the smoke-filled air betrayed both Zivy's bad habit and her rebellion against Carter's rules.

"Jesus," JJ moaned, relieved. "When you didn't come out that window, we figured you were done for."

"Not dead, done for, mind you," Zivy added, her empty fingers still worrying an absent ciggy. "But...you know, off the case or whatever."

"Good to see you too," I said, heading straight for the fridge. I needed water to flush away the sickening sweetness of the whiskey.

"Hey!" JJ said. "I told you to go before me."

Finding the fridge devoid of bottled water, I settled for apple juice.

"Chill," I replied as I chugged. "Everything's still a go."

Zivy mimed wiping her brow. "Whew. Not sure I'd be comfortable sticking around with half the team missing."

"Don't worry. I'm staying."

JJ peered at me, cocking his head as he did so.

"What is it?"

"Hmm?" Time to let *him* sweat.

"What happened up there? What aren't you telling us?"

Now Zivy was on alert as well.

"Spill it, chick."

I'd like to chalk their deductive powers up to psychic phenomena, but sometimes I had to admit others were privy to some secret interpersonal language to which I was not.

"Fine. I told Carter to wake Utter up."

I threw back a shot of apple juice—a move that probably felt more authoritative than it looked.

"Why?" JJ asked.

Before I could answer, something on the floor caught my eye, a flash of color, and I bent to examine it. Red. One remaining bit of the vexing stained glass. I picked it up and rolled it between my forefinger and thumb.

"Because I don't like being lied to," I said, slipping the nugget of glass into my pocket.

29

The clock on the microwave read two thirty when Mr. Carter came a-calling.

"We're set."

The three of us followed him into the library, our footfalls breaking the stillness. Once inside, Carter fiddled with the TV monitor while the rest of us stood by in silence. The only sound other than Carter's last minute technical finagling was the *scritch-scritch* of Zivy's nails on her jeans. The girl needed nicotine bad.

JJ leaned in close.

"What do you plan on asking?"

"First off, I'll ask why we can't just bop in and chat with him face-to-face." I nodded toward the locked door to the South Wing as I said this.

"But if he's so sick—"

"If he's so sick, you'd think there would be a couple of

spare N95s around. Did everybody just forget Covid? Besides, Zoom calls suck. Everything gets lost in translation."

JJ didn't have an answer to this, but I did notice him glancing over at the door more than once before Carter took a step back from the TV.

"We're live."

Live. Alive. Living.

Didn't quite seem apropos at the moment.

The screen glowed warmly. An image of Utter's study awakened, the fire snap, crackle, and popping in the background.

As we stood awaiting our host's arrival, I couldn't help but remember those intricate, CGI winter scenes folks had become so annoyingly fond of—those computer-generated videos of idyllic mountain cabins accompanied by gentle piano music that fooled viewers into thinking they were nestled snug in a Colorado mountain hideaway.

Carter headed for the exit.

"You're not going to stay, Mr. Carter?" I asked, already knowing the answer.

He smiled wanly. "It's your party."

He strode to the foyer, opened the front door, and slammed it shut behind him.

We were alone with the TV.

"Are we being stood up?" Zivy asked.

I was wondering the same thing. The flickering flame in the fireplace was the only on-screen sign of life. Perhaps Carter had gotten his signals crossed; the man did seem to be running on one cylinder.

Before I could answer Zivy, Utter stepped into view.

"Give me just a moment," he said, walking to the fireplace and tossing a log on the blaze. "I simply love black oak. Burns forever."

When he turned back, I saw he was wearing the same robe as during our previous chat; however, he had ditched his genteel demeanor. This James Utter was most assuredly pissed off.

"Dr. West tells me that, above and beyond the treatments she's prescribed, rest is the best medicine for my condition, and plenty of it. Now, Ms. Marx, if you would be so kind, please inform me why the hell we're meeting in the middle of the goddamned night."

Why was he so bent out of shape? He agreed to meet. Heck, it was he who called Carter to get the ball rolling. I don't know how he knew to call but call he did.

But I said nothing of the sort.

"Why don't we cut to the chase, Mr. Utter?"

"I appreciate your directness, Ms. Marx."

"I only have one question for you."

Utter frowned. "One question that couldn't wait until morning?"

I countered his frown with a grin. "That's not a gas fireplace, is it?"

The man had obviously steeled himself for any number of intrusive queries, but my simple question flustered him.

"The fireplace?" He turned back to it as if seeing it for the first time. "Why, it's wood-burning, of course."

"Right," I said, slapping my forehead with my palm. "The black oak. Burns forever, you said."

"Where are you going with this?" JJ whispered to me.

"Shush."

Utter aggressively cleared his throat. "I really don't see what you're getting at."

"Me either," Zivy added.

"It's odd," I said, allowing myself the freedom to wander about the room. "You see, not too long ago, I paid Mr. Carter a visit in the carriage house. Or rather, he *caught* me in the carriage house."

"Yes, yes?"

"Before popping back in here, I strolled the grounds, taking in the night. The Hudson Valley is quite beautiful, and your little corner of it is to die for. Our hills in Iowa can't hold a candle to yours. Ours are more like mounds. October evenings in New York have their own distinct flavor, wouldn't you say? A mix of pumpkin, dead leaves, and—"

"Ms. Marx!"

"Smoke."

I whirled on the TV monitor. Those detectives on TV would have been proud. "That's a fine fire you've got going there, Mr. Utter. I don't know anything about black oak, but I suspect it would take a while to build a blaze like that." I was in the zone. "What I don't understand is why, when I was outside, I didn't catch so much as a whiff of smoke rising from this building. Didn't see any, either. That's not a question, by the way; just an observation."

Utter stared at me open-mouthed. Then, a flush rose from

his neck to the top of his head. If he were in the room with me, I'd consider stepping out of slapping range.

Just when I thought the man was about to explode, he turned some inner pressure relief valve. His anger quickly dissipated—damned if he didn't even chuckle. He turned back to his fire and stoked it with a poker.

"I told Carter we had a good batch this time. Smart, unique..." He flashed Zivy a grin. "Easy on the eyes." He held onto the poker, letting it sway back and forth like a metronome. "You didn't really want to ask me about my fireplace. You'd already worked that part out. So why don't you ask what you really want to ask?"

Go big or go home.

"You're not here at Utter Hall at all, are you?"

His grin widened and his eyes narrowed.

"Which," I continued, "begs the question: if you're not here, where are you?"

He pointed the poker directly at me.

"Oh, and you were doing so well. I'm sorry to disappoint you, but contrary to your suspicions, I am in fact right here in the South Wing."

I nodded toward the locked door.

"Why not let us in and prove me wrong?"

"Yeah!" JJ interjected.

"You're too tricky by half, I'm afraid. That would be... inadvisable."

"For you or for us?" Zivy asked.

"Both, I'd say."

"We read your book," I said. "*Sorrow's Leap.*"

"I'm flattered." I wished he would drop the damned poker. It was distracting me. "I suppose you want it autographed?"

This last bit carried a tone I recognized from my childhood days. Snide contempt. It was one of Mother's favorites.

"I'd rather you explain why the ghostly woman who attacked Quan appears to have been ripped from its pages."

The flicker of anger was back, and this time it bled into Utter's voice. "I thought that's what I was paying you quite handsomely to uncover."

A sharp laugh caught me off guard. Zivy slapped her hands on her thighs.

"Who the fuck cares about your money, dude? I've been broke before and I'll be broke again. What really ticks me off is that you've been holding back on us. Cockblocking Ellen when all she's trying to do is get some answers out of you. You may have been some big-time author back in the day, but all I see is an old man getting off on playing a fucking game of cat and mouse."

"Fuck, yeah," JJ added.

"No one's keeping you here," Utter growled.

The gloves were off. At last. Maybe now I could finally get to the bottom of—

A harsh squeal sounded from outside the room. A fire alarm? Burglar alarm? Some other fucking sort of alarm?

"What the hell?" Zivy said.

"Fire?" JJ shrilled. "Is there a fire?"

Ignoring them, I bolted from the room. I was determined not to let anything interrupt *just* when I was about to get down to the nitty gritty.

This whole place is a spiderweb of faulty wiring. Carter probably triggered some sensor when he slammed that door.

But I was wrong.

Dead wrong.

Quan's device sat just where we'd left it, neat and orderly next to the front door.

And it was screaming.

30

L ED lights blinked red and yellow in rapid succession as the ghost monitoring/luring mechanism threw a preternatural fit as if it housed a gremlin that was doing its best to eat its way out.

Remembering what had happened after the first time the device had come to life, I whirled on the stairs, expecting to find the Dark Lady bearing down on me, her nipping shadows chittering by her side.

But no. The stairs were empty. Why then was Quan's mechanism sounding the alarm?

The cries from the library answered my question.

"Ellen!" JJ shouted. "Get in here!"

I flew back to the library. JJ and Zivy stood mesmerized, eyes locked on the TV monitor. James Utter still stood in the middle of the frame, poker in hand. He was wielding the tool in self-defense.

The giggles of little children issued from the TV speakers. Utter's eyes were wide and searching.

"What's that?" Utter spat. "Who's there?"

Gleeful laughter was the only response.

"Shit," JJ said. "It's happening again..."

From every corner of his study, shadows emerged. They stretched across the screen like dark sunspots, eating up pixels as they invaded Utter's inner sanctuary.

The author, for his part, was screaming his damn head off, swiping at the advancing shades.

"This can't be happening!"

I had the sudden urge to change the channel, as if that might save our host from his fate. Instead, I chose the only course of action I could think of.

Abandoning the library once more, I dashed back to the foyer. Quan's device was short-circuiting, its piercing alarm morphing into yelps of transistor death. I kicked it to the corner where it whimpered in muted agony.

I grabbed the Bakelite phone from its cubby.

Carter picked up at once.

"Yes?"

"If you plan on having a job tomorrow, get the hell over here. Now!"

I slammed the phone down and rushed back to the library, my calves suffering the cost of neglect. If I made it out of there alive, I was *definitely* rejoining the gym.

Utter had taken to swinging at the insubstantial shadows like some crazed baseball slugger.

"You don't belong! Back...back, you filth! You *don't belong!*"

One particularly feisty shadow squirmed around his neck, cutting off his air. Utter stumbled, gasping for breath.

"They're going to kill him," JJ cried, taking an impulsive step toward the TV, pulling the box cutter from his pocket as if prepared to dive through the screen.

"*Better him than us.*"

I shot Zivy a sideways glance. The surprised look on her face confirmed that she was as taken aback by Byrd's sudden interjection as I was.

JJ broke ranks and rushed the door to the South Wing. He tugged at the door, but his failed efforts made it clear—it was firmly locked. He took a few steps back, then threw himself at it with all the gusto of a linebacker. His shoulder hit hard wood, and something cracked. Door or bone? I wasn't sure.

"Fuuuuuck..."

JJ sank to the ground, cradling his arm.

Zivy dropped to his side and rubbed his shoulder, as if friction might miraculously undo the damage.

Utter spat venom. "Don't just stand there, Ms. Marx. You're supposed to be the expert. Do something!"

"Open the door and I'll think about it."

"Go to hell."

I relaxed back on my heels. If he wasn't willing to aid in his own rescue, what was there for me to do but enjoy the show?

My body language must have spoken volumes because he relented.

"Fine! Fine! I'll buzz you in."

But just as he made a move toward his desk, the lights in the room fluttered and blinked out, leaving him silhouetted in the fireplace's glow.

"No..." Desperation crept into his voice. "No, no, no, no, no..."

The shades circled him, the scene like something out of a Balinese shadow play. There were more of them than before, and their numbers were growing. I got the disturbing sense that once their darkness filled the screen, something quite awful would happen to James Utter. Might the shadows pry his lips apart and burrow down his throat? Would they squeeze him like half-mad boa constrictors until his ribs splintered? Or would they simply consume him, digesting him until he became one with their inky blackness? The truth, I feared, would be far worse.

Chunky was right: it was time to break down the door. We just needed something more effective than his beefy shoulder.

But what?

The kitchen...

I was moving before the thought was fully formed in my head. Images of Charles Laughton as The Hunchback swam through my head, swinging from the parapets, calling down, "Sanctuary! Sanctuary!" as the mob stormed the cathedral doors. I didn't have a mob or a battering ram, but I didn't need either to get past Utter Hall's locked doors.

All I needed was the island in the kitchen. It had wheels.

Upon entering the kitchen, I shoved the stools aside and grabbed the island with both hands, tugging it backward toward the door. The rolling table just managed to squeak through the doorframe, and with a few determined yanks, I soon had it out.

When I shoved the island into the library, my cohorts instantly picked up on the play.

"Here," Zivy said, coming to my side, "let's line it up first."

"My damn shoulder..." JJ whined.

"Push with your back," I suggested.

"Good idea."

"No, a good idea would be diet, big guy."

"Shut up, Byrd!"

We were running out of time. The screen was all but black. Utter's screams sounded muffled. The damned things were smothering him.

Once we were locked on target, I gave the signal.

"Let's roll."

At that, we charged the door.

Our footsteps thundered as we sped across the wood floor, barbarians coming for the king's hold. Soon would come the collision: marble countertop versus mahogany door.

When the island struck home, all romantic ideas of us as a battering brigade shattered along with the front edge of the stone top. Although we'd cut a deep gash in the wood, the door remained solidly in place.

"Let's go again," I said.

We backed up halfway across the room and, upon the count of three, charged the island once more toward the locked door. This time hinges groaned, and the door's inner locking mechanism snapped like a walnut.

"Lemme try it!" JJ offered, jumping at the chance to swing wide the door.

The decorative handle simply spun in his hand, wrenched clear of its latch.

Zivy, perspiration-dampened hair plastered to her forehead like orange lightning bolts, turned to me with raised eyebrows.

"Third time's the charm?"

"It'd better fucking be." I helped her reposition the island. "JJ! Leave it."

JJ, who was still trying to Houdini his way around the broken lock, rejoined our attack group.

The sounds coming out of the TV speakers were the stuff of nightmares.

"Ready?" I asked.

"Uno," Zivy said.

"Dos," I added.

"Tres! *¡Vamos, vamos!*"

We leaned into JJ's war cry and shot toward the door. This time, we were an unstoppable force, the mahogany slab proving less than immovable.

The island collided with the door, ripping it from its hinges and sending it flying into the hallway beyond.

The South Wing lay before us.

The shift from active construction site to refined elegance caught me off guard. The South Wing's renovation had taken precedence over all else. The intricately woven floor runner, the crystal globes emitting warm illumination, and the ruby-red wallpaper made it clear that we, the workers, were staying in a Motel 6 while the boss had booked a room at The Plaza.

Still, we weren't the one screaming.

I didn't have to tell the others to follow; they were close at my heels.

"All right, you Great and Terrible Oz, here we come," Zivy shouted.

"Huh?"

"Jesus, JJ. When we get outta here, I gotta sit you down and make you watch some goddamned movies."

We passed three or four rooms flanking the hallway as we traveled its length, each of them empty. The main event lay ahead, and there was no stopping us. At the far end of the hall sat a door not unlike the one we'd just demolished. Would we have to break it down as well?

Utter's cries had grown hoarse, and even though we were mere steps away from the room at the end of the hall, I feared we were too late.

JJ stopped short of opening the door.

"Are we sure we want to do this?" he asked.

I nodded, Zivy nodded, and JJ's nod made three.

He grabbed the doorknob, gritted his teeth, and turned.

Light flooded into the hall as the door swung open, temporarily blinding me. It was all I could do to keep from tearing up.

Utter was moaning, but that wasn't the sound that disturbed me as I struggled to regain my eyesight. No, it was the familiar, rhythmic sound playing beneath his pained vocalizations that cut me to the quick.

Bleep...bleep...bleep...

Son of a bitch...

"Mama's gone to heaven. Sad day. Say goodbye, now—I have things I need to do for her."

James Utter lay in a hospital bed, tubes in his veins, wires on his skin. His head was shaved as was his face. His eyes were closed and sunken to a depth I didn't know possible. He was blue in pallor, and his bones stuck out in sharp relief. The scent of industrial cleaner and shit pervaded the air, as did the incessant beeping of his heart monitor.

This wasn't the man I'd gone toe to toe with via our Zoom call. This was a living corpse.

A young woman in a bright nurse's top stepped between us and her patient as he howled and howled and howled.

"Mr. Utter must *not* be disturbed!"

31

Utter's nurse raised a warning hand. She needn't have worried. I had no intention of getting any closer to the shrieking cadaver in the hospital bed.

"Jesus..." Zivy whispered, grabbing my hand.

The shriveled man squealed through vocal cords long out of commission, sounding like a strangling newborn. His skin was weathered parchment, his teeth, kernels of shoepeg corn. He was as gaunt as dehydrated roadkill, and the smell wafting up from beneath these sheets did nothing to dispel that image. He'd be right at home among the victims of any number of the world's atrocities.

No, he wasn't the man we'd chatted with via Zoom. But then again, he was. Just like an apple is still the same apple even if you leave it in the sun to rot.

This was our Mr. Utter...only rotten.

"Shut him up, will you?"

The voice came from thin air, and at first, I was convinced a new spirit had entered the fray. But it was JJ who quickly cracked the case.

"Guys," he said.

I turned toward him, forcefully muting the nurse's protestations, and followed his gaze.

Positioned on the wall next to the door and opposite the bed was a TV monitor, twin to the one in the empty library.

On its screen was the room we'd just left, its shelves devoid of books. But it wasn't the main image that drew my attention. It was the smaller screen-in-screen video feed in the lower right corner. Within that rectangle, Utter did battle with the shadows, swinging his poker wildly despite his obvious terror.

I looked from the man on the screen to the man in the bed and back again. My brain seized as it did when trying to lock in those 3-D images that required blurring your vision in order to see its depth. My mind was trying to piece together two competing realities and was doing a remarkably bad job of it.

The nurse, responding to her boss's voice on the TV, produced a syringe and small vial from her bag on the nightstand. Old memories pulled at me once more: Mom in bed, the smell of death, a sea of syringes.

The woman slipped the needle into an IV port leading into the man's scrawny arm, and his howling ceased almost at once.

"Leave now or I'm calling Mr. Carter," the nurse said, clearly flustered by the chaos. Up until now, her job had no doubt consisted of sitting watch at the shrunken author's bedside, monitoring his vitals between games of Candy Crush.

"No need," I said. "I already did."

The TV flickered, possibly in reaction to the sedative now

coursing through Utter's veins, and the man on the screen cried out, both angry and alarmed, "They bite!"

The three of us stared at the monitor, watching helplessly, the small screen in the corner now nothing but swirling blackness.

"He's beset, he's beset, he's beset!" Byrd cackled.

"Shut up!" Zivy slapped herself hard across the cheek. An angry blush rose to the surface of her skin.

Byrd shut up.

"Can you hear us?" JJ shouted at the screen.

"Of course I can!"

JJ shook his head, unsure what to do with the information.

I pressed ahead. "Where are you?"

"You know damn well where I am!"

For someone being "beset," as Byrd so aptly put it, he wasn't being very gracious to those trying to help.

But he was also right.

I *did* know where he was.

A figure burst into the room, and for a moment, I was certain the Dark Lady was making her entrance.

"What the hell are you doing in here?" Carter yelled, causing JJ to yip and Zivy to grab my hand yet again.

I stood my ground and pointed an accusing finger at the screen. "I think the real question is: what the hell is *he* doing *in there?*"

Carter stared at the monitor. It took a moment for him to process the scene, but when his confusion lifted and he saw his boss flailing at the shades, his jaw dropped. He stood there stammering, and I could smell schnapps hot and heavy in the air.

"What do we do?" he finally said, his face ashen.

"I was really hoping you'd tell me."

The voice on the TV laughed manically. "Carter! If one of them doesn't do something soon, so help me God—"

JJ and Zivy stood stymied, both of them muttering possible solutions under their breath.

Shit.

It was up to me, wasn't it?

Without a second thought, I placed my hand on the screen. It was warm with a hint of electricity running through it. But as I closed my eyes, its temperature dropped. The glass turned to ice, and I feared if I pulled my hand away, I'd leave a layer of skin behind.

"Ellen?"

I wasn't sure who said my name, but it sounded as if they were a million miles away as I...

Breathed...

Focused...

And reached out.

My life has been filled with unusual experiences. One of the earliest I can recall is when a pair of roller skates followed me home.

Mother was a thrift store, bargain basement, garage sale kind of gal, and she lugged me around every weekend to rifle through other people's belongings. Early one Saturday morning—Saturdays always started early in my household so

Mom could get a jump on the rest of the buyers—we visited a yard sale in a nearby town.

I spotted a pair of roller skates with what I thought was a reasonable price, but Mom didn't see it that way and ended up bickering her way out of the purchase.

"Overpriced garbage," she said as we pulled away from the sale.

I bit my tongue. I'd learned from experience that even a whisper of discontent would leave me fending for myself the next time while she contentedly made her rounds of the sales solo.

I stared through the rear window at the receding yard sale, wishing I had those skates. Not aloud, of course, lest my mother shoot back with something like, "If wishes were fishes, we'd all swim in riches!"

As the house disappeared from view, I glimpsed something on the road behind us. Following us. It was the skates. And wearing them was a translucent girl about my own age.

I waved at her, and she waved back. She followed us for another block until Mom peeled off, leaving the neighborhood and the girl with the skates behind.

It was the first of many dark detours on the path to Utter Hall, my palm pressed to the icy surface of a TV screen, peering into another world. Just another day at the office for Ellen Marx.

A second later, a shock of intense electrical energy threw me backward into the room. I tripped over my own feet and went tumbling onto my butt with a *whump*.

As I sat there breathing through the pain of the fall, I had the distinct sense I wasn't in Kansas anymore. It was the scent in the room that gave it away—it had shifted. No longer dank and medicinal, the air took on a toasted quality.

Black oak. Utter's words in my head. *Burns forever.*

I opened my eyes.

JJ? Gone. Zivy? Gone. Carter, the nurse, and the man in the bed? Gone, gone, and gone.

"Welcome, Ms. Marx!"

I turned slowly. Standing behind me, poker upraised, was James Utter, white-haired and full of fire.

"Welcome to Sorrow's Leap."

32

Something swished past me, scraping my neck like catfish whiskers. It passed before my eyes, temporarily blocking Utter from view.

Oh, yeah...the shadows.

Utter swung at my head—not actually *at* it but above it—and the iron implement swooshed over my crown.

"Are you trying to brain me?" I shouted.

"It was coming for you!"

Better the nip of an ethereal shadow than the all-too-solid whack of a poker, I thought.

"They're scared of you," Utter whispered in awe.

"I don't think so."

"Look!"

The shadow flitted past to join its fellows. No longer did they fill the air as they had while we watched via the TV. Now, they gathered together in a corner of the room. A cluster of spiders waiting to pounce.

As the shadows amassed, I caught a glimpse of a group of people standing opposite me. Just a glimpse, mind you—here one minute, gone the next. An image burned on the retina, already beginning to fade.

Zivy. I saw Zivy. And JJ and Carter and...

Me. For that split second, I saw myself from behind. My hand plastered to the screen.

I was seeing split versions of the room, one in which nasty shadows plotted their next move, another in which the team watched on as I communed with the TV.

I was in Utter Hall *and* Sorrow's Leap. I was in both and in neither. I was between.

Utter abruptly interrupted my thoughts by throwing the poker, javelin-like, toward the clustered shadows.

"Take that, you filth!" he cried.

The shadows didn't react, even though Utter's throw was powerful enough to embed the poker into the wall. They simply swirled about it in a dark and dreadful maypole dance.

I whipped around to face Utter. He was there, he wasn't— he was in bed, he wasn't.

"So..." I said, giving voice to the absurdity that was the only conclusion I could muster. "We're trapped in your book? *Sorrow's Leap?*"

He reached over and pinched me. Hard.

"Book? Does that feel like a book?"

My first instinct was to slap him. Nobody pinched me. Not anymore. It was the physical version of "fuck you"—mean, disrespectful, and a thing my mother had done on a regular basis.

Cooling my jets, I pressed on.

"Then what is this place?"

Utter laughed, full of bile and contempt. "Right where she stuck me, the bitch."

"I don't understand. You're in bed, hooked up to—"

"Yes, yes, yes," he said, growing frustrated. "She didn't steal my body. Had no use for it. Just the ghost rattling around inside." He slapped his chest to drive the point home.

"She stole your spirit?"

"Stole it, trapped it. But I'm going to get out. You hear me?" He was no longer addressing me. "You hear me?!?"

A painful white light slipped through my brain, threatening to split the two hemispheres. The two realities were not playing nice, each increasingly covetous of my presence.

The Ellen at the TV slumped, then fell to the ground. JJ hunkered down at her side, trying to wake her.

"Ellen!" Zivy cried.

Staring at my crumpled body, I made a sickening realization. It wasn't just Utter who'd been separated from his physical form. I'd joined the population of Sorrow's Leap as well. I held a hand in front of my face. Sure enough, I could see the room beyond as if I were nothing but a layer in Photoshop at fifty percent opacity.

Great thumps echoed throughout the house, and the room bucked like a ship in a storm. All, I supposed, in anticipation of *her* arrival.

"You said 'she' stuck you here?" I shouted over the cacophony around me. "The Dark Lady? Who is she?"

Utter stared as if seeing me for the first time. "You...you got past her," he whispered, a smile dawning on his face. "You got in! And ripped a damn hole between the two versions of this place." His laugh curdled into a chuckle, low and careful and full of ill humor. "You got in. That means I can get *out*."

"You mean *we*, don't you? *We* can get out?"

"Of course, of course."

I wasn't sure I believed him. What if I lent him a hand, dragged him back to our world only to have him slam the door in my face? Roaches check in but they don't check out.

I was about to lay down some ground rules for helping him when death passed over his face.

"Oh, fuck. She's here."

I turned ever so slowly, incrementally, as if doing so might make me invisible.

No such luck.

The Dark Lady stood in the doorway, eyes trained not on Utter but me.

She was ghastly in appearance, even more so in the light of Utter's study *his hospital room, his study, his hospital room, his study* but she was also beautiful. Robed in the night, she moved like one submerged. Her skin was moon-kissed and pale. She was elegance and more. Much more. She was vengeance and sex and want and need and...and...

And she was stepping through the door.

The whole room bent toward her, iron filings to a magnet. My vision blurred in synchrony with the rise and fall of her imitated breathing. There was nothing as dead as the thing standing before me. The air stank of spoiled meat, the sickly-sweet scent of offal, the moist putrescence of an unquiet grave.

"We can't beat her," Utter sobbed. "Not here."

Loath as I was to believe him, I did.

The Dark Lady glided into the room. Which room? Both rooms, or at least that's what I believed. Her shadows joined her as she came, hungering to be near her, to embrace her.

She raised her arms, and as she did so, her shadowy companions morphed into strands, then into strings, then into tubes filled with dark and vile liquid. They pierced her arms, her neck, dangling like fetid vines.

Or IVs...

The Dark Lady shed her clothing as she approached in a terrible striptease, dropping her black garments, revealing a pale hospital gown beneath stained brown with ancient blood.

No.

Her IVs floated upward as she moved, causing her to look like some diabolical marionette torn free from its puppeteer.

Get back.

She caressed her face with her hands as if applying cream for the night, and when she brought them back to her side, her face had changed...

Dear God, dear God...

...into that of my mother.

"Stay with me, Ellen."

I instinctively backed away, bumping into Utter who was standing behind me.

"The only way to beat her..." Utter said, mouth so close I felt the heat of his breath on my ear.

"Sta-a-ay..."

Utter gripped my shoulders.

"...is to get out!"

He wrapped his arms around me and pulled me close. He was stronger than I expected, crushing my boobs, squeezing the breath out of me, causing my ribs to click in succession.

"Stop it!" I tried to say, but my lungs were under assault, so all that came out was, "Op!"

The Dark Lady...no...Mother leaned over the two of us, entwined like teen lovers caught in the act, and she whispered in a tone that boiled my guts in guilt.

"Mommy needs a hug!"

33

The woman reached out a gnarled hand and caressed my cheek. My nerves popped and jumped under her cold and poisonous touch.

Mommy needs a hug? Mommy's going to be disappointed.

Utter gripped me even harder. If I couldn't free myself, at least I could put him in between me and the thing with my mother's face.

I spun around, shifting Utter's position so that the Dark Lady and I formed an Utter sandwich.

The man squealed as his back brushed up against the ghost and he loosened his grip just enough for me to wriggle out of his arms.

The Dark Lady snaked around the author, whispering IVs wrapping about him like tentacles. And how he screamed. I don't know if his pain was mental or physical, but I felt it in my teeth.

Zivy turned at the sound. She had become much more

tangible. As a matter of fact, the hospital room itself was becoming more present, more solid. The swap between worlds was underway, Sorrow's Leap bowing to Utter Hall.

But the spirit had no intention of leaving. She was enjoying herself.

She dropped her disguise, sloughing off Mom's face for her own, her inky garments reconstituting. Before I could comprehend what was happening, she was the Dark Lady once more.

The version of James Utter in her arms faded along with the rest of the study in a final flicker, like a birthday candle being blown out.

All was as it had been.

Save for the looming nightmare dressed in black.

No one should ever have to see out of two pairs of eyes at once. There's unnatural and then there's un-fucking-natural. I was lying on the floor staring up at the Dark Lady, but I was also standing at the TV looking back at myself. One me; four eyes. Something had to give.

The angry phantom reached for me once more, and I let go. I snuffed my gift as I had done upon seeing my mother's corpse. I closed in on myself, dowsing the flame, drawing back.

And then, with that horrible falling feeling one has in a dream, I slipped back into my body, surrounded by JJ, Zivy, and Carter.

"She's coming around!" JJ cried.

I struggled to my feet, helped up by half a dozen hands.

"Oh, shit," Zivy said.

Not content to remain in that other place, the Dark Lady

had followed me back and now stood at Utter's bedside, giving the Ghost of Christmas Future a run for his money.

And the future did *not* look good.

The nurse bolted past us and out the door. Whatever duties she'd been hired to perform obviously did not include facing the wrath of a supernatural being. I thought Carter might follow, but to his credit he remained with our huddled group. We watched helplessly as the Dark Lady bent over Utter's shriveled body and began to keen.

The sound of it was horrific, like the mournful call of some deep-sea creature, rage and sorrow echoing through the murky depths.

Utter's eyes fluttered open, and he squinted against the light.

"You," he said in a broken voice.

His heart monitor burbled to life, unaccustomed to the rapid beats it detected.

The spirit replied with even louder wails, reaching out its ashen hands as if to bestow a dark blessing. Or a curse.

"We can't let her," JJ whispered.

Let her what? Whatever she had in store for the helpless husk of a man would no doubt defy comprehension.

I was about to tell JJ that yes, we *could* let her, and better Utter than us, but he was running on a different current than me.

He wielded the box cutter, his muscles tense. At that moment, JJ Gadzinski was heroism incarnate, misguided though it may have been.

He was also about to get his ass handed to him.

JJ took a single step toward the bed. The dark thing made a simple motion with her hand, like shooing a fly, and one of her shadows shot forward like a dart, striking him in the sternum. He dropped the blade and clutched his chest. I have no doubt his heart skipped a few beats.

The Dark Lady hadn't even looked up.

Carter leaned in. "Do something!"

"Such as?"

"I don't know. Exorcize her! Send her forth! Whatever the hell you do with things like this."

I'd done just that to countless restless spirits over the course of my career. But this? This was different. I'd sensed that much in her touch. Any rituals, tricks, or traps I'd used in the past would be of no avail. The Dark Lady was something quite new. Something unique. Something intent on getting its way.

Utter shrieked once more, forcing his lungs to work harder.

"*Eee-ahh* she's *ahh-hh*, it hurts, it hurts *ahh-hh!*"

My last efforts had landed me in a fractured reality filled with ghoulies galore, but I had to try something.

Perhaps, simplicity was required.

Ghostbusting 101: Make Your Demand.

I cleared my throat. "You may not harm this man," I began. "This is his home, and you are not welcome. It's time for you to move on."

Utter paused mid-shriek and stared at me, as if to say, *What the fuck? Is that all you got?*

The black-cloaked thing did likewise.

Great. They both think I'm nuts.

Their focus turned from me back to each other. The Dark

Lady engulfed Utter, surprise limbs reaching from beneath her skirts and grasping him. One hand tugged open his jaw while another probed his mouth. Soon, he would be enveloped in the ectoplasmic nightmare in black.

Black...

The others went stiff by my side, resigned to standing witness.

No...not black.

Utter's lips pulled back, exposing yellowed teeth, his gums inflamed and swollen and...

Red!

I plunged my hand in my pocket, fingers searching desperately and coming up short. Where was it? Lint? Check. A spare quarter? Check! But the thing I sought? Nowhere to be found—

Ah!

The nail on my forefinger clicked against the tiny object wedged in a crease of fabric. Slowly, carefully, I extracted it— the nugget of stained glass I'd found on the kitchen floor.

I held it up between my thumb and forefinger, wielding it like one of the Weird Sisters' crystals.

"Is this yours?" I called.

The moment I held that scarlet shard aloft, I had the Dark Lady's complete attention.

Shit. Now what?

The spirit congealed, withdrawing her sinuous appendages from Utter's frame, until she was once more recognizable as a woman. Dead, maybe, but definitely a woman.

We stood staring at each other, both waiting to find out what I would do next.

"Ellen, what's the plan?" JJ asked.

"Beats me."

He looked flummoxed. "But you've got her attention."

"That I do."

"And...?"

Shut up, Chunky. Let me think!

Perhaps it was my furrowed brow or my whispered conversation with JJ or the fact I was simply standing there like a jerk, arm upraised with a niblet of glass between my fingers. In any case, the Dark Lady must have sensed my bluff and made her move.

The moment before she lashed out, her face twisted and her eyes grew sharp. She was my Gollum; the bit of glass her precious. And she meant to have it. Come hell or high water.

Which is exactly why I swallowed it.

34

I didn't feel the bit of glass as it slid down my throat. I'd seen magicians chew and swallow entire lightbulbs, so what harm really could a piece of glass smaller than a pea do?

The Dark Lady's reaction was such that I realized while there may have been no harm in swallowing the glass, there definitely might be in its extraction.

She rushed me, knocking me flat on my back, the roar of savage winds blasting in my ears as she locked her hands around my neck. Out of the frying pan and all that.

If ever I'd hoped Carter might come to my aid, I was sorely disappointed. He was cowering in the corner of the room.

My vision began to dim as her fingers tightened around my throat. Her face was inches from mine, and it was once again beautiful in its fury. Her pupils expanded, turning her eyes a shiny obsidian. Her eyebrows tilted inward in a venomous *V*. Her mouth, a flexing black hole, closed in, and I finally realized her game plan.

She meant to suck the glass from my gullet.

Her lips encircled mine in a kiss of death, her mouth as dank as an open grave.

The others were shouting, but they might as well have been on the moon for all it mattered. I'd played my last card and gone bust. Now, the Dark Lady was collecting her winnings.

A sharp pain filled my chest, then my throat. The thing's method was working, the glass reluctantly rising in my gorge, rending my tissues as it came like a sharpened cat's claw.

My vision went from dim to dark to black. My world was growing smaller, and I feared soon enough, it would disappear entirely.

At the very moment the glass nugget crested the back of my tongue—a ruby red tonsillolith being hoovered up by my supernatural oppressor—I was released.

The shutters covering my eyes flew open, and I took a deep, involuntary breath. Luckily, the bit of glass caught the side of my tongue instead of traveling down my windpipe to my lungs where God knows what damage it would do. I plucked it from my mouth and held it firmly in hand as I tried to assess what the fuck had just happened.

Zivy.

Zivy is what happened.

"You wanna play, asshole?" she said.

"Ziv, no!" JJ shouted.

Zivy had swiped the box cutter from JJ and was now holding its razor-sharp blade against the meat of her forearm.

Whatever you're thinking of doing don't do it, dear God, don't do it—

"Let's play!"

Zivy drew the knife easily across her skin in a practiced stroke. Gouts of blood appeared like a magic trick, followed by a pulsing gush. Gore streamed down her arm, pooled at her elbow, and fell like a crimson cascade. Great droplets splattered on the floor, and I was unable to escape the spray.

"What did you do? What did you do?" JJ was in a panic, but Zivy was as calm and as sure as I'd ever seen her. She held her arm up in defiance, shooting daggers with her eyes at the swirling Dark Lady, who, for the time being, had paused her attack.

The "whys" overwhelmed me. Why the self-inflicted injury? Why the spirit's sudden reluctance to advance? Why—

The slurping cries bubbling from the blood-drenched floor wiped my mind clean of all questions.

Rising from the growing pool of blood—more than had fallen—was the hint of a nose, the suggestion of a brow, and the outline of a mouth open wide in utter fear and pain.

"Why?"

I was glad someone else was beset by that question. Too bad that someone was Byrd.

"Why!" he demanded, a bloody face birthed from Zivy's spillage.

Without thinking twice—thinking had gone out the window the moment I laid eyes on the emaciated author in his bed—I tossed the speck of glass into the bloody Byrd pond where it disappeared, red hiding within red.

The Dark Lady knocked me aside, her arm striking me like

a tornadic gust. She reached a hand into the pool and felt about, causing Byrd to scream even louder.

And when the ghost couldn't find her prize, she went after Zivy.

"Back!" was all JJ managed to say before he too was batted aside.

The Dark Lady rose to full height and beyond, towering over the bleeding girl. Then, ever so slowly, like a spider closing in on its prey, she pulled Zivy to her breast.

In a flash, JJ was back on his feet and ready to do battle, David to the spirit's Goliath. Only JJ didn't even have a slingshot. If he rushed the Dark Lady again, she would end him then and there.

"Zivy!" he cried. "Do you trust me?"

He was fixing to do his little trick again. Swoop in and spirit Zivy away to his neck of the netherworld where an overturned car was forever ablaze and the child within was in constant danger of burning.

And then what? The ghost had so wrapped herself around our friend that the two were blending into one. The blood no longer fell but instead joined the swirling darkness that was the Dark Lady's body, red mingling with black.

If JJ plucked Zivy from this room, no doubt the spirit would follow. New location—same problem. Although now it would be so much worse. Little Julian, trapped in the backseat of his parents' car, would be no match for the Dark Lady.

I couldn't let him do it.

Zivy and I locked eyes, and whether it was intuition or

some other hooky spooky shit, I knew the same thought had crossed her mind as well.

"Do you trust me?" JJ yelled, hand outstretched.

Ignoring him, Zivy nodded at me. "Keep him away from me."

I'm not proud to say I obeyed.

"Please..." JJ gasped, trying to wriggle free as I dragged him to the corner. "Don't stop me. I helped you, Ellen. I can help her too..."

But there would be no visit to the side of the New Jersey highway for Zivy. I held him firm. He writhed in my grip, screaming for me to release him, peppering his language with words I didn't know he knew.

The dark specter placed a hand on Zivy's head. She threw me a last look that said, "Ain't it just typical..."

The Dark Lady's palm passed through Zivy's skull like hot coals on ice. My friend's mouth went slack as the spirit wrenched her essence from her. There was a sudden *pop* like the uncorking of a bottle as the ghost drew back her hand. Zivy's body, now bereft of everything that made her *her*, went slack.

The dark thing turned toward me and smiled. She dabbed at the corner of her mouth as if to tell me she'd not only taken Zivy's soul, but it was delicious.

The air pressure in the room rapidly shifted, the whole room taking a deep breath. The scene held a moment, balanced between life and death. And when the exhale finally came, the Dark Lady rode it into the ether and was gone.

Zivy's unconscious body crumpled in a heap, her soul's departure leaving the room all that much smaller for its exit.

JJ wrenched free and knelt at her side. He glared back at me, betrayal incarnate.

"How could you?"

"She told me to save you—"

"What about *her*?"

His words were flame, and my cheeks reddened beneath their heat.

"It was a no-win situation—"

"Fuck your no-win situation!" With every word he punctuated, I suffered an unnatural blast of heat, as if he were channeling the blaze that had engulfed his family's car. Another such outburst, and I was afraid I might actually go up in flames.

"It's over," Carter said.

It *was* over. And there was no one in that room more too blame than me.

Utter, the wheezing wonder, was the only one in the room who actually looked better for the mayhem. He was sitting up like some grotesque mannequin, his gown having slipped off his shoulders, exposing a concave chest and starved ribcage.

"Thank you," he hissed as he saw me.

"Screw you," I replied.

Blood soaked into the knees of JJ's cargo pants. He cradled Zivy's head and whispered to her softly, but it was no use. Although her eyes were open, there was nothing of Zivy left in them. Zivy had gone to Sorrow's Leap.

JJ looked up, his eyes rimmed with angry tears.

"You did this."

"Carter," Utter wheezed, beckoning his manservant to his side. "Get the doctor."

His gaze landed on me.

"And get these people out of here."

35

By the time Dr. West arrived with her medical team, it was five in the morning. Carter hadn't called an ambulance or the police. The good doctor simply had him place Zivy in the backseat of her assistant's car before sending them down the hill. "To St. Luke's," Carter said. The main attraction was the newly revived Mr. Utter. Zivy, it seemed, was an afterthought.

Carter herded JJ and me back to the main living quarters. Once we hit the entryway, he turned to face us.

"Get your things together," he said, distracted by the arrival of two uniformed guards. Their car announced them as members of the A-1 Security Group.

"What's with the rent-a-cops?" I asked.

"Boss's orders." Carter wouldn't meet my eye.

"And what about Zivy? What's going to happen to her?" Gone was any hint of good-natured JJ. His demeanor had changed from sugar to steel.

"Oh...that reminds me," Carter said. "Would you mind collecting her belongings and bringing them down here?"

JJ shot across the room with a speed I didn't know he had in him. He grabbed Carter by his shirtfront, buttons popping, and slammed him against the wall.

"What the hell?" Carter whined, struggling to be free of this new and improved JJ.

"Maybe you didn't hear me the first time. What...about... Zivy?" With each emphasized word, JJ stabbed Carter in the chest with his forefinger.

One of the security guards had exited his vehicle and was watching the encounter with interest. "Is there an issue here, Mr. Carter?"

"No," Carter assured him, waving him off.

"You sent her to St. Luke's—"

"That's where Dr. West sent her—"

"Then that's where you're taking us."

Carter balked, but I stepped in next to JJ, forming a united front. Even in his frazzled and semi-drunk state, Carter could do the math.

"Get your things," he said.

JJ wouldn't speak to me. We packed in silence. By the time I was finished, he was already busy neatly folding clothes Zivy had never once folded herself. When I mentioned this to him, he gave me a look that said something between "how dare you" and "go take a flying leap."

Back into the van we went. It felt cavernous with only two passengers, but I didn't dare mention this to JJ. He might have bitten my head off.

"A quick detour to the hospital and then I'll get you home."

"Quite a scorecard you've got going, eh Carter?" JJ said.

"Come again?"

"As far as workplace injuries, you're two for four. You and that boss of yours."

Carter revved the engine. "I think you'll find Mr. Utter is more than generous. He's authorized me to double your fee."

JJ's laugh was cold and bitter. "Well, isn't he a fucking prince?"

I wanted to speak up, but I felt like anything I said would keep the tension brewing. It was almost overflowing as it was.

Carter pulled away from Utter Hall, the taillights casting a momentary red glow across its face, and I felt a wave of something I'd never experienced at the conclusion of any investigation: defeat. Utter defeat, if you'll excuse the pun.

We snaked down the drive, through the fields, and back to the main road. Delivery trucks were already zipping north and south, and we joined the ranks of predawn travelers envious of those still abed.

I blame my nodding off en route to the hospital on the dissipation of adrenaline. The drive couldn't have been more than forty-five minutes. My nap lasted only half that long, but the dream it produced packed a wallop.

I was sitting in the back of the van, JJ had hunkered down in the middle row, and Carter...he was nowhere to be seen. Instead, Quan was our driver. His hair was white as snow.

"I'll get you back home in no time," Quan called out reassuringly, and I took him at face value.

Unfortunately, just as nature abhors a vacuum, dreams abhor cohesion.

A split second after Quan spoke, he was gone, replaced by none other than Utter himself. The corpsicle version.

"Hang on!" he shrilled, boney hands spinning the steering wheel like a carnival game.

The van's wheel screamed, and the vehicle flipped, landing on its roof, sparks flying as metal hit blacktop. I tumbled to the ceiling which was now the floor—yes, I had a sense where this was going—while JJ remained belted in and dangling. Flames lit up the interior even as we continued speeding and spinning down the road.

Finally, JJ glanced down at me and said through bared teeth, "I hope you burn."

If it wasn't for the crater-sized pothole we hit at that very moment, shaking me from the dream, I had no doubt that I would indeed burn. And upside-down JJ would have smiled as I did.

I must have let out a noise as I woke; both Carter and JJ looked back in alarm. I gave them a little wave to assure them I was okay. Carter's eyes returned to the road, but JJ's remained fixed on me.

"You okay?" he asked.

I nodded, and he went back to staring out the window.

I wanted to ask him if *we* were okay, but I supposed I'd find out soon enough. I joined him in staring out at the scenery whipping past, suddenly homesick for my drab little apartment in Iowa City, my local Indian restaurant, and my public library. Maybe this is what came of unbottling my personal genie. Maybe the silence was better.

From the outside, St. Luke's looked more like an office building than a hospital. Dark brick, evenly-spaced windows, with a large blue banner that informed all who might want to know that medical office space was currently for lease.

"Wait here while I see what's up," Carter said as he parked the van in the sparsely populated visitor's section.

I wasn't going to argue. A fine mist had crept in, and my breath fogged the window. The weather had turned ugly. Gray, wet, bone-chilling.

As Carter made his way toward the main entrance, darting to avoid an arriving ambulance, I figured if JJ and I were ever going to speak to each other again, it was now or never.

"I'm sorry."

They were words I didn't often use. Not because I never felt regret—I had that by the bucketful. It just wasn't a phrase this narcissist's daughter was taught.

At first, not a peep out of JJ, and I figured that was that. Another bridge burned. How many had I left in my wake?

"I know you are." He finally turned to face me. "But I'm not the one you should be saying it to."

Maybe this bridge was still salvageable after all.

"I don't really feel like waiting in this van," I said.

"Me neither."

With that, JJ slid open the door, and the two of us stepped out into the murky morning.

"I have one question for you," JJ said as we headed for the hospital's main doors.

"Shoot."

"Why did you eat the glass?"

I'd been prepared to answer any number of questions—that wasn't one of them.

"I...I'm not sure."

"Seriously?"

How could I put into words what had felt like such a natural thing to do? My gifts didn't come with an instruction manual. I had to rely on instinct. And instinct told me to scarf it down.

"It stopped her from attacking Utter, didn't it?"

"Better him than Zivy."

I stopped short. It was time to settle this. "I didn't ask her to save me. I didn't ask her to slice herself up like an Easter ham. That was all her. And when she told me to get you out of the room—"

"You shouldn't have done that—"

"Shut up and listen!" A cop who was leaning up against the wall near the doors looked up from his coffee. I opted to lower my tone. "She was trying to save you, you idiot. So was I."

"I didn't need saving."

"Yes, you did. I'm sorry to break it to you, JJ, but you're a big puppy."

"Excuse me?"

Shit. I wasn't explaining myself very well.

"Puppies have big hearts. They'll jump into any fray. But you don't let a puppy take on a mountain lion, do you?"

"What are you trying to say? That all this time, you've seen me as nothing but a helpless little puppy—"

I grabbed him by the arm. "What I'm trying to say—and failing badly—is that I care about you. So does Zivy. And we weren't about to let you get hurt on account of us."

JJ considered this a moment. We weren't finished, but at least we'd ripped off the Band-Aid. A wicked breeze had picked up causing the mist to slap us sideways, and he gestured toward the door. I bid the watchful cop goodbye with a nod as we slipped into the hospital lobby.

"Why is she in restraints?"

JJ said aloud what we were both thinking as we stared in at our friend lying in her hospital bed. Carter had finagled an off-hours visit, albeit from the "safe" vantage point of the hall outside Zivy's room.

The nurse flipped through a chart.

"She was brought in with self-inflicted wounds. Restraints are standard."

She looked worse than I imagined she would—swollen eyes, purple and yellow bruises on her neck. But who looked anything but awful in a hospital? It was the bandage on her injured arm that got me. The injury she'd done to herself to save me. I had the sudden urge to bolt. If I never set foot in another one of these places, it would be fine with me.

JJ let out a quiet moan as tears streamed down his cheeks. I put a hand on his back, hoping he wouldn't shrug it off. He didn't.

"Hey," the nurse said, his tone softening. "She's stable. That's something."

Carter, who'd been conferring with staff, returned. Hungover as he was, he'd look right at home in the empty bed next to Zivy.

"That's it," he said, directing us toward the elevator at the end of the hall. "They want us out. Dr. West's pull only goes so far."

As we headed back down to the lobby, my stomach rumbled loud enough for all to hear.

"I'm sure the cafeteria is open by now," Carter said, checking his phone. "It's just about seven."

"No," I shot back. If I had to have one more meal in a hospital cafeteria, I think I'd lose my mind.

"I saw a little coffee shop in Cold Spring," JJ said.

Carter sighed. "I'd kind of like to hit the road."

"And I'd kind of like to beat the living shit out of you," JJ replied. He was *way* past the point of giving a fuck. "But I'll settle for a coffee and croissant."

Carter regarded us both warily, as if he hadn't realized he was sharing an elevator with wild creatures.

"Coffee it is," he said as the doors slid open.

———

Cold Spring's Hot Coffee was supposed to open at seven, but it was forty-five minutes later when the owner finally put out the sandwich board and flipped the open/closed sign.

"Sorry!" she said as we exited the van. "My sister hit a deer on the way to work, and I had to give her a ride."

Not even the wildlife was safe around here.

We took the two tables in front with a view of the street. The rain had stopped, leaving Main Street awash in freshly fallen leaves. The sun was doing its best to come out, but maybe the weight of the past twenty-four hours was just too much for it to bear.

JJ and I sat at one two-top, Carter sat alone at the other. When our drinks came, and they were damn good, Carter tried to elicit conversation.

"I'm going to quit, you know."

Quit booze or quit Utter Hall, I wondered. Either way, he sounded like an addict making a commitment that would be broken by the end of day.

We ignored him and wolfed down our respective baked goods.

Outside the fogged-up windows, Main Street was coming to life. Workers making deliveries, locals walking their dogs. It was a place I could really get used to. If it wasn't for the mad author on the hill and his house full of horrors.

"You gonna finish that?"

Part of me knew it was the last of my quiche that JJ was asking about, but I didn't answer. My attention was on the steady flow of people walking past the shop.

Actually, it was on one person in particular.

I crumpled my napkin and threw it on the table. JJ asked me where I was going, but I was already out the door. I had to get outside before the person who had caught my eye vanished.

"Quan!" I called out.

The young man with the white hair stopped dead in his tracks and turned to face me.

"Ellen?" he croaked.

By now, both JJ and Carter had exited the coffee shop behind me.

Quan glanced from them to me, apprehension slowly dawning on his face.

"Wh-where's...?"

He swallowed hard, speaking clearly a chore. This old goth's heart softened at his concern.

I held up a hand to stop his efforts.

"Where's Zivy? Taken."

36

We sat on the bench outside Hot Coffee, Quan assuring us that despite his ravaged vocal cords and snow-white hair, Utter Hall had not gotten the best of him.

"I'm g-gonna keep it," he said, tugging at his ivory locks.

Why not? His groupies would go bananas over his newly acquired gravitas.

JJ and I gave him a quick rundown on what he'd missed, slowing only to give him a full account of our absent fourth.

"P-p-poor girl," he said with the tentative pronunciation of a stroke victim.

"So?" I asked. "What's new with you?"

He smirked at my flippancy and filled us in, sometimes aloud, sometimes typing his thoughts on his phone when his voice failed him. After his abrupt exit from the investigation, he'd been put up for the night —as Carter had assured us—at the Riverview Hotel. Sleep evaded him, and so he'd spent the hours online, digging deeper into Utter and his hall.

"EVEN WOKE MY TEAM," Quan typed, using his phone as his own personal captioning device. "NOT HAPPY. TOLD THEM TO CANCEL OUR NYC GIG."

"What did you find?" JJ asked.

"C-c-contradictions," Quan stammered before tap-tap-tapping on his phone. "WENT THROUGH HIS CAREER PAST TWO DECADES. END OF THE NINETIES, NO MORE HITS. HAD A COUPLE TV MOVIES ADAPTED FROM OLD BOOKS, BUT NEW STUFF NOT SELLING."

"I think I saw one of those movies," JJ said. "B-list actors and a lousy script."

"IN 2015, THINGS PICK UP. SHIFTED FOCUS TO PERIOD PIECES. PUT OUT A SHORT STORY COLLECTION, BUT NEW NOVELS WERE MAIN MONEY."

"You're saying he rebranded himself?" I asked. Why not? If his style was getting stale, best course of action, in my opinion.

"RAN EARLY BOOKS THROUGH AI ALONG WITH NEW."

"Someone did that with Shakespeare's plays." JJ nodded furiously. "To see which were legit."

I was aware folks used AI to cheat on their schoolwork and create photorealistic images of politicians in their underwear, but I hadn't so much as dabbled. It was the "artificial" bit that turned me off.

"Well?" I was ready for the punch line.

"STRONG POSSIBILITY NOT THE SAME AUTHOR."

"If Mr. Utter isn't the author of Mr. Utter's books, who is?"

"Gho...gho...ghostwriter."

There it was. The same thought he'd been trying to spit out before Carter and Dr. West ushered him down the hill.

Ghooo...Ghooo...

He must have touched upon the truth when the Dark Lady grabbed him. Did he remember? My guess was no.

"Hey, guys? Where'd Mr. Carter go?" JJ rose, looking up and down the street.

Shit.

The van was still there, but there was no sign of our driver.

"He was pretty shook up," JJ said.

"Maybe he needed something a little stronger than coffee," I replied.

"At this hour?"

For guys like Carter, any hour was happy hour.

Quan typed frantically. "SPLIT UP. NOT MANY BARS HERE. I'LL CHECK HOTEL. BARTENDER HIS FRIEND."

"I'll head down Main Street," JJ offered.

"And I guess I'll head up," I said. "Meet back here in ten?"

We were agreed. Quan and JJ walked west toward the river's edge while I headed in the opposite direction. Quan was right—Cold Spring catered more to antiquers than drinkers. I passed half a dozen still-closed shops, their windows filled with old movie posters and peopled by mannequins wearing furs. The only bar on my route had been closed by the health department, and by the time I reached the end of the block, I'd ventured into more residential territory.

I doubled back on the opposite side of the street. Just more antique shops and a cooking supply store. Ebb's Mercantile, where I'd picked up my Cold Spring hoodie, which was in desperate need of a wash, was coming up on the left. I was about to walk on by when the thin woman who'd rung me up, now sporting an autumnal vest, popped out of the store and waved me down.

"Miss?"

Perhaps she had intel on our AWOL driver.

"Yes?"

"I thought I recognized you." She held up a finger and quickly slipped back into the store. When she returned, she was holding a framed photo. "You got me thinking about that photo I mentioned."

It felt like years had passed since I'd last spoken to the woman, but I did recall her telling me something about the photo of Utter.

She proudly held it out.

"It was hanging in my sewing room. I still have to replace the glass, but there you go."

I took the piece in both hands and stared down at the black and white image, encased behind a pane of cracked glass.

James Utter—a much younger and much healthier version —sat laughing at a wide table in the middle of Ebb's Mercantile. A leaning stack of books sat next to him. He held a felt marker in his hand, the photo catching him waving it about like a conductor.

The stack of books? *Sorrow's Leap*, of course. And who was that standing behind him, her arms filled with more volumes of the same?

I almost dropped the photo.

Behind Utter and to his left was a young woman in thin-rimmed glasses and a thick sweater who bore a remarkable resemblance to...

"The Dark Lady," I said aloud.

"Come again?"

"When was this taken?"

"Around 2012. Why?"

I placed my finger on the image of the young woman with the stack of books. The crack ran straight through her torso. "Who's this?"

The woman craned her neck to look at the photo in my hands, examining it carefully. "Her? That's his assistant. She used to keep my local authors section stocked with his books. Sweet thing. Can't remember her name. Haven't seen her since Mr. Utter went into seclusion. Left for greener pastures, I suppose."

"May I borrow it?" I asked.

"No."

"All right..." I said, thinking quickly. "Can I buy it?"

"No."

I reached for my phone. No need for the original if I could take a photo. But then I remembered I'd ditched my company phone back at the Hooky Spooky.

The woman in the pumpkin vest and I were at an impasse.

It was time for a little fancy footwork.

"I understand," I said, passing back the photo. "Thanks for showing it to me. It's a cool piece. I just spent the night up there, did you know that?"

"Up...?"

"At Utter Hall. Mr. Carter took us. I'm sure you know Mr. Carter. He was with us when we stopped in yesterday. Thought he might have mentioned it."

The woman gave me a look not unlike those I'd received trying to pawn off the Weird Sisters' discount dreamcatchers.

"Glenn took you up there?"

"Glenn? He sure did. Good ol' Glenn Carter." I flashed her a smile and made to leave. "That was some night, believe me. Thanks anyway!"

"What was it like?"

Bingo. I'd hooked her.

"It was...God, how do I explain this? It was...haunting."

The woman nodded vigorously. Everyone loves a good ghost story.

"Did you see anything?"

I nodded right back at her. "The more apt question is did anything see *me?*"

This sent a shudder through her, and she stepped closer.

"So Mr. Utter's still up there. Is he writing?"

"Is he writing?" I paused just long enough to get her salivating. "He's hard at work on an autobiography. It's going to feature his time here in Cold Spring."

"Oh, my."

"That's why I was so taken with your photo. I'm sure he'd

love to include it in his book. Giving you and Ebb's credit, of course."

The woman in the vest stared down at her prize.

"That would really be..."

Come on! Spill it, spill it.

"...something," she finished. After a split-second mental wrestling match, she held out the photo. "I'd like that. Can you get it back to me later this week?"

I smiled so broadly my face quivered.

"I'll even replace the glass for you."

This last bit clinched the deal. She tucked her business card in the back of the frame and handed it over.

As I started back down the street, evidence in tow, she shouted after me, "Wait! What's your name?"

"Zivy!" I called back. "Zivy Wilde. I'll have it back before you know it."

I quickened my steps, examining the image of Utter's assistant as I dodged the piles of wet leaves and dog poop littering the sidewalk.

Who are you?

Or better still...

What's your story?

The way the woman glared at Utter spoke volumes. She was harried, a stark contrast to her boss's ebullient nature. She looked efficient and prepared to keep passing him books as long as he had a mind to sign them. But there was something else about her that eluded me.

I cast my mind toward the woman in the thick sweater, hoping I could pick up some hint of what was on her mind.

A single word hit me like a blast.

Hate.

I stopped dead, one foot in a puddle, my shoe soaking up last night's rain.

Though she hid it well, the young woman standing behind Utter was filled with hate, practically oozing with it.

"Ellen!"

I spotted JJ halfway down the street waving his arm with so much gusto he could have been shooing off death itself.

"We found him! We found Mr. Carter!"

37

The stench of sour beer hit my nose the moment I entered Pickle's Pub. An old jukebox flickered in the corner; its glass yellowed from decades of cigarette smoke. In fact, the whole place had a bottom-of-an-ashtray feel about it— gray and gritty with a hint of disease.

Carter sat alone at a table in the black heart of the joint, a glass of whiskey in his trembling hands.

The unshaved man tending bar glanced up at the new arrivals, and spoke those words uttered by bartenders immemorial.

"What'll you have?"

"I'm good," I said.

The man shrugged and returned to the business of opening up. No skin off his nose.

We approached Carter as a united front, the guys one step behind me, subtly positioning me as their spokesperson. I set the picture frame on the sticky tabletop next to Carter's yet to be downed drink.

"Who is this?" I tapped on the image of Utter's assistant, feeling the crack in the glass.

"So, you found her," he sighed, taking his first sip of booze. He was as nervous as those Dateline murder suspects when confronted about a dead body secreted away in a storage unit.

I chose not to repeat my question.

Carter took another gulp, emptying the glass, before taking the framed photo in both hands and holding it up to the light. Red light danced across his face, reflected from the Miller High Life lamp overhead.

"Where'd you find this?" Carter whispered.

Again, I opted for silence.

After a long moment, he looked up from the photo.

"What do you want to know?"

"Her name, for starters," I replied.

Carrie Underwood's "Two Black Cadillacs" exploded from the sound system.

"Sorry," the bartender called out as he scurried to cut the volume down to a fraction of its initial earsplitting level.

"Well?" I was done waiting.

"Gemma." Carter spoke so low, I thought I'd have to ask him to repeat it. "Her name was Gemma."

"Just Gemma?" I prodded. "Like Prince? Cher? Our friend is lying unconscious in a hospital bed, Glenn. Spill it."

I'd thought of him as just Carter for a while, but my informal use of his name snapped him to attention.

"Reid. Gemma Reid," he said. Saying her name aloud took a toll on him, and his hand reached for his empty whiskey glass.

He raised a finger to order another, and I grabbed it hard and twisted.

"Jesus H. Christ!" he protested.

"No more drinks for you until I'm satisfied." I sat in the chair across from him, my boys flanking me. Like I said, a united front.

"Who was she and what the fuck happened to her?"

Carter licked his lips and stared down into his empty glass. "She was Utter's assistant. He brought her on a few years before launching the renovation. Fresh out of grad school, I think she was. I didn't hire her, you see. That was all Utter's doing."

Quan held out his phone. "EIGHT YEARS AGO, RIGHT? SAME TIME HIS PUBLISHER REJECTED HIS LATEST NOVEL?"

This was news to me, but then again, while we'd been facing off with the thing up the hill, Quan had been holed up in a hotel room doing research.

"Yes," Carter moaned. "Please, this will go a lot easier if you let me have another drink."

It was JJ's turn to play bad cop. "You heard Ellen. No info, no drink."

"Fine." Carter sucked on his lip and stared us down. Our faces must have been enough to convince him he wasn't getting out of here without an absolute confession. "Gemma was talented; Utter liked that. She was young; he liked that even more. After six months of helping him reorganize his back catalogue and marking up his newest manuscripts, she finally got up the courage to show him her own work. She'd zipped through the Creative Writing Program at Cornell and landed in New York City. Just in time to catch the once-famous James Utter at one of his rare appearances, a reading at the Tempest Bookshop.

"After the event, they had friendly conversation over dinner. The next thing I knew, she was on the payroll and moving her shit into Utter Hall. She'd gotten the boss out of his slump, and soon the place was alive with talk of a new book. Soon, fresh chapters started popping up on the dining room table."

"His chapters?" Quan asked.

"No."

"B-but with his name on them?"

"Yes."

So, Utter hadn't written *Sorrow's Leap*. So what? I bet the number of people who'd slapped their names on other people's work would astonish the reading public. It's not like Utter had a deficit of bestselling titles. If he needed to lean on one cribbed book, was it really the end of the world? Was it enough for him to—

"He killed her, didn't he?" JJ, jumping the gun. "He stole her work and got rid of her."

"What? God, no," Carter scoffed. "Do you think I'd work for a man who'd do something like that?" Tears formed, forcing him to remove his glasses to wipe them away.

"I don't know, would you?" I asked, just to keep him talking.

"Gemma knew the score, even as she shifted from beta reader to collaborator to ghostwriter." That last word hung in the air like the Dark Lady herself. "He had connections, and she had none. He paid well, and she was capable of writing James Utter novels in her sleep. It was a win-win situation... until it wasn't."

By now, the man was so unnerved by his tale that he gaped like a Hungry Hungry Hippo. I nodded for Quan to keep him here while I rose and approached the bar. The bartender had given up stocking the shelves and was instead watching football replays on his phone. He grudgingly glanced up as I approached.

"Change your mind?"

"What's he drinking?" I asked.

"Glenn? House whiskey. The fool drinks it straight."

"Pour him another."

"We should call the cops," JJ whispered in my ear, making me jump.

"Damn, JJ! Creep much?"

"How does any of this help Zivy?"

"Just give me one more minute with him."

"Ellen—"

I picked up the proffered drink with a quick nod to my bartender friend and fixed my eyes on JJ's.

"Do you trust me?"

He opened his mouth, realizing I'd stolen his line, and fell silent. I walked Carter's drink back to the table.

"What happened in the end?" I asked, setting the rot gut in front of him.

He held the glass gingerly, understanding the bargain: take a drink, spill the beans. Every single one.

He drank...

"As I mentioned, she was young."

...and he spilled.

"I told myself it was harmless flirtation on his part. One creative mind meeting another. But when she came to me at the carriage house that night..."

Another drink.

"...it was obvious he'd pushed too far. Idiot that I am, I hadn't seen the signs. Or I didn't want to see them. I'm good at keeping my head down."

We'd come to the meat of it, but Carter struggled to continue. Maybe he didn't have it in him. Maybe I'd have to help.

I reached a hand across the table and took his in mine. He flinched—perhaps just muscle memory recalling how I'd twisted his finger—but he didn't pull away. Warmth passed between us, drawing us closer. I whispered with an inner voice both cool and insistent, urging him to speak aloud what I'd already seen hiding in the back of his mind.

"She was troubled, but who isn't at that age? She was also..."

Yes?

"How do I put this?"

Just say it.

Carter pulled back his hand and wiped his nose.

"She was like you." And then, "She was like all of you."

"She had gifts besides writing?" I asked.

"Gifts?" Carter let loose a pained laugh. "I guess that's one way to put it."

JJ, restless and eager to put a period on the end of this conversation, stood abruptly, his chair toppling over.

"What happened to her?"

Carter slumped back in his chair, the horror of it finally coming home to roost.

"She jumped! From the cliffs surrounding Utter Hall. God help me, but she jumped!"

38

One minute Carter was sitting in front of me, the next he was making a dash for the restroom.

"Gemma Reid." I rolled the name around on my tongue, feeling the shape of it. It didn't have the weight of "Dark Lady." It sounded almost perky, like it belonged to someone who might invite you to join their sorority.

"Hmm." Quan had his nose in his phone.

"What'd you find?" I asked.

"NOT MUCH RE: HER AFTER CORNELL. AN AWARD OR TWO," he typed. Pausing, he gave a phlegmy chuckle. "ANY GUESS WHAT THE NAME GEMMA REID MEANS?"

I had no idea and didn't care. "Girl who reads?"

He held out the screen. His favorite AI app had cheerily spat out: SURE! I CAN HELP YOU WITH THAT. THERE ARE MANY WAYS TO INTERPRET GEMMA REID. GEMMA: JEWEL, DIAMOND, PRECIOUS STONE OR

SPROUT; REID: RED, RED-HAIRED, OR CLEARING
IN THE WOODS...

Clearly not "sprout in the woods." Despite my loathing for
the tech, it had stumbled upon a valuable insight.

Gemma Reid.

Red Diamond.

The image of the sorority sister vanished from my mind.
The gal was sly, her wordplay sneaky. What other tricks did she
have up her sleeve?

The sound of Carter puking echoed from the men's room,
triggering JJ's sympathetic gag reflex. I headed to the back and
threw open the door, the foul scent hitting me full-on.

"How was Utter able to communicate?"

Carter, doubled over inside a toilet stall with no door,
offered up a wet burp and a frantic gesture for me to leave the
room.

Sorry, no can do.

"The TVs. The Zoom meetings. How does a man on his
deathbed run a conference call?"

"Wasn't in bed. Was..."

"Yes?"

"...in the other place. The place she made. Dragged him
there. Left his...his body behind. Like your friend. Like Ziv—"
Errp. "Like Zivy."

"Come on, how does someone in the other place take
delivery from Best Buy?"

The retching man said something, but his words were lost
in the toilet bowl.

What? Fin?

"What's 'fin' mean?"

"Thin!" Carter managed to gurgle. "Some parts of...Utter Hall...thinner than others."

"Meaning?"

"Jesus, can't you let me barf in peace?"

"Meaning?"

He flushed down his sick. "You can pass things back and forth. Places where both meet..." He puked again. This time I could almost taste the whiskey.

He hadn't given me much to work with, what with his truncated thoughts and distracting regurgitation, but I grasped the sense of it. Utter Hall was wearing thin in places, spots where Sorrow's Leap had eaten through.

"Not just objects, but signals too. Phone, Wi-Fi. Bounced through the ether."

"But not people," I deduced. "Not Utter."

"Not until you pulled him out. Guess that way out is reserved for folks like you."

"Where are these thin spots?"

"His study...now hospital room. Also up...up..."

"In the turret." I clapped him on the back, setting off a horking spasm. I abandoned the nasty place, cured forever of my affinity for bathrooms.

I'd gotten all I needed from Mr. Glenn Carter.

JJ looked up from the pint of seltzer he'd procured. "Well? He spill anything?"

"Other than his breakfast, lunch, and dinner?"

Quan held out his phone. A young woman smiled back.

"Gemma," he confirmed.

She looked lighter than she did in the framed photo. Almost buoyant. No doubt a school ID photo, but even in that institutional format, something secret shined through. I enlarged the image, and as I did so, I felt an electric tingle. Was it static from Quan's phone? Perhaps, but my gut told me that was not the case.

What did Gemma Reid have in her quiver besides the ability to create an entire phantom world?

Guess I'll have to ask you when I see you.

"Boys," I said, "let's go get Zivy."

JJ and I retrieved our luggage from the van in case Carter decided to take up permanent residence at Pickle's Pub and followed Quan down Main Street toward the Riverview Hotel.

We strategized as we walked. I explained what Carter had told me about Utter Hall's thin spaces and described what it had been like to slip through.

"It's like stepping into another version of the place," I explained. "Or a memory of it, complete with imperfections and additions."

"We're never going to be able to sneak in," JJ huffed under the weight of his backpack. "Not with those hired guns patrolling the place."

"We don't have to."

Quan gave me a confused look. "Exc-cuse me?"

"We don't have to get into Utter Hall. We have to get into

Sorrow's Leap." I threw an arm around JJ's shoulders. "That is, if you'll oblige."

JJ kept walking, but he had caught my drift.

"I d-don't understand," Quan said.

"You will."

We followed Main Street as it dipped under the commuter rail line at the edge of the town proper and emerged at a promenade on the banks of the Hudson. Looking out over the great river and the high, dark cliffs on the Jersey side, sat the Riverview Hotel. Our base of operations.

Having charmed the front desk clerk into arranging a late checkout, Quan led us to the second floor and the room Carter had acquired for him. It sat at the southwest corner, with a brilliant view of the river. After bringing Quan up to speed, I promptly drew the shades and got down to business.

"Let's set this table in the middle of the room."

I'd already begun emptying it of Quan's notepads and such, but he swept in and cleared it himself. JJ and I shifted the bed against the wall, giving us more room in the center of the space while Quan placed two chairs and a small settee around the table. Between the antique décor and the centered table, the room looked ready for a séance. Which, I suppose, wasn't that far off.

"Okay, here's the plan," I said, choosing the comfy settee. "I pay a visit to your younger self and get him to point me in the direction of Sorrow's Leap. I'll slip in and slip back out with Zivy. Easy peasy, lemon squeezy."

Quan didn't look convinced. "J-just like that?"

"Why not? I pulled Utter out. Why not Zivy?"

"Don't you think—"

"The plan is solid. And JJ's my failsafe."

"I am?"

"Sure. You yanked me back, safe and sound, didn't you?"

The guys both grumbled. Why were they fighting me on this?

"Yeah," JJ said, "but I sent you away and brought you right back. This is different. And bringing two people to the highway? I don't know if I can do it. Heck, I didn't even know I could do one until I tried."

I was confused. "What do you mean two?"

JJ looked from me to Quan and back again. "Quan's going too, right?"

"Obviously." Apparently, Quan and JJ were on the same page.

"Like hell you are."

"Don't be silly, Ellen." JJ was trying to manage me; I *hated* being managed.

"I've got this," I insisted. "Do you really want this thing to turn into a big dumb dog?" This was met with blank stares. "The bigger the dog, the dumber it is. Hence, the more people going, the more chance someone's going to fuck up."

"Excuse me?" Quan folded his arms. The dude actually folded his arms! "I'm g-going."

I threw up my hands in defeat. "Fine! Whatever. Let's get to it, shall we?"

JJ trained those damn puppy dog eyes on me.

"I don't know if I can—"

"You can."

"I mean, who knows what could happen? What if something goes wrong?"

No need to sugarcoat it—what he needed was the blunt truth.

"Then Zivy is gone. For good."

JJ nodded. He didn't have to ask us to trust him. We did. I took one of his hands, Quan took the other.

"If my phone c-comes through with me, I'm t-taking all the pics I can. P-pulitzer prize, baby."

"What are you going to tell him...me to focus on?" JJ asked.

Good question.

"Hate." Quan suggested. "Anger."

"How about red diamonds?" JJ asked.

"No," I said. "I'll tell him to send us to our friend. To Zivy."

JJ smiled. As with most questions, the simplest answer is often the best.

"Zivy," JJ whispered and closed his eyes. "Dear God, please bless these, our efforts. Let us not succumb to fear but walk in your grace. And"—he glanced up from his prayer—"if it isn't too much trouble, keep these jokers from doing anything stupid."

"Amen," Quan said.

The room, already dimmed by the drawn shades, darkened even further, the antique-scented air replaced by the sharp cold of a winter's breeze. The transition from Cold Spring to the side of the New Jersey interstate was instantaneous, like going from sleeping to waking.

"Damn," Quan said, his voice vapor on the wind. He showed me his empty hands. His phone hadn't made the trip.

All was as it had been the last time I'd journeyed there. The overturned car, the boy in the backseat, his stuffed dog Jersey half-buried in a snowdrift.

I picked up the pup, approached the car—its wheels forever spinning in the air—and squatted down to peer inside. The mini version of JJ stared back at me with startled eyes.

"Hey, Julian." I handed him his dog. "Do you think you can help us?"

39

The boy with JJ's face clutched the stuffed dog with an affection reserved for loved ones and nuzzled the toy's ear.

"You were here before...I think."

"I was. I'm Ellen. You remember me?"

"Kinda."

It dawned on me that I should have delved deeper into the mechanics of this little trick. If I mentioned something to JJ, would Julian know it as well? Only one way to find out.

"You showed me the way out of here. I was wondering if we could try something different this time—"

"Who's that?" The boy was staring at Quan, who was taking in the scene for the first time. With Julian hanging upside down as he was, I couldn't tell if he was curious or frightened by Quan's presence. Best to put him at ease.

"That's Quan. He's a friend."

"Quan?"

"Quan's my last name. It's William, actually." Quan offered the boy a comforting smile. "But you can call me Bill."

"Hi, Bill."

"You never told me I could call you Bill," I said.

"You never asked."

The ice-covered asphalt rumbled under my feet, causing me to lose my balance. Squatting as I was, my knees gave out and I soon found myself sitting in a pool of slush.

"What's happening?" the boy cried.

"I...I don't know," I said.

Quan helped me up, and I felt my backside. Yup, soaked through and through. The metal Exit 46 sign swayed back and forth, its undulations caused no doubt by the same quake that knocked me on my ass.

The ice hissed as an aftershock rolled in, doing its best to send us sprawling yet succeeding only in setting the car to rocking.

"Ellen!" the boy wailed.

"I take it the tremors are new," Quan said. He paused, humming a bit to test his vocal cords. "Hey, my voice is back." His hair, however, remained as white as the landscape.

"I think sending two of us is overwhelming JJ." Another massive rumble drove home my point.

It was time to make our ask.

"Julian?"

"Yeah?" The boy was trembling.

"The last time I was here, you performed a cool magic trick. I was really impressed."

"You were?"

"I was. Do you think you could show my friend Quan—"

"Bill?"

"Yeah, Bill. Do you think you could show him how it works?"

Tears flowed down his forehead. "Are you leaving?"

The kid was breaking my heart.

I knelt before him and looked him square in the eye. He was JJ, all right, or would be down the road. Kind, helpful, loyal JJ who didn't deserve the fate that awaited him if I didn't hurry this up.

"We have to. Because if we stay—"

"I know."

The exit sign crumpled like an aluminum can, as if a great hand had caught it in its grip. This was not a world in which to loiter. Heaven knew what that invisible hand might do to flesh and bone.

"We need to go somewhere else this time. Is that okay? We need to find Zivy. Do you understand? Zivy?"

A quizzical look passed over his face. Zivy? Who was Zivy? For a moment I thought we were sunk. But then, as I knelt there with wet snow melting beneath my knees, his mouth opened in an *O* of recognition.

"Zivy." The voice wasn't just his but JJ's as well, the two intermingled in atonal harmony. "She's pretty."

"Yes, she is."

"But her hair's always messy."

"That's right."

"You need to go to Sorrow's Leap."

A thunderclap rocked the night, perhaps in an attempt to shake itself loose of the interlopers.

"Can you do it?" I asked.

Quan tapped me on the shoulder. "This place is falling apart. We need to get him out of there, pronto."

"Quan—"

"Let's pull him out, then we can talk."

"Give me a second—"

"Jesus, Ellen, what are you waiting for?"

I didn't have time to explain.

"Julian? Can you do it?"

The upside-down boy closed his eyes and frowned. A shudder ran through me, as if his efforts had brought the very air to life. The harder the kid concentrated, the more the fabric of this peculiar reality wavered.

Quan tried to muscle past me. I grabbed his arm, and he whirled on me so violently I thought he might shove me into the icy puddle.

"Quan, listen to me—"

"I smell gas. Don't you? The car could go up any second—"

"Be quiet. Both of you."

The boy spoke with a calm assurance that stopped Quan in his tracks.

He scrunched his eyes tight, releasing another wave of vibrations. Quan was ready to pounce, but he kept his distance. If the kid couldn't pull it off before the flames came to life, there would be no stopping Quan from pulling him free and spoiling the trick.

"I see something..."

I nodded, urging him on. "Yes?"

"I see...red."

The headlights sparked to life—not halogen white like last time but emergency red—turning the side of the overturned semi into a bloodbath. Dark shapes began to form within the scarlet swirl. Silhouetted trees stretched across the improvised screen in a skeletal dance. Hills rose and fell, massive blocks of black against the sanguine sky. But the image failed to coalesce, the landscape rushing past like an express train to Hell.

"I feel it, but I can't *see* it."

The car let loose a metallic *pop*.

Oh, shit...

"Fire. Jesus, Ellen, the car's on fire!"

Time's up.

I had to give the boy a boost.

I took his hand in mine and did my own eye-scrunching, drowning out Quan's protestations and the sound of the car's sizzling innards. I flooded my mind with overlapping images: Zivy with her orange mop of hair, the Dark Lady draped in black, framing my memories in a perimeter of pulsing red diamonds.

The boy's hand squeezed mine, grasping at the pictures I was sending him.

"Ellen!"

"For the love of God, Quan, shut the fuck up!"

The kid loosened his grip, releasing a great sigh. I glanced over at the projection. An image shimmered in the rising smoke. At first, I mistook the structure emerging from the ether as Utter Hall. But as it came into focus, I realized I was looking at Sorrow's Leap, the great mansion undulating in the smoke like something alive.

"Good job! Good job, JJ!" I cried.

"You have to go." The boy was insistent.

"I know."

"Ellen?" He held out his ragged dog. "Will you take Jersey with you?"

If there had been a spare second to give the kid a kiss, I would have done so. Instead, I gently took the stuffed animal from him.

"Of course I will."

I rose, placing my hand on the car's side for leverage. The vehicle was hot to the touch.

Quan watched on in horror as the flames spread. Dark billows of burning rubber filled the air, making it all the more difficult to grab his attention.

"We have to go!"

"No."

"Now!"

I grabbed Quan's shirtfront, latching onto chest hair as well. He yelped, and the momentary jolt of pain distracted him just enough for me to yank him forward and into the reddened smoke.

Quan cried out for me to stop, but I had momentum on my side. I dragged him into the wavering image, and, gripping Jersey like a football, I made my way downfield.

The boy might have screamed as we passed from his world into the next. He did in my nightmares. But before I had the chance to wallow in guilt, darkness overwhelmed me.

I'd expected to simply pass from one world to the next as I had the first time I'd visited JJ's secret domain. This time, the journey was not so instantaneous.

The air congealed to gelatin around me, forcing me to hold my breath. It was slimy as shit and stung the skin, causing me to lose my grip on Quan. I dared not open my eyes, and yet, a brilliant, red light seeped through my eyelids, my only indication that I was heading in the right direction. The air thickened further still, and I swam through the bloody muck, the taste of copper in my mouth.

My fingertips touched a cool membrane. I tried to push through but was denied. I pushed harder, but with nowhere for my feet to find purchase, I failed again and again.

With my lungs screaming and panic running wild, I did the only thing I could think of: I opened my mouth, bared my teeth, and bit.

My taste buds howled in revolt and revulsion. The flavor of the foulness that rushed into my mouth must have been the same as that of the putrid goo that lined coffins once their bodies had begun to break down.

And yet, I bit, I tore, I gnashed until I caught a thin ribbon of flesh in my teeth. With my brain crying out for oxygen, I whipped my head back and forth, tearing open a ragged orifice through which to escape.

The membrane gave and gravity took over. I dropped to the rocky ground like a newly birthed foal.

I lay there, heaving like a college kid after their first night out on the town, and waited for my head to stop spinning. When I'd regained a semblance of stability, I opened my eyes and took in the view.

There on the horizon, rising twice as high as Utter Hall, was Sorrow's Leap.

40

I t was night in this world. I got the sense it was *always* night in Sorrow's Leap. If I were creating my own supernatural realm, I'd likely banish sunlight as well.

A groan rose from a patch of dead grass to my left, and Quan stood, frantically swiping at his clothes. Trying to wipe away the filth we'd traveled through. He soon realized the paranormal gunk hadn't followed us through. Apparently the same was true for JJ's childhood toy. I'd lost the stuffed animal somewhere between my entrance into the barrier realm and my expulsion.

"I'm not sure if I'm built for this," Quan said.

"I don't think anyone is."

"Whatever happened to simple hauntings?"

I wanted to tell him that such things didn't exist, especially if you were investigating correctly, but we'd have plenty of time to debate methods should we get out of here in one piece.

We surveyed the massive stone structure sitting on the hill.

Although it held echoes of James Utter's mansion, it was more a half-remembered glimpse of the place. It kept shifting in appearance as memories often do. One moment the place was two stories tall, the next, it was three. Spires appeared and disappeared on a whim, and the number of windows varied from minute to minute.

The road leading up to the place had been designed by a lunatic. It snaked around trees and rocks, nonsensically doubling the distance to the great house.

I'd have preferred landing closer to the house, but at least we hadn't dropped into a sinkhole. Besides, the hike up to the house would allow Quan and me to strategize.

"Hold up."

Quan stopped me with an outstretched arm. "Check it out."

I followed Quan's gaze to the view behind us. Or rather the lack thereof. The way we'd come held nothing but darkness. This world was home to one thing and one thing only: the house on the hill.

It was as much of a narcissist as dear old Mom.

Setting my sights on the most direct route, I took a step forward.

"What do you think you're doing?"

"Huh?"

"We're not going through the field."

"That drive is a meandering nightmare."

"We are *not* going through the field, Ellen."

What the hell is his damage?

"Why not?"

"I gave myself a crash course on Utter's post-*Sorrow's Leap* titles."

"You mean Gemma Reid's titles."

"Bingo. One was a short story collection, each tale more fucked up than the last. The title story, *Children of Woe*, describes a scene just like this. Open field, looping drive."

"So?"

"There were things hiding in the brush. Bad things. If I had my equipment with me, maybe I could suss them out—"

"You want a piece of professional advice?" I was done with the niceties. "The best equipment a paranormal investigator has is their gut. And right now, my gut is telling me to *mush*."

"You want to take the shortcut? Count me out."

We were at an impasse.

"You win. We'll take the damn yellow brick road."

I took off down the drive at fast clip, gravel crunching underfoot. Quan raced to catch up.

We walked on in silence. Flanking the road on either side, the ground gave way to the occasional hole dug into its surface. Sorrow's Leap was apparently populated by oversized gophers. As we proceeded, the holes grew larger and larger.

Those must be some gophers.

Maybe we were right to keep to the road.

"You never told me how you passed Utter's test."

The hell?

"What do you care?"

"I just think it's funny. You're usually such a straight shooter. Hell, you're a regular sniper. What are you hiding?"

I stopped dead. "You wanna know? Fine. I have no fucking clue."

"I was just curious—"

"Well, so am I. Maybe that makes me a fraud, who knows." He'd tripped a wire, and I couldn't contain myself. "You happy? Maybe it would have been better if I'd minded my own fucking business. Maybe if I…Quan, are you listening to me?"

He was not. His attention was focused on a spot far out in the field.

"What the—"

A hundred feet out, two figures perched on a rock. They were as indistinct as the mansion—fading, appearing, fading again. No doubt we'd stumbled upon another of Gemma's fictions: *The Men of the Moors*, perhaps.

I turned to ask Quan if this was indeed the case and found him transfixed, his jaw hanging open.

"Billy!" one of the figures called out. A young man's voice.

"Bill!" the other cried.

Tears welled up in Quan's eyes. He took a lurching step toward the newcomers.

"Thomas? Mark?"

"Quan, what are you—"

He was off in a flash, tearing across the field, leaving the safety of the drive behind.

"Quan!"

I was shocked; it wasn't like Quan to abandon reason. Yet there he was, sprinting through the grass, gopher holes be damned.

He'd just about reached the twin figures when he tripped,

hitting the ground with a yelp. The moment he dropped, the men flickered out as if someone had turned the channel.

Damn it, Quan...

"You okay?"

"I don't think so."

"I'm coming to get you."

"Don't you dare."

"Fuck you."

I followed the path of trampled grass until I stood over him. I gulped at the sight. Quan sat dead still, one foot sunk deep in a freshly dug hole. He looked like a soldier who'd stumbled upon a landmine.

"Are you hurt?"

Quan was inconsolable. "Where'd they go?"

"I don't know." I held out a hand. "Let's get you up—"

The force of his scream shattered the night.

"Come back! Come back!"

Grief flooded from him. The grass in which he'd fallen withered at the sound of his cries and the clouds let loose a rumbled warning.

I waited for his sobs to subside, and when they didn't, I crouched and put my arms about him. His chest heaved up and down with the violence of his sorrow.

"I know it wasn't them," he whimpered. "But I couldn't help myself. I'm sorry. I'm so sorry."

"You've got no reason to be sorry—"

"Remember that story I told you about? *Children of Woe*?"

"Yeah?"

"They burrow underground and wait."

"Wait for what?"

"For some dumb bunny like me to step into their nest."

I stared at his trapped foot.

"You could be wrong."

"I wish I was." He flashed me a frightened smile. "Ellen, one of them is touching me."

Time froze; Quan unable to move, me unwilling to leave him.

"Jesus—"

"Hush, will you? I need you to listen very carefully." He shifted his weight, trying to make his uncomfortable position more tolerable. "They're carnivorous. At least they are in the story."

"What the hell are they?"

"Remember those little footsteps we heard in the foyer? They belonged to toddlers. Toddlers with teeth."

A muffled giggle rose from the hole. Quan joined in, laughing at the absurdity of his fate.

"When you get to the house, keep clear of the walls. There may be things inside. In her story, *The Walls Have Eyes*—"

"Stop talking like I'm going alone."

"Pay attention. I need to give you a crash course." Sweat appeared on his brow. "Steer clear of the cellar, you hear me? There's something particularly foul down there. And should you come across a billiard room—"

"Stop it!"

Quan took my hand in his. "See what going with my gut got me?"

"I'm getting you out."

"Get back to the road. You can outrun them."

"I'll drag you if I have to—"

Quan cut me off with an anguished howl. Whatever dwelt below had grown impatient of its meal.

Quan's leg bent backward, snapping like a dry tree branch. His howls turned to shrieks, and he instinctively reached for me—a drowning man grasping at straws.

His leg twisted and popped as it accommodated itself to the hole. His hips folded inward, his pelvis now a grotesque accordion. The tight squeeze forced his innards upward, and his face reddened under the pressure.

He spat out one final thought.

"Bring her home!"

And then, he disappeared, his body dragged below, bones snapping like kindling, his screams snuffed out.

I won't describe the sounds coming from below. Suffice it to say that Quan did not die instantly.

I stood there, my guts churning; I was stunned into indecision. I'd sure stepped into it. Who knew how many of those things were out there, what deadly game of whack-a-mole I'd have to play moving forward.

As I frantically pondered my next step, the subterranean munching ceased. Now, streams of dirt tumbled into the open maw as something dug its way to the surface.

The creature that broke the surface also broke my nerve. A pale-domed head appeared, smeared red with my companion's blood. Its eyes were silver dollars shining in the night. It grinned at me through fanged teeth, as if remembering the punchline to a nasty joke.

The deformed infant pulled itself from the hole, naked and sexless, its body filthy with mud and gore. Upon spotting me, it snapped its jaws hungrily. Quan had been the appetizer; I was the intended main course.

You can outrun them.

I sure hoped he was right.

A wave of unsettling titters rose about me. The beastly baby had friends, and by the sound of it they were eager to join in on the fun.

Shit.

Mom had been a font of aphorisms, mangled and otherwise. She gleefully peppered everyday conversation with gems like, "You can lead a whore to culture, but you can't make her think." But one of her favorites seemed quite apt at this moment.

Shit or get off the pot.

With the swift attack of a ravenous rodent, the monstrous infant suddenly skittered forward, crawling with confounding speed.

I picked up a rock, prepared to bash the baby's brains in, when something brushed past me from behind. I didn't see it clearly, simply caught the barest of glimpses. It was all fur and growls and pounding feet. It grabbed the infant by the neck and shook, the little fucker's laughter turning to squeals of pain.

Crack-crack!

Neck bones shattered in the newcomer's jaws, and the wee

beastie went limp. My mysterious savior released its prey, the little corpse dropping to the ground with a sickening *plop*.

Before I could assess my new situation, the newcomer turned my way and lifted his ears, assessing the situation. When our eyes met, he opened his bloodied jaws and damned if he didn't smile, his tail wagging in overdrive.

"Jersey?" I asked, dumfounded.

The floppy Golden Retriever galumphed toward me, lapping my hands with urgent relief.

How the fuck...?

"Hold up! Wait for me!"

That voice...

JJ emerged from the darkness, picking his way carefully toward me.

"Good boy, Jersey!" he called.

Good boy in-fucking-deed.

41

A month ago, I'd been content with my solitary life. No one forced me to socialize, no one asked me to help them move, no one cluttered up my calendar with endless movie nights and Sunday brunches. But the moment I saw JJ step into view, my heart leaped with gratitude.

"You sonofabitch!" I sighed.

"Good to see you, too."

Jersey danced around his person with the enthusiasm only dogs possess. His remarkable transformation baffled me, but his boundless joy was infectious. JJ knelt before the animal, scratching his ears in wonder. "I can't believe this. This is unreal. How the heck did this happen?"

"Look around you. How is any of this possible?"

"You have no idea...no idea at all." JJ loved on the dog, happily accepting his sloppy kisses. "All my childhood, he was there. After the accident, during the damned TV circuit." He stared directly in the dog's eyes. "Mom and Dad weren't there for me, but you were, weren't you, boy."

Jersey favored him with a barrage of tail wags.

I couldn't imagine what JJ must feel like. My childhood toy was a stuffed bear named Zip my mother had picked up at a flea market. Zip was missing an eye and smelled like cat piss. Zip had no business coming to life.

"Quan told me what happened."

"He's okay?"

"No thanks to this place, but yeah, he's fine."

I'd expected to carry Quan's death with me forever, but now? What a sweet reprieve.

"He said he got picked off by a baby. Did I hear him right? Anyway, after he woke up at the hotel, I figured you could use a hand."

"You didn't have to—"

"Yeah, Ellen, I did."

There was no reason hiding my relief, and I threw my arms around him, giving him one of the few hugs I've ever instigated myself.

"It's good to see you, Chunky."

"Good to see you too, weirdo."

I drew back, instantly nervous. "If you're here, how do we get back?"

JJ's face instilled zero confidence. "I was hoping you might have an idea."

I didn't, but we'd have to cross that bridge when we came to it.

"Let's play it by ear."

JJ chuckled. "That's what Quan suggested."

"He did?"

"Yeah, he said, 'Just go with your gut.'"

That Quan was growing on me. Perhaps he was ready to see it my way after all.

I gave Jersey a scratch for good luck. His fur was not quite fully formed—he still felt like Julian's stuffed animal. But his teeth had been real enough to rip apart a Child of Woe, so I had no complaints.

"Let's get going," I said. "Mind the holes."

We opted to head back to the drive, the two of us walking side by side as Jersey ranged ahead, sniffing out trouble. We passed a few pockets of hidden laughter, but one snarl out of JJ's dog silenced them.

Thankfully, we made it to the blacktop in one piece. The drive was ancient and shattered, and from its cracks, odd weeds sprouted. They followed us as we passed, leaves curling as if desirous of our company. Quan had made no mention of any Weeds of Woe in the short story collection, so I ignored them.

The hill upon which Sorrow's Leap sat trumped that of Utter's mansion, its angle of ascent far steeper. Step too close to the edge and the asphalt gave way, resentful of travelers. My calf muscles complained the entire way. Once we finally reached the top, we got our first clear view of the house that Gemma Reid built.

The façade of the great stone building was cratered and cracked. No wall-hugging ivy here; the stone was worn and faded to the jaundiced hue of an old man's skin. Massive double doors were set in the middle of the structure, their carved pattern shifting and shifting again. One moment, they were ornate, Bavarian; the next, they looked like a kid had taken an axe to them.

Great windows lined the second floor, and these held particular interest. Stained glass, each and every one of them. Red was the dominant color. And the pattern? Diamond, of course.

The place was Utter Hall's bastard child.

"It's hard keeping it in focus," JJ said. He was right; details of the building kept shifting. Take your eyes off a window and it popped up someplace else. Sorrow's Leap suffered from a serious identity crisis.

The large double doors shuddered, then slowly swung open to greet us. Jersey whined his concern.

"It seems we're expected," JJ whispered.

"I guess that's it for the element of surprise."

"What now?"

"We stick to the plan. Find Zivy, get her out, get back home."

Even Jersey had his reservations; he gave me a look that said, "Are you f-ing kidding me?"

"I wish I had your confidence," JJ said.

"You don't need it. I've got plenty for both of us."

I thought I was being serious, but JJ cracked up at this. He stepped toward the door and bowed with mock gallantry.

"Then, you first."

"Fuck that."

Jersey surprised us by taking the lead. He stepped through

the doorway, a low and wary growl in his throat. Humbled, JJ and I followed.

The moment we passed the threshold, the great doors closed behind us with the finality of a coffin lid slamming shut.

"I give you a D for originality," I told the empty room, despite having jumped at the sound.

"Don't antagonize her," JJ hissed.

"Why not? I feel pretty goddamned antagonized myself, don't you?"

"Yeah, but—"

"But nothing."

The foyer, like the rest of the house, was a funhouse mirror image of that in Utter Hall. Maroon curtains hung from the lofty ceiling, cascading to the floor like bloody waterfalls. Twin suits of armor stood guard at the foot of the massive staircase, and I had no doubt that if I rapped on their metal chests, they would rap me back.

"I'm sorry," I said, flirting with danger, "but your place looks more Munster than mysterious. A tad overwritten, wouldn't you say? But then again, you were the one who wrote that abomination, *Sorrow's Leap*."

I hadn't seen storm clouds on the horizon, so I took the thunder that followed for a tantrum. It was easy getting under her cold, dead skin.

JJ hissed at me. "That's enough."

"Oh, I'm just getting started." I stepped to the middle of the room, cupped my hands to my mouth, and shouted, "If you speak of the devil, he doth appear. What's your excuse?"

"Ellen!"

"I think you're scared. I felt it when we bumped into each other in the tower. Is that it, Gemma? Are you scared? Scared I'll uncover all those dirty little secrets you thought you'd taken to the grave?"

Jersey let loose a howl that could wake the dead.

And, for good or for ill, that was exactly its effect.

The wall sconces flickered with rage.

Excellent.

We had the bitch's attention.

42

Somewhere overhead, a large piece of furniture crashed to the floor. A patch of ceiling plaster broke loose, missing my head by inches and striking the floor with a percussive crash.

"That all you got?"

JJ pulled me aside, whispering hotly in my ear. "Stop showboating, will you?"

"I've never showboated in my life."

"Then what do you think you're doing?"

God, working with others was such a chore. You had to explain everything.

"I'm taking the heat. I'm drawing her out so you and Jersey can go sniff out Zivy."

JJ looked like I'd slapped him across the face. "No. No! I'm not going anywhere."

"Divide and conquer. It's the only way."

"You're *not* facing her alone."

"Watch me." I turned my attention back to the owner of the house. "Gemma, you incredible hack, take off that ridiculous Dark Lady suit and show yourself!"

The timbers trembled and plaster filtered down like snow. I'd hit a nerve, disrespecting her writing skills and her alter ego. At least she wasn't ignoring me.

The effect of my insults was immediate. The empty knights collapsed with a clatter, dismembered pieces scattering across the floor. Perhaps I was being given a preview of my fate should I continue poking her.

"Get going!" I tried to nudge JJ along, but he remained immovable.

"Jersey? What's the matter, boy?"

What now?

The pup stumbled, took a step, stumbled again. With a plaintive whine, he fell over sideways, a puppet with its strings cut.

"Is he okay?"

"I don't think so," JJ said.

Jersey lay panting at the foot of one of the towering curtains. Had he been a real dog, I might have thought he'd succumbed to exhaustion.

But real dogs didn't give off smoke.

"Oh, God..." JJ rushed to Jersey's side and knelt beside him. "Please, God, no."

The floor trembled as if a train passed beneath. The house was fully awake. JJ had to get moving. The Dark Lady was on her way.

"Leave him with me," I said. "Go find Zivy."

JJ raised a hand. His fingertips glowed like lit candles.

"I'm sorry."

Wisps of smoke rose from his hair.

"I guess there's no escaping the flames."

I stepped forward; he held out a warning hand. The next minute, both he and his dog burst into flames.

I hadn't taken the heat; JJ had.

I shielded my eyes.

"It's okay!" JJ screamed.

It wasn't. It was fucking far from okay.

JJ and his dog were a runaway furnace.

"Save Zivy!"

Despite the smell of burning flesh and scorched hair, I had to look.

He'll disappear any minute. Just like Quan. He'll be okay. He'll be okay.

Young Julian sat in the center of the blaze, hugging Jersey —once more a ragged stuffed animal—and rocking back and forth.

The boy stared back at me; JJ's sorrow reflected on his small face. He was leaving me alone in this madhouse on the hill, and there was nothing he could do about it.

With one last eruption of blue-orange flame, he and his toy dog blinked out of sight.

He's back at the hotel. He's back with Quan. He's back at the hotel...

If wishing could only make it so.

My hands shook...*calm down*...my mouth went dry...

swallow, dammit ...and my vision blurred...*he's okay he's okay*
HE'S OKAY!

Embers rose from the spot where JJ had vanished, dancing upward until they touched the highest reaches of the drapery. The wine-colored fabric welcomed their arrival, offering ample fuel. With a flash and a *whuff*, the curtain burst into flames.

A shriek from the top of the stairs whirled me about. Staring down at me with a mix of horror and loathing was the Dark Lady herself, awesome and dreadful to behold.

43

Back at Utter Hall, the Dark Lady had appeared as a garden-variety ghost, all *Wuthering Heights* and shit. Here in her domain, she was something else entirely.

She stood on the landing as if affixed to it, her gown no longer mere fabric but a part of her very essence. Her hair crackled with static, and her eyes glowed like twin moons. She formed, dissolved, and formed again; one minute glamorous and gothic, the next, fetid and foul. Her skin was dull gray, and there wasn't enough of it to go around, allowing patches of skull to peek through. No beaded necklace for this woman. Her décolletage dripped with maggots instead.

Her eyes darted from me to the rising conflagration and back. Someone had set her world on fire, and she was *pissed*.

"Ell-llen!" she cried, her voice full of catarrh and contempt.

"Gemm-mma!" I called back, my voice dripping with mockery.

I paused.

With JJ hopefully on his way home, my role was no longer to taunt the haunt. I was now the lone member of the rescue team.

Time to zip my lip.

The dead woman descended. Those pesky little shades appeared, circling her, caught in her gravity. They were as unnerving as they were swift. What kind of twisted mind had conjured such unpleasant things?

The same mind that had conjured all of this.

I had no intention of making my final stand here and now, and so, hoping to impede the woman's progress, I grabbed hold of the blazing drapery and pulled with everything I had.

The thick material had thinned where the flames had eaten away at it, and the curtain tore loose with a great rending sound. It fell in slow motion, and as it did, I leaned in hard, for once thankful for the extra pounds I'd been lugging around. I forced it to land across the staircase, creating a flaming barrier.

The spirit howled. I didn't stick around to see how my barricade fared. I took off down the nearest hallway, heart pounding and tears falling in a torrent.

Please be okay, JJ. Please.

The hallway twisted and turned this way and that, giving the Minotaur's labyrinth a run for its money. Right, left, right, right, left!

I ran on, past artwork hung in a haphazard manner, each more insidious than the last. Portraits featuring stern and sour men gave way to paintings depicting all manner of depravity. Antique surgeries, cannibal feasts, torture devices the Marquis de Sade could only dream of.

The velvet wallpaper peeled away like sloughing skin, and beneath, huge rolling eyes marked my progress. Each pounding step brought me closer to madness, each sharp turn took me farther from my goal.

What the hell was I looking for anyway?

I passed an open door, the first I'd seen, and if I didn't dive through it, I might run on forever, trapped in this hypnotic hallway. And so, in I went, slamming the door behind me.

I doubled over, panting, trying to wrangle my wits. Bit by bit, I recovered my senses and took stock of my situation.

Great. You're in a closet, Ellen.

A closet with only one way out: the way I'd come in.

The light fixture overhead glowed brighter now that I'd arrived, orange and sputtering like a fuse about to break. Valet rods empty save for wire hangers encircled the cramped room, the hangers swinging slightly as if recently relieved of their clothing.

Is the room getting smaller?

No. It's just your imagination.

But the light is definitely getting brighter.

On that point, we agree.

The bulb in the fixture began to buzz like a bug zapper, its warm orange glow cooling to a blue green. I shied away, its glare threatening to fry my corneas.

Something struck the back wall.

I retreated, pressing my back against the door. Whatever was on the other side had hit the wall with such force, the wallpaper had buckled inward.

Wham! Wham-wham!

The reports came one after another. Each time they did, the light overhead buzzed even louder.

Wait...that's not the lightbulb buzzing.

The pounding stopped. Maybe this was just a boo scare not a bite scare.

The bone-dry wallpaper bulged and tore. Something was coming through.

Pretty sure you didn't tell me about this story, Quan!

The paper peeled back, the surprise unwrapping itself. The thing burrowed its way into the closet, mandibles clicking and antennae searching.

It was a fucking giant wasp.

A wasp with a human skull for a face.

Of course, it was.

44

The insect pulled itself through the hole it had created, and when its wings were clear, they commenced beating an angry rhythm I could feel in my chest.

"Who the fuck comes up with a giant wasp?"

Having freed its abdomen, the droning beast dropped to the floor. It scrambled about, looking for flesh in which to sink its stinger. It approached, hollow eyes searching out any movement. I stood stock-still, even when it crawled over my foot. I had once considered getting a cat. I nixed that idea once and for all.

It rose into the air once more, wings razor-sharp and flapping incomprehensibly fast until it hovered in front of me, smelling me out with its antennae.

Rancid venom dripped from its stinger. This was the end. I'd failed my friend. Once the wasp sank its dagger in me, Zivy would be on her own, trapped as Utter had been.

But if it kills me, won't I wake up with JJ and Quan?

Logic said that made sense. But I was beginning to suspect the ghostwriter was a lot cleverer than I gave her credit for.

And though she begged for death, the accursed insect's venom rendered that impossible. First came paralysis, then came the eggs, and finally...eternity itself.

If that were the case, I was well and truly fucked.

It was enough to make you laugh.

Almost.

I reached for the doorknob, but the wasp moved with such speed that I never reached it. The creature latched onto my chest, its skull-face staring dumbly into mine. I retched at the stink of it—sweet and rotting flesh.

I raised my hands in self-defense, and then...

I was falling backward into the hall.

Someone pulled me through the doorway and slammed the door closed a moment before the mighty wasp struck.

"Thanks," I said, still gagging.

"No problem, chick."

My rescuer stood over me, hair spilling around her face like a great red mane.

"Zivy?"

45

Zivy grabbed my hand and pulled me up. I was face-to-face with my damsel in distress.

Or am I the damsel?

Either way, it was damn good to see her.

"Jeez." Zivy looked me up and down. "You're the first thing in this damn place I'm happy to see."

"Thanks for the save."

"Anytime."

Zivy threw her arms around me and squeezed me hard. I heard a sharp *crack*. Not my back giving way but the closet door. The wasp was attempting a breakout, using its stinger as a pickaxe.

"What is that thing?" she asked.

"You don't want to know."

"I'll take your word for it. Come on, these halls aren't safe."

"You're telling me."

She took off, and I followed at her heels.

She led me through a series of zigs and zags until the house opened up into a cavernous room. It echoed with the dissonant chords of an untuned piano.

We slowed to keep from drawing unnecessary attention. The room was large—an oversized parlor with ferns that grew wild. They reached out in all directions, searching in vain for sunlight.

Jesus. She walked us straight into a funeral.

Mourners sat motionless in their chairs, dressed in the blackest of blacks. No electric or gas lamps here; banks of candles set the mood. Potted lilies tried and failed to mask the scent of death.

The casket had slid off its bier and lay open on the parquet floor, the deceased half in, half out.

The mourners were as dead as the mourned, their faces locked in rigor mortis grins. The pianist was the only one who showed any signs of life. He sat hunched over the keyboard, pounding away at the keys with skeletal hands.

This is why I hate fiction. The lack of rules is appalling.

"This way," Zivy called, drawing my attention from the grisly scene.

"Where are we going?"

"My hiding place."

We raced on, through what seemed like an endless supply of adjoining rooms, each with its own horror on display. From a nursery with a crib containing a limbless man to a washroom filled with bloodied sheets.

Don't look, just move.

"How'd you get in?" Zivy asked, rounding yet another corner.

"I piggybacked with JJ. Long story. Tell it to you later."

"So, you're on your own? Where are the guys?"

I had no interest telling her that JJ had gone up in flames and Quan had been eaten by babies.

"You expected a battalion?"

Zivy snorted. "Har-dee-har. This way."

We came to a room devoid of light. I paid special heed to the sound of Zivy's footfalls, blocking out the snuffling and wheezing that started the moment we entered the space. Something big and slimy was following us—*whump-splat-whump-splat*—but we soon left it behind.

We exited the darkness and entered a dimly lit anteroom. We stopped there, and Zivy cautiously approached the door. I was fighting off a massive stitch in my side, but Zivy? She'd barely broken a sweat.

"Here we are." She smiled and turned the doorknob.

I stepped inside and the penny dropped. This was not just any room—it was a writer's room. Its bookcases were as stuffed as Utter's library had been bereft. A worn Persian rug covered the floor, and a humble oak desk sat at the far end of the room, piled high with manuscripts.

Situated on the wall behind the desk was a lone window stretching to the ceiling. The glass sported a jagged hole, as if someone had tossed a large stone through it. The floor was littered with fallen shards.

I walked to the center of the room, picked up one of the

broken pieces and held it aloft. The light caught the fragment, accenting its sharp edges.

Red glass.

Hate. Anger. Rage.

The pattern of the stained glass? Diamond, of course.

The door swung shut behind me.

"I think that piece is too big for you to swallow."

I dared not turn around. I could have kicked myself for being so blind, but when one finds oneself pursued by a giant wasp, one takes whatever form of escape available.

"Utter stole more than just my stories. He took everything. *Everything*. I thought he valued me. I thought I was safe."

I dropped the shard. It shattered at my feet, bits of glass scattering. She'd led me right where she wanted me, and I hadn't put up a fuss. Fuck, I'd come willingly! And now, I was all hers.

"It's hard to feel safe when your bedroom door creaks open in the middle of the night. He'd always splash on extra cologne before paying me a visit. The smell of it made me sick. I'd spend hours washing his stink away—shower on full blast until my skin was raw."

She'd gotten me, gotten me good.

"He told me he loved me."

The lock clicked.

"He had a funny way of showing it."

I turned ever so slowly. The woman who had looked like Zivy no longer did. She flashed a viper's grin.

"You win," I said.

"It would seem so."

Something stirred behind me, and one of the stacks of manuscripts slipped off the desk and to the floor.

"Holy Christ...Ellen?"

I chanced a glance. Peeking out from behind the writing desk was Zivy—my Zivy. Her face was drawn, dark circles encasing those bug eyes of hers. She looked positively Gorey-esque.

"Stay put," I told her.

"Oh, Ellen." She looked positively pained. "You shouldn't have come."

"She's right," faux Zivy said. "But now that you're here, why don't we stir things up a bit?"

She was shedding her Zivy persona piece by piece. The flame-red hair dulled, skin pulled tight over bones. Her breathing grew labored, as if each breath might be her last.

I could only be so lucky.

The glass shard pulsed in my hand like one of those beepers restaurants give you to let you know your table is ready. It held a steady beat, a rhythm reminiscent of...

I'm still standing. Even after the burning boy, the biting shadows. But nothing has prepared me for this.

...a heart monitor.

Zivy's doppelganger was gone. In her place stood a withered figure, hospital gown hanging off one shoulder, IV lines spilling from her arms. The old woman regarded me with abject betrayal.

"You left me."

"Mom?"

"You left me to die."

46

Mother—*not Mom not Mom*—raised an arthritic hand, her arm trembling with the effort.

"I needed you..."

"Why are you doing this?"

"...and you weren't there."

"Stop it!"

The room grew uncomfortably warm.

I heard Zivy's voice behind me but not her words. My head was swimming, my attention drawn to the talking sinkhole in front of me.

"I died in pain. No one answered the call button."

Fuck fuck fuck...

"I died alone, Ellen."

Not real not real not real...

"No one should die alone."

I was no longer in control of my body. Like a deer in the headlights or a kid on the train tracks, I could only stare in horror as the figure in front of me blossomed into the person I had tried so hard to forget. With every second that passed, she honed the details, perfecting her impersonation until there was no discerning her from the original.

"They put me in a ba-aa-aag!" she wailed, smothering me in waves of emotion I hadn't known possible. Her emotions or mine? Was there any difference? Everything blurred beneath her withering gaze.

"You're...not..." I tested out my voice, finding it lacking in both volume and conviction.

This tickled Not-Mom to no end, and she leapfrogged toward me, Spring-Heeled Jane.

"You're not going out in that, are you?" she screamed. She was no longer Hospital-Mom but High School-Mom, roiling in disgust. "That top's too tight and you're too fat. If you wanted to look like a clown, join the circus!" She practically sang this, an amalgam of all of her golden oldies.

The moment was getting away from me. There was something very important I was supposed to do, but for the life of me, I couldn't pin that important something down. It didn't help that I had a fly buzzing in my ear, telling me to stand back and stand down. I tried swatting it away, but it kept coming back.

"Ellen! Get away from her!"

Pesky, pesky fly!

"Your fly's undone, you stupid girl! I hope you didn't plan on going to the library like that!" Another Mom, ever-watchful, ever-critical, like a lighthouse shining its beam on me and me alone. "You don't want the world seeing your paa-aanties, do you?"

"Shut up," I whispered.

This only enraged her more.

"You know that library is full of perverts, don't you? Touching themselves in the stacks. Waiting for stupid little girls like you to wander too close—"

"Shut up!"

She shifted again. Now she was part Mom, part crab. Appendages threatened and snapped.

"I bet that's why you go there in the first place. You're too dumb to get anything out of all those books. It's those men, isn't it? It's those pervs! Fumbling around in the reference section, looking you up, looking you down, looking anywhere they please."

My knees buckled and I crumpled to the floor. The assaults weren't just verbal, there was a physical element as well, and every insult, every jab came complete with a healthy bite. The choir of shadows accented each spiteful phrase with syncopated attacks.

"Strange men in dark shirts..."

Snap-bite!

"Waiting and wanting..."

Bite-snap!

"And stupid little Ellen falling for it hook..."

"You're wrong."

"Line..."

"It only happened once, and I told the librarian."

"And sinker!"

"I told the librarian, and they kicked him out!"

"Ellen! Back...the fuck...away!"

Hands grabbed me—*it's the man in the stacks, the man in the stacks*—and yanked me back. I landed on my ass—*where's the librarian? I need the librarian!*—before being dragged forcibly away from Mother.

In a flash, I was face-to-face with the stranger. No...not a stranger. Not the man in the stacks but a vision with red hair.

"Snap out of it!"

But I couldn't. I knew it was Zivy who had pulled me from the line of fire, but the ties to the poison-spitting woman were deep—bone deep. The more I resisted, the tighter those ties pulled.

"Ellen!"

"ELLEN!"

There was no room in my head for both voices; fuck, there was barely enough room for *me*. And so, I shoved Zivy aside and clambered to my feet, legs trembling, ready for her to do her worst.

And damned if I wasn't disappointed.

"My head hurts!" she shrieked.

The tumor grabbing hold.

"The man next door is trying to kill me!"

The dementia settling in.

"And you don't care..."

I took you to every appointment...

"You don't care..."

To every specialist...

"You don't CARE!"

And they all came back with the same answer. She was going to die. She was going to—

"Hold on," I said. Words not for her or for me but for this construct, this lie. The world was slipping away from me save for that simple imperative. "Hold on!"

Even the menacing thing in front of me had to obey. My insistence had put a crack in the spell it held over me, but that was all I needed. I had been a good girl. I had done the right things. And I didn't deserve this. Not one bit.

"You *hate* me!"

The raging tempest before me tried to regain its footing, but the chat had ended, the line had been cut, and whatever momentum it had on its side spun itself into oblivion.

"I don't hate you."

Mom howled. Sorrow's Leap shook.

"I don't love you."

"No no no no no no no!"

I could barely hear myself above the blood pounding in my ears, but I finally got down to it, distilled the truth I had been hiding even from myself.

"But I forgive you."

I thought the woman in front of me might explode with rage. She retreated within herself, shrinking once more into the hospital gowned mummy my mother had become in her final days. Her multiple IVs—an impossible number, an insane number—shot forward, piercing my arms, my neck, my chest, dragging me toward her outstretched arms, gnarled hands ready to rip me to pieces.

I didn't resist.

Neither Zivy's cries nor the shadows' gnashing teeth could keep me from doing the one thing I'd never done, swore I'd *never* do.

I stopped fighting back.

Crossing the few feet between us, I reached out and embraced the crazed thing and pulled her close.

"I forgive you."

One moment, I was holding a corpse in my arms, cold and rotten; the next, the form shrunk further still in my embrace. No longer cold, no longer eager for my demise. The scent of doomed flesh transformed into the subtle sweetness of spring flowers. Roses? Perhaps. Definitely something red.

"I'm sorry."

Warm tears hit my neck. Mine and hers intermingled.

I leaned back, putting space between us while still holding tight.

"Gemma?"

47

"Watch yourself," Zivy warned.

I took a step back to get a better look at the woman. Gemma struck me as drab and lifeless, which is saying a lot for a ghost. She hovered just this side of emaciation, obviously starved of whatever passed for sustenance on this side of reality. She shivered beneath my gaze, a Jenga tower on the verge of collapse.

"I'm good," I called back. Then, upon further reflection, "The question is: are *we* good?"

Gemma nodded. Gone was any trace of malevolence, replaced by fragility and remorse. She tried to speak, but the words caught in her throat.

Best to help her out.

"Where did your 'friend' go?"

Gemma's brow furrowed. She was either loath to admit any relationship to the Dark Lady whatsoever, or she didn't know.

I thought I'd have to drag it out of her when she managed, "Back inside."

"Inside the main house or..."

"Back inside." She placed a hand over her chest.

Good. Time to take advantage of the temporary détente.

"We need to leave before she gets out again."

She wiped at her eyes. "I'm not sure I'm in control anymore. I poured so much...hate into her, there's less of me every day."

"All the more reason to help us while you can."

She pondered this, then hit me with a curveball. "She loved you."

The thought was so foreign it snapped my wits.

"She?"

"As much as she was able."

Gemma stepped forward. I instinctively jumped back.

"The problem was..."

The pale woman closed the distance between us.

"...she was her own Dark Lady. She failed to tame her, but she tried."

Shellshocked, I stood my ground.

"She's still trying."

Gemma placed a hand at her mouth, the universal signal of secrets being passed, and whispered in my ear...

"Who do you think sent that text?"

My mind reeled. The text. My ticket into this nuthouse. The single word that unlocked all those little doors in my head.

Hate.

My answer to the riddle of the stained glass wasn't *my* answer at all.

It was Mom's.

"But why?"

"Because the only true Hell is being alone."

She flinched and clenched her fists. Her muscles tensed and her lips pulled back. I'd seen pain in my life, the kind not even morphine can quell. The woman before me was in agony, and the room pulsed in sympathy.

Suspecting our ceasefire would soon be at an end, I pressed her. "How do we get out of here?"

She opened her mouth, but another voice answered, echoing wetly from her gullet. "Only one way out."

Gemma clamped her mouth closed and tried swallowing the other's words. It was a struggle she was destined to lose.

"I..." she said, eyes wide with the recognition that these words would be her last. "I wrote her too fucking well."

Black liquid, oily and shimmering, poured from Gemma's mouth. She was an erupting geyser, and as the flow increased, Gemma Reid retreated until there was nothing left but a cascading fountain of despair.

I heeded Zivy's advice and dove behind the desk.

"About time you came to your senses," Zivy said.

"What can I say? I'm a slow learner."

I peered out from the safety of the oak desk to find the liquid solidifying into flesh, weaving itself into fabric. Gemma was no more. In her place stood a newly emboldened Dark Lady, angry as fuck.

"One way out!"

Stained glass trembled and cracked in its frame, showering the room in a fresh rain of red shards. She was anger, she was hate, the discard of a life lived in sorrow and fear.

"Shall I obli-i-ige?"

48

"Screw you."

The Dark Lady exploded with laughter—half hyena, half child falling down the stairs.

"One way out?" Zivy asked. "What does she mean?"

There was no time to explain. The Dark Lady was expanding. She'd put down roots in the wood floor, and the planks soaked up her murky essence. Like watercolors on thirsty paper, she flowed into the room, becoming the room, making it over in her own image.

Books, grown heavy absorbing her, caused their shelves to bow and crack, spilling to the floor with overripe *splats*. The wallpaper morphed from faded foliage to desiccated wastelands. She infected all, drawing joy from the illness she spread.

The desk behind which we hunkered no longer offered shelter; it too drank deep of the Dark Lady's offering. I pulled Zivy back as the oak desk drowned in darkness.

"All around the Mulberry Bush," the Dark Lady shrieked. "The monkey chased the weasel! The monkey stopped to pull up his sock. Pop!"

On "pop," she tossed the desk aside with the sweep of a clawed hand. Even physics bowed down to the Dark Lady in this realm.

"Goes the weasel!"

"What's the play, coach?" Zivy held tight to my arm, her fear threatening to melt into me.

There was no getting out of this. Not in one piece. The room had become a big, black box, the three of us actors in search of an ending.

As the black tide rolled in, spreading toward us across the floor, ripples of death lapping at our feet, I could see clearly the ending the Dark Lady had in mind.

Too bad I had to disappoint her.

The dark current had overflowed most of the wood floor, yet a few square feet remained untouched. Spread across its planks, catching the light like frozen blood, were the last remnants of the stained-glass window.

I grabbed the largest shard I could find and held it firmly.

"Zivy," I whispered, my eyes fixed on Gemma's nightmare. "Do you trust me?"

"Huh?"

"Do you *trust* me?"

My message was clear and my urgency true. It felt like a lifetime before Zivy answered with a resounding yes.

"I do!" she cried. "Whatever you're going to do, just do it!"

Slipping behind her, I wrapped my free hand about her

chest and pulled her to me. The Dark Lady sang on as I placed the shard's edge against Zivy's neck.

"Pop goes the weasel!"

"Fuck the weasel." I pressed my forehead to the back of Zivy's head. "Say hey to the boys for me."

With that, I drew the glass across Zivy's throat. I pressed hard, cartilage cracking beneath the makeshift blade.

Blood flowed hot over my hand and down Zivy's front. Droplets hit the floor with the sound of a snare drum. Zivy gave a single surprised yelp. I'd cut deep, and her silence thereafter brought the finality of my act home.

The spectacle of one of her victims doing violence to another caught the spirit off guard. As the coppery scent of spilled blood rose, the Dark Lady looked at me with a mix of shock and betrayal.

She was fuming. "You actually did it."

"I did. And not only that," I said, darkly amused. "I killed two birds with one stone."

Zivy let out a final gasp and fell face first into a pool of her own blood. The next second, she was gone. No whoosh of smoke or pop goes the weasel...just gone.

A disembodied voice that rose from the bloody puddle pierced the moment with a forlorn cry.

"No-o-o!"

I almost felt sorry for the thing that had called Zivy home. His grief rivaled mine when my mother died. Loss, yes, but more than that...abandonment.

"Ahhhhhhhhhhh!"

Blood rose in twin columns, forming legs. A cataract of

gore flowed in reverse, knitting itself muscles and sinew until the outline of a man took shape.

Byrd was loose.

Fearing his ire, I dropped the shard, letting it shatter. Best not to be caught holding the weapon that killed his host.

Byrd knelt before the pool from which he sprang and searched longingly with his hands.

"Where's Zivy?" His anguish was unmistakable. "Whe-ere?"

I grabbed hold of the narrative.

"She's gone!" I spat, pointing an accusing finger toward the dark spirit. "And *she's* to blame."

He turned on me.

"No. You!"

"I would never hurt Zivy," I insisted. "I saved her. I released her. Just like I released you."

He lurched toward me, gore-covered hands hungry for my neck. My gambit had failed.

That was, until the Dark Lady opened her big, fat mouth.

"You did your friend a favor," she giggled. "I would have made her scream. Scream forever!"

Byrd paused, his jelly eyes inches from my face. He smacked his raw lips and turned toward her, neckbones clicking as he did so.

"You," Byrd said, swapping allegiances in the blink of an eye.

I can't tell you how gratifying it was to see the look of panic on the Dark Lady's face.

Caught in Byrd's sights, the spirit shifted, activating self-preservation mode. She melted, liquefying and reforming into

the only shape she thought might keep the bloody thing at bay:
Zivy.

In her haste, she got *a lot* wrong. The face was sideways, for
one thing, tilted at nine o'clock. Her hair was a solid mass of
red-orange, and her fingers just as comfortable curling one way
as the other.

"My little Byrr-rrd..." she crooned. "You wouldn't hurt me,
would you?"

The sinewy, skinless abomination dove at the Dark Lady,
arms outstretched, wailing in his sorrow. He latched onto her
with all the ferocity of a crazed jackal, shredding her dead flesh.
Bits of gown filled the air.

Byrd's attack was less about inflicting damage than it was
about going *home.* He'd been robbed of his comfy hidey-hole,
and he meant to have it back, even if it meant boring his way
inside the Dark Lady.

Her minions swarmed the two combatants like famished
mosquitoes, biting indiscriminately. The snapping shades bit
red and black alike, equal opportunity scavengers frenzied by
the clash.

D. Ellis Byrd ripped a wide gash in the woman's side. He
slipped through the wound he'd inflicted, entering the Dark
Lady with a terrible sucking sound.

I ducked out the door and into the smoke-filled hallway.
The fire ignited by JJ's conflagratory exit had spread. Flame
ripped through the house like a fever.

The house's hallways had shifted since I'd last traversed
them, so I relied on my inner GPS. This proved to be a good

strategy. A few lefts and rights, and I once more found myself in the funeral of the undead.

The maestro of the keyboards pounded the ivories with mad abandon. His song was as tuneless as a rockslide, but its meter was unmistakable: ragtime. The gathered throng twitched in syncopated rhythm with the piano. Even the dearly departed, their legs pinned beneath the upended coffin, rapped their skull against the floor to the lunatic beat.

My condolences.

Dashing through the door at the far end of the room, I skidded hard in an attempt to avoid slamming into a wall that hadn't been there before and passed through it, as if it were water.

Sorrow's Leap was losing its coherence.

I found myself in the middle of a smoking room, replete with floor to ceiling humidors. A corpse in the corner puffed away at a Churchill cigar as rats nestled deep in his innards.

He offered me a cadaverous grin and crumbled to dust, leaving the rats to scatter.

How long until the construct dissolved entirely, taking me with it? With Mommy and Daddy fighting, I had but a narrow window for escape.

Window!

Perhaps I had a way out that didn't involve slitting my wrists.

I had thought to follow Zivy by making my own exit, but wildly Sorrow's Leap had rekindled my sense of self-preservation. It had succeeded where every therapist in Iowa had failed.

Carter had spoken about places where Utter Hall grew thin. Spots through which he could pass things to his employer. If I could find one of those spots, maybe I could slip out unnoticed.

The turret.

I gathered my wits, reset my inner compass, and shot off in search of the spiral staircase.

49

Finding the turret proved next to impossible. The house, unwilling to let me slip through its fingers, pulled out all the stops. It threw up horrors left and right, determined to obstruct my progress.

Despite having only read part of one of Gemma's tales, every nasty encounter taught me more about the creative monster living inside her head.

The kitchen I passed through? Stocked with marbled torsos hanging from hooks. The sewing room I snuck past? Home to a sinister seamstress fashioning a suit out of skin. Each room I encountered held depravities worse than the one before. I flipped past these chapters, eager to get to the fucking end.

I tumbled into the foyer, ruining my knees in the process.

Flames engulfed the entryway. I couldn't leave by the front door if I'd wanted to. It wasn't just fire that deterred me.

It was the knights. They'd pulled themselves together, so to speak, and now stood ready to do battle.

It seemed Sorrow's Leap still had some tricks up its sleeves.

There was nothing inside the clanking armor, yet that didn't seem to stop them from attacking. Heat had warped the metal. The disfigured tin men jumped me, their gauntlets leaving searing blister marks on my skin.

The pain kept me moving.

Outflanking the metal men, I dove through a wall of flame and into a side room as yet untouched by fire or fictional beastie.

The room was bare save for a single closed door. I held no illusions about making it safely to the door—*the floorboards are rotten, the ceiling will fall*—and yet I managed it in record time despite screaming knees.

A sudden rumble rocked the house, and a gust of burning creosote pressed me against the wall. A far wing of the house had just collapsed. No doubt the battle royale I'd initiated had come to an end, and the victor would soon be heading my way.

Even money says the Dark Lady came out on top.

It was time to blow this popsicle stand.

I threw open the door. I'd never been so happy to see a staircase in my life.

I took a step, and my leg buckled beneath me. I grabbed hold of my thigh and inched my fingers downward. My kneecap had split in half.

Oh, shit...

I hobbled through the door and mounted the first step.

Lightning shot from my knee to my groin. My stomach cramped, and I dry heaved in pain.

Another wave of heat blasted me, and I glanced over my shoulder to find the fire had reached the room behind me, its floorboards igniting like aged kindling.

You found the turret. Nothing left to do but climb.

That was easier said than done. My knee had swollen to the size of a cantaloupe, the slightest movement causing it to howl.

I'd been an abysmal hopscotch player in my youth, and my sense of balance hadn't matured since. But the stairs were my only option. And so, I hopped from one rickety step to the next.

The smoke rose much faster than I, and by the time I was halfway up the spiraled height, I was sweating and coughing like a miner. The flames had reached the bottom step, yet on I hopped, each impact jolting my injured knee awake.

One more minute. One more, and I'm up.

I focused on one step at a time, doing my best to ignore the sound of popping wood as the flames devoured the supports.

But there was another sound riding above the crackling fire, and I had to pause momentarily to suss it out. Rising from the hungry inferno, youthful laughter echoed loud and clear.

The climax, apparently, called for the return of the Children of Woe.

I quickened my pace.

Don't look down.

I didn't.

Keep moving.

I did.

Keep moving!

"I am, goddammit!"

The creatures following me snickered as they leaped from step to step. Were they getting closer? Damn right, they were.

Just get to the top, get to the top, get to the top...

And what would happen if I did? When I had climbed the turret in Utter's mansion, I'd seen embers floating behind a lone pane of glass. The same embers now alighted on my skin. Would the window prove to be one of the thin places between worlds? If I climbed through it, might I find myself back at Utter Hall?

Maybe, maybe not. But I'd limited my options dramatically by taking the stairs.

A ferocious roar shook the stones like thunder.

"Too late, Ellen Marx."

The Dark Lady was now imbedded within the very fabric of the house. She had become Sorrow's Leap.

I took two steps with a single hop and...*there!* Up above. A single rectangle of light appeared, offering a view unlike the others.

It was the window home.

The pain's not real. Use both legs. Pick it up!

But the moment I obeyed that little voice, I nearly lost my footing. I came crashing down on my kneecap, shattering the remaining pieces.

I hadn't felt such pain since my mother backed over my foot with the car. She hadn't given the rearview mirror a second glance.

My agony returned me to my childhood, and I cried out,

my voice echoing about the tower, returning to me again and again.

"Mommy!"

Unhinged laughter answered my cry.

"Mommy's dead."

The world thrummed with her voice. The walls reaching upward soaked her up, fading to black at her insistence.

The darkness moved past me, over me, *through* me. I'd never reach the window in time. Shadows rose to the top of the turret, singeing the windows black.

The first pair of little hands latched upon my ankle. The first teeth sank deep. I was out of moves. Soon, the Children of Woe would swarm me like piranhas as their dark mother screamed with glee.

"Let go."

The words came to me on a cool breeze. There was none of the usual mockery or insinuation, but I recognized my mother's voice nonetheless.

"Let go, honey."

My clothes caught fire. The babies screamed, and the Dark Lady rejoiced.

And me? I did something I hadn't done since I was a girl.

I obeyed my mom.

I let go of the railing and plummeted into the heart of the blaze.

50

I woke with a start face down on the hotel room's carpeted floor, the sensation of falling still alive in my gut.

"I let go."

"Easy," JJ crooned as he came to my side. "Quan, grab that water."

I took baby sips, relishing the cool liquid on my parched throat. When I'd drunk my fill, I opened my eyes. The guys stood by, anxious and attentive.

"Is it done?" Quan asked. "Did you find her?"

"It's done."

JJ hugged me tight. "I thought we'd lost you there for a minute."

"That makes two of us."

I rose and sat on the settee. I found I was crying, and the realization made me weep all the harder.

JJ and Quan kept quiet, patting my back, offering more water. Typical men.

When I'd had my fill of tears, I wiped my face clean.

"Let's go get our girl."

———————

Zivy's eyes were closed when we entered the hospital room, but they fluttered open as we crowded around her bed.

"Is it time for my sponge bath?"

JJ laughed, relief spilling out of him. "Thank God."

"I think I'll save my thanks for Ellen."

She reached for my hand. I took it, wondering how I had ever found discomfort in human touch.

"Don't mention it."

"We got you a present," JJ said, handing her the stuffed rabbit he'd found in the gift shop. "We thought you could use a lucky rabbit."

Zivy took the toy with trembling hands.

"Looks more like a poodle. I think I'll call him Mr. Awful."

She gazed lovingly at us, one after the other.

"I had the strangest dream. You were in it. And you, and you."

"Really?" JJ asked.

Zivy hit him in the face with the rabbit-poodle.

"I'm going to make you watch that movie if it kills me."

She took a deep breath. It would be a long time until she was free of Sorrow's Leap. Its shadow hung over her face.

"Is she gone? I mean really gone?"

I didn't know how to answer. In my experience, the dead

had a tendency to come back. Over and over again. And so, I lied.

"Absolutely."

EPILOGUE

The smell coming from my pantry was something awful. I'd opened all the windows in my apartment, but the stench remained.

My first thought was that a mouse had crawled underneath the refrigerator and died, but after pulling the fridge away from the wall, all I found were empty ramen packages and a dozen Yuengling bottle caps.

Yuengling...damn. I'd forgotten to buy beer. But didn't guests usually bring their own? Surely that was what the acronym BYOB was for.

Utter's money had eventually made its way into my account. After going AWOL for a few weeks, Carter had finally returned my call. The funds were available the next day. He'd obviously forgotten his earlier announcement about leaving Utter's employ, but I got the sense from our conversation he was genuinely sorry for his part in our "adventure." Not sorry enough to tear up the NDAs we'd signed, but hopefully that would be moot soon enough.

As I awaited the arrival of my guests, I glanced out the kitchen window. The Lincoln Tunnel's evening traffic had crawled to a stop. Frustrated drivers laid on their horns. I liked my little apartment above the tunnel. The steady rumble of cars and trucks lulled me to sleep quite nicely.

Half a year had passed since I'd ditched Iowa City for Weehawken, New Jersey. All I really missed were the pork chop sandwiches the Kiwanis used to sell outside my neighborhood supermarket. It was a small price to pay for gaining access to fresh bagels, pizza you could fold, and the delicacy locals called "dirty water dogs."

One World Trade Center was visible from my window as well—a glass shard towering at the south end of Manhattan, anchoring the city. There had been two towers once; now, there was one. There was a lonely poetry to that.

The image changed on one of the electronic billboards flanking the tunnel, drawing my attention.

"JAMES UTTER RETURNS WITH A TERRIFYING NEW TALE!"

"Enjoy it while you can, douchebag."

The doorbell buzzed, rousing me, and I scurried to answer it.

My visitor shoved a bottle of champagne in my face. Apparently BYOC was a thing as well.

"Happy housewarming, chick!"

Zivy swooped past me and made herself at home, tossing her coat in the corner and checking out my sparse furnishings:

my futon that doubled as my couch, the green bookcase I'd gotten off Craigslist, and my collection of over-watered plants, sick and yellowing on the windowsill.

"Love what you haven't done to the place."

"You're too kind."

She'd chopped off most of her hair, opting for a bob. I hated the new do. She asked me how I liked it.

"It's great. I bet you use a lot less shampoo."

"Not quite the ringing endorsement I was hoping for."

I was saved by the buzzer. I ran to the door. JJ stood on the stoop, a massive, oil-soaked box in his hands.

"Someone order a pizza?" he chirped. Then, glancing over at Zivy, "Nice hair!"

"Now, *that's* an endorsement."

Zivy bounded over to JJ and planted a kiss on his cheek. She swiped the pizza from him and shuttled it to the kitchen table—thirty bucks on Facebook Marketplace.

"Oh, my God."

Zivy stared wide-eyed at the photo on the wall.

"Yeah, I should probably return that."

It was the photo I'd borrowed from Ebb's, although "borrowed" was looking a lot like "stolen." Utter sat at his table, basking in admirers' attention. Gemma watched on as he signed the book she'd written.

"Feels like a million years ago, doesn't it?" I said, testing Zivy's mood.

She traced the crack in the glass.

"No. It doesn't." Her shoulder trembled. "I miss him. Is that crazy?"

"Utter?"

"Not him."

I'd been slow on the uptake. She was talking about Byrd.

"We were together for so long. I feel empty, like there's not enough me to fill in the holes. I guess it's like kicking a habit. Once it's gone, all you're left with is yourself."

I put an arm around her. She was trembling.

"Yeah. It's just like that."

I got out plates, and we divvied up the pizza. We squished together on the futon, the TV trays I'd found on trash day coming in quite handy.

"All right, it's movie time," Zivy announced. She was feigning excitement, but at least she was trying.

She grabbed the remote and brought up the movie app. She pressed a button, and up popped a smaller window, embedded in the lower corner. The guy inside the window waved.

"Hey, Quan!" we said in unison.

"Hey, people." Quan's voice still sounded like he'd spent a lifetime smoking unfiltered cigarettes, but other than that he seemed much recovered. "What's the feature presentation?"

"Patience!" Zivy said. "You'll know soon enough."

"Hey, Quan. How's the book coming?" JJ asked.

Quan leaned closer to the camera. "Slow but steady. Mr. Carter has *a lot* to say. It's good having a man on the inside. By the way, my lawyer says he should have those NDAs cracked by the end of the week. Utter won't know what hit him."

"Any ideas for a title?" I asked.

"I don't want to put the cart before the horse, but"—he

grinned mischievously—"I was thinking something like, *The Ghostwriter of Sorrow's Leap.* Or should I keep it simple? *James Utter: Haunted Hack?* Or maybe—"

Zivy popped the champagne. "Guys, how about we just watch the movie?"

Her sudden change in tone made it clear: tonight was not about stirring up old ghosts, it was about watching a bad movie and drinking too much.

She hit play.

The Metro-Goldwyn-Mayer lion roared to life, accompanied by the strains of a Hollywood orchestra. When the sepia-toned title sequence began, we roared louder than the lion.

"Not again!" Quan moaned.

"What?" Zivy cried.

"We watched this three movie nights ago," JJ complained.

"Come on. It's always time for *The Wizard of Oz.*"

We shouted her down.

"Fine. Spoilsports."

She flipped back to the menu and loaded a movie from her library. The thumbnail showed a wormlike creature rising from a swamp, its circular mouth filled with razor-sharp teeth. *Suckerville* it was.

"Happy?"

The B-movie was everything I imagined it would be. Bloody, bawdy, and required zero concentration.

Good choice.

We chatted back and forth, enjoying each other's company more than the movie.

A foul odor hit my nose. The stink from the pantry had returned.

I glanced at the others, but they'd taken no note of it. They were engrossed in the flick.

I turned my head in time to see the pantry room door swing open.

A man in his underwear hung from the ceiling, his neck in a noose, twirling slowly. I watched him spin as the watch party howled at the CGI leeches. I couldn't discern his age, but I could tell he was deader than dead, despite twitching fingers and toes.

He spun gracefully, unhurried—a life ending in melancholy.

When he opened his eyes, I put a finger to my lips. We were watching a movie, after all.

"I'll deal with you later," I promised.

ALSO BY CHRIS SORENSEN

If you enjoyed this book, please check out...

THE MESSY MAN TRILOGY

The Nightmare Room

The Hungry Ones

The Messy Man

CREATURE FEATURES

Suckerville

Bee Tornado

SPECIAL THANKS

I couldn't have brough this book to light without the help of some wonderful folks: Nick Sullivan, Angela Sylvaine, Mark Aldrich, Matt Shale, Leslie Farrell, Matthew Ballen, Gretchen Douglas, and of course Deborah Graybill and JoAnne Sorensen. You guys rock!

ABOUT THE AUTHOR

Chris Sorensen is the bestselling author of *The Nightmare Room, The Hungry Ones, The Messy Man, Suckerville,* and *Bee Tornado*. He's penned over fifteen plays for Thin Air Theatre Company and the Butte Theater of Colorado, including *A Haunting at the Old Homestead, The Vampire of Cripple Creek,* and *Dr. Jekyll's Medicine Show*. He lives with his wife and pups in Colorado, where he splits his time between writing spooky stories and narrating audiobooks. Chris has narrated 300 titles for Audible, Tantor Audio, Hachette, Podium, Bee Audio, Recorded Books, and many others. He studied under William Esper at the Rutgers Professional Actor Training Program and has taught/directed at Cornell University, the American Academy of Dramatic Arts, the Atlantic Theatre Company School, Interlochen Center for the Arts. Additional credits: original company member of The Present Company Theatre (Edinburgh Fringe First Award) and a member of SAG-AFTRA and the Horror Writers Association.